A Murderous Intent
Kit McKenna

McKenna Publishing, LLC

Other Books By Kit McKenna

THE OKLAHOMA SKIES SERIES

All Sorrows Are Less

https://mybook.to/AllSorrowsKitMcKenna

Paint the Earth Red

https://mybook.to/PaintEarthKitMcKenna

The Heart That Returns

https://mybook.to/HeartReturnsKitMcKenna

Perfect As You Are

https://mybook.to/PerfectKitMcKenna

The Art of Passion

https://mybook.to/ArtPassionKitMcKenna

A Matter of Trust

https://mybook.to/MatterTrustKitMcKenna

Get a FREE copy of the Valentine Short Mr. Wrong door

https://dl.bookfunnel.com/myptwbvjh0

THE BELLADONNA SOCIETY SERIES

A Pointed End

https://mybook.to/PointedKitMcKenna

A Murderous Intent

https://mybook.to/MurderousKitMcKenna

A Secret Revealed

https://mybook.to/RevealedKitMcKenna

A Devil's Snare

https://mybook.to/SnareKitMcKenna

A Predator's Threat

https://mybook.to/ThreatKitMcKenna

THE MORRIGAN MAFIA SERIES

Crossed

https://mybook.to/CrossedMcKenna

Coup

https://mybook.to/CoupKitMcKenna

Crashed

https://mybook.to/CrashedKitMcKenna

Dedication

This book is dedicated to anyone who has been forced to carry secrets they were too young to handle.

I see you.

I love you.

I am you.

May you find the help and healing you need to discover life beyond the trauma.

Trigger Warning

This book contains instances of assault and recounted childhood
trauma which may be triggering for some readers.

Prologue

Gabriella

Three Years Earlier

I tapped my foot as the phone rang.

Pick up, pick up, pick up, you fucking asshole.

I heard a click and just when hope started to flush through me, it was dashed when his voicemail message started to play. "Where are you?" I hissed into the phone. "You have a meeting with the Sandersons that was supposed to have started seven minutes ago. I cannot believe you've done this to me again."

I hung up the phone. Okay, so I slammed it down on the receiver. That sonofabitch had done it again.

He was probably perched on a barstool somewhere in Bricktown, yucking it up with a group of his cronies. For the millionth time this week, I thought about walking out the door and leaving him high and dry. I used to love this job, but now, I loathed it.

Oh, who was I kidding? I still loved this job; I loathed the environment. And my boss.

And I loathed doing absolutely everything while Fucking Franklin Harper had whittled down his job duties as owner to taking the profits and occasionally showing up in the office while sometimes remembering to pay me. I thought for sure he'd show up for this meeting. I loathed him, but I needed him, too.

Oh well. Nothing to be done about it now.

I squared my shoulders, took a deep breath, and plastered a fake smile on my face before I went back to the conference room where the clients were waiting.

"I'm so sorry. Frank got into a little fender bender and asked me to go over the plans with you," I lied.

Mrs. Sanderson's face was overcome with concern. "Oh no! I hope he's okay!"

"Yes, yes, he's fine. He just won't be able to make this meeting. Not to worry, though, I know the plans and proposal front to back so I can answer any questions you might have," I assured her as I made eye contact with her, then her husband.

When my gaze landed on their contractor, his cool blue stare pinned me in place. He raised an eyebrow at me, letting me know he knew I was full of shit.

My neck grew warm. I turned away from his laser beam stare and began the presentation. Once I spread out the renderings, I began to walk them through the design while pointing out the items that were left open for them to decide. Additional drawings are also presented as overlays to the originals to show how things would look with each option.

We went through the projected costs and timelines. Mrs. Sanderson wanted to look at the drawings closely while Mr. Sanderson talked low with the contractor.

Mr. Sanderson would ask questions of the contractor who relayed the questions to me. I appreciated him asking for my input rather than assuming I wouldn't have any idea about the technical aspects.

Every time I looked at the contractor, my stomach would do a flip-flop. My eyes were drawn to his every move. He was relaxed, but emanated power.

As they talked, I studied his hands, his knuckles dusted with hair. When he turned his hand while talking, I noticed his palms were rough with callouses.

I could see a few lines of ink peeking out from the cuffs of his crisp white shirt. I wondered what images he had desired to have permanently painted onto his skin with ink and needle.

"Miss Carmichael?"

I had been so lost in my contemplation of body art that I completely lost track of the conversation. "I'm sorry. What was that?" My eyes snapped up.

One side of the contractor's mouth tilted up. What was his name again? Something with an M. Mason? No. Martin? No, that's not it either. Mr. M repeated the question, his eyes dancing with amusement.

I flipped through the pages to the electrical schematic and showed them the details of the electrical wiring plan. This contractor was sharp, and I was probably showing him too much information.

Frank liked to keep a lot of the information to himself, hoping to land the project management gig for the added income.

He wouldn't have shown them half of the drawings that I included in the presentation. Someone sharp could simply pay close attention and then have their own drawings done, cutting our company out completely.

I would blame it on this contractor. Milton? No, that's not it either. Morgan. Yes, I think that's it. Something about this man, this Morgan, made me want to lay out all of my cards and show him everything in my hand.

Mrs. Sanderson asked me about the finishes, so I turned to her and flipped to the color board pages. The men went back to talking as I spoke with Mrs. Sanderson. She was very sweet, but indecisive. I assured her that the wood tones and other finishes could blend with a variety of color palettes, showing her the options pages.

The men had grown quiet, so I looked back over to find the contractor, *Morgan, his name is Morgan*, staring at me. He had one arm across his chest, the other hand raised to a contemplative position where it stroked a thumb over his lips.

I swallowed. He was so intense. "Are there any other questions I can answer?"

He raised an eyebrow.

"I think I have all of my questions answered," Mr. Sanderson said, "What about you, dear?"

"Oh no, I can't think of anything else right now," Mrs. Sanderson told her husband.

"Mrs. Carmichael, if there's anything else that comes up, I'll get back in touch. For now, give us a few days to discuss what you've shown us, and we'll get back to you by the end of next week," Mr. Sanderson said.

When he said Mrs., Morgan's eyes had flicked to the naked ring finger on my left hand. I wasn't married, but I didn't feel the need to correct the older man.

"That will be fine, Mr. Sanderson. Feel free to call me at any time. We'd love to work on this project with you and your wife."

Mr. Sanderson rose and offered his hand to his wife to help her stand. I smiled at the gentlemanly courtesy and stood as she did. Moving ahead, I walked to the door of the conference room to hold it open for them.

When they passed through, Morgan the Contractor said, "Robert, you go on ahead. I'll follow in a moment."

Mr. Sanderson nodded his head at the younger man. "Call me this afternoon, Morgan, so we can discuss your thoughts more in-depth."

"I'll do that."

Once they had left the office, Morgan looked down at me. "Why are you still here?"

My brow furrowed. "I'm sorry? I don't know what you mean."

"With Frank. It's obvious that presentation was all you from the design to the renderings and possibly even the technical drawings. Why are you still working for a... for someone like Frank?"

I frowned, unsure how to respond.

"People in the industry know that he has been checked out of the business for some time. I can see now that the only reason his company's still around is because of you. You're quite talented."

The heat in my neck returned and flamed up to my scalp. I looked down. "Thank you, but all the contacts are Frank's. We wouldn't have any business if it wasn't for the people he knows."

"That may have been true in the beginning, but that's not what brings them in now."

I couldn't look at him. His laser blue gaze would turn me to ash. "It's complicated."

"Pity," he said. His voice was low and filled with gravel. It sent ripples of sensation across my skin. "You should uncomplicate it." With that, he opened the door and left.

For the rest of the day, his words rolled through my mind. He didn't know the entire story. Frank was a lousy boss and Morgan might be right about the company, but I needed Frank as much as he needed me.

Hours later, I woke from a deep sleep unable to breathe, clawing at the hand around my throat. "You stupid cunt, you should know better than to use that tone with me," a raspy voice hissed into my ear.

I relaxed, realizing it was Frank. The pungent smell of alcohol surrounded him like a cloud, but mostly he stank of sweat and stale cigarettes. My lip curled from the stench.

He wasn't acting his usual drunk self. This was something different. His naked body settled between my legs, and he started pumping against me, trying to hit the right spot. I slipped my hand down to guide him, and he squeezed harder.

"Leave it alone," he growled. "Your gash is so big that I don't need any help to hit your hole."

This is why I needed Frank. He knew what I needed. He knew I preferred humiliation and shame to the numbness that usually accompanied my sexual experiences. Feeling something, even if it was horrible, was better than feeling nothing.

After several attempts, he finally slid into me. He was almost frenzied in his thrusts, his body slapping against mine. I wondered if he'd moved on from booze to something harder.

"Goddamn," he panted, "your pussy's so loose you're never going to be able to make me cum."

He pulled out and, without warning, flipped me onto my stomach. I knew what was coming. I gripped the sheets and tried to crawl away, but he grabbed me by the hair and pulled me back.

"Frank, no, stop!" I cried, but he didn't. Usually if I said an absolute no to something, he would stop. Whatever he was on had him ignoring me.

He yanked my hair. "Shut up, you stupid bitch. It's your fault that I have to fuck you in the ass. If your cunt wasn't so useless, I wouldn't have to."

Breathe. Just breathe. It will be over soon. Just get through this.

An eternity later, he was finally finished. As soon as he pulled away, I got off the bed and ran to the bathroom to throw up. He came in and wet a washcloth to clean himself up.

"Quit being so goddamn dramatic, Gabby. It wasn't that bad," he said as he looked down at me with obvious disdain.

I hated when he called me that and he knew it. "Get out," I said, but it was so low that he didn't understand me. I was hoarse from screaming.

"What's that?"

I pushed up to stand on shaky legs. With clenched fists, I swallowed to wet my throat and repeated, "Get out."

"What the fuck is wrong with you?"

He was genuinely confused and didn't know why I was upset. "Get out, Frank, and don't come back," my demand was stronger.

He laughed at me. The mother fucker actually laughed at me. When he saw I was serious, he sneered and, without warning, backhanded me. The blow took me by surprise and knocked me off balance. I hit the wall and slid to the floor.

He pulled back a foot and kicked me. The wind was knocked out of me. *Sonofabitch, it feels like he cracked a rib.* I gasped, trying to get my breath back.

"What did I tell you about talking to me that way? Fuck, you really are stupid."

"Get out," I wheezed from the floor, "Get out!" I lamely swiped a foot at him, my voice rising as the tears started again. "Get out or I'm going to call the cops and tell them you assaulted me."

"Whatever," he said, dismissing my threat. "Get over yourself. You need me and you know it." I sagged with relief when I heard him slam the door as he left.

I got back onto my feet and looked at myself in the mirror. My cheekbone was angry red close to my eye, and I figured I'd have a black eye by the morning. Once I cleaned myself up, I used a mirror to see how much damage Frank had done with his backdoor assault.

Thankfully, I wasn't as bad as I had feared. I treated the area with some cream, washed my hands, washed my face, then went back to bed, even though I doubted I would sleep anymore that night.

As I lay awake in bed after Frank left, I had an epiphany. Morgan was right.

The next morning, I went into the office early to avoid seeing anyone in the building. I didn't want to show off the shiner Frank had given me the night before when he backhanded me. Although I was sore, I still didn't think anything was bad enough to warrant a visit to the hospital. At least I hoped not.

I left a letter of resignation on Frank's desk and gathered up my few personal belongings. After a moment's hesitation, I also took some files that were mine.

For the past few years, I had done all the design work, as well as all the technical drawings. Frank might have had all of the contacts in the beginning, but he hadn't brought anyone new in for a long time.

Every project we had won over the past three or four years had been because of my efforts, because Frank had stopped showing up. Word of mouth from clients satisfied with my work had drawn new clients in.

He might have served a purpose in my fucked up brand of sexual crazy, but last night Frank had gone too far. It was time to cut ties personally and professionally.

Chapter 1

Gabriella

It's right there, hovering on the edge of my senses, waiting for just the right moment to overtake me. Casually, taking my time, I move his hand upward. First, placing it on my breast.

His touch is enthusiastic there, squeezing and molding the flesh. Although enthusiastic, it's too gentle. Placing my hand over his, I try to firm his touch, but he moves his hand to my shoulder, resisting the guidance.

This puts me that much closer to my goal. I pull his hand to my lips and kiss it, then pull it down, gently putting it on my neck and letting it rest there. After a few heartbeats, I put my hand over his and squeeze.

He freezes. Just stops. Stops moving, stops fucking me, and he might even stop breathing. Then there's a flurry of motion.

I roll to get out of the bed as Dwayne does the same on the other side, moving away from me as quickly as he can. "For fuck's sake, Gabriella, I told you I'm not into that shit." He starts getting dressed, his anger palpable in the room.

"I know. Sorry. I won't do it again." I had hoped that he would warm up to the idea and could do at least some things I need when it comes to sex. Obviously not.

Shame rolls over me like it always does. I hate myself in these moments, but my history is something that is not easily overcome. If I could flip a switch and make myself normal, I would do it in a heartbeat. Instead, I stay broken and unable to move on.

"That's what you said last time. You should go find some BDSM club to hang out at. Maybe then you'll find someone who's into that weird stuff."

He sits on the bed to put his shoes on. I sit on the other side of the bed, my head hung low. There's a pause before he opens the door and I look up, hopeful.

His head drops and his shoulders sag. Without looking at me, with a low voice, he says, "Lose my number, Gabriella." Then he leaves. Another one gone.

I should probably feel sad, but as usual, once the shame fades, I just feel numb. And empty.

You've blown it again, Gabs, you stupid, ridiculous idiot. At this rate, you're going to fuck your way through the whole of Oklahoma City in no time and probably still end up alone because you can't find anyone to put up with your shit.

It has been almost three years since that last night with Frank and replacing him sexually has been more difficult than I had expected. Unbeknownst to Dwayne, I've been to plenty of BDSM clubs.

However, it seems that most of the men who think they're a Dominant really just want to be justified in treating someone like crap all the time and calling it a lifestyle. There might be certain things I need, but I refuse to go back to being treated like shit ever again.

With a sigh, I get moving. I might as well shower and go home. Tomorrow is a workday and I'll face it better after sleeping in my own bed.

Standing under the hot water, I try to muster some tears for Dwayne, but I can't. I don't even feel a little bit sad, more than anything, under the numbness, I feel a little relieved.

If I ever did find someone who warmed up to the small things I need, it would eventually lead to needing more. That would mean opening up to them even more and showing another person exactly how fucked up I am is a horrifying thought.

It's so scary that I push it out of my thoughts and run back to safe ideas. If I'm going to have unfulfilling sex, I might as well go back to normal relationships. There is something to be said for being held and having someone to lean on, even if the sex is simply a matter of going through the motions.

I'm good at those motions. I know all the right moves and all the right noises to get them off and make them think I'm right there with them, even though I don't actually feel a thing.

That's it. I'll go back to boring, blah, vanilla. In fact, there's a guy I've been putting off meeting. He didn't seem to be my type at all, but maybe I should give him a chance.

I dry off and dress, trading the sexy lingerie and professional dress I came into the room wearing for comfy yoga pants and an oversized sweater. After one last circuit of the room, I am sure I have all my things and stuff it all into my overnight bag. Leaving the key cards on the nightstand, I go into the hallway and head for the side exit of the hotel where no one will see my departure.

When I get home, I email Ralph, the guy who's been wanting to meet, and set up a time to say hello over drinks. I choose a bar across town rather than near my neighborhood.

I like to keep a little distance until I know a little something about them. A short meet and greet will give us both a chance to see if there's any level of connection, but mostly gives me a chance to start to make sure they are who they say they are.

It probably shouldn't, but it still surprises me how many people on online dating sites out-and-out lie and then try to make excuses when they're found out. I mean, we were all cute when we were twenty.

However, trying to pass yourself off as looking exactly the same when you're twice that age and sometimes twice that weight now is ridiculous. Also, if you're supposedly pulling in over six figures a year, why are you still living in your mom's basement and can't afford gas money to show up to a meeting?

Why is it so difficult to find someone?

Chapter 2

Gabriella

I show up at the Belladonna Society the next evening to have dinner with friends. Five of us met during orientation our first night as members of the club and have kept a running engagement to have dinner on Thursday evenings as often as possible. Sometimes it is all of us, but most often, it's just Caitlyn Foster and me.

Cait and I are the only ones without extensive family commitments to draw us away from the weekly date. Caitlyn is recently widowed and all her children are grown, strewn to various parts of the country. She has a boyfriend, but as a detective for the OKCPD, he stays busy much of the time.

I'm married to my job and haven't had children. Yet. If ever. Because I had such a screwed-up childhood, I often think it will be best if I don't ever have kids.

I would probably screw them up, too. However, one thing I do know is that I would never treat them as if they were unwanted or like an outsider in their own family. I struggled with that aspect of my childhood for years and finally cut ties with my family because of it.

I see Cait wave at me from our table. It looks like it will be just her and me again. That's okay with me. I enjoy Cait's company.

Over the past few months, we've become fast friends. She's about ten years older than me, although you'd never know it by looking at her, and she's starting to feel a bit like an older sister.

Cait is elegant and classy. She comes from money, but she's not pretentious at all. Women like her are the reason I joined the Society. I wanted to build connections and friendships with women of quality, and it's turning out better than I'd hoped.

She rises and hugs me when I reach our table. "Good evening, Ella! That red is a gorgeous color on you."

"Thank you Cait," I say as I take a seat next to her at the table. "You look lovely, as always. I hope you haven't been waiting long."

"Not at all. I came in early to exercise so I've been relaxing with a glass of wine. It's been nice to just sit and be still for a little while. I feel like I have been running full steam ahead for weeks now, trying to track down a house."

"A house?" I ask, surprised. "I know you and Ford have been looking for a house, but it sounds like you have something specific in mind."

"Yes. I have loved living with Ford, and he was so gracious to have me move in when my house sold..." She tapers off and pauses.

"But..." I prompt.

She lets out a breath. "But his place is great for a bachelor or even a young couple starting out. However, for the two of us, it is small, and he's had some objection to every home we've looked at possibly buying. He says he doesn't care and that I should just pick one, but I hate to do that. I want it to be our place, something that suits both of us, not just me. I've asked him about the places he grew up in to get an idea of the type of house he might like, but the last house he remembers is his grandparent's home."

"Is it in this area?" I ask.

"It is, but he doesn't remember where. He was just a small boy when his grandparents passed away and all he can remember is that it wasn't far from Oklahoma City, somewhere on the outskirts of town."

I know a few things about land records and might have a few tricks to track the house down if she has some basic information for me.

"Do you know his grandparent's names?"

She brightens. "I do. There must be a way to find it through the information I have, but I have no idea how."

I put my hand over hers, then pull a notepad out of my purse.

"That's okay, I do. Give me their names and I'll see what I can find at the County Clerk's office."

"Oh, Ella! I would be so appreciative of anything you can discover."

"Leave it to me and I'll see what I can dig up."

We linger after dinner for a while. I can tell that Cait isn't eager to go home. She says that Ford is in the middle of a big case and is gone quite a bit. I don't have anything or anyone to go home to, either, but eventually we get up and head toward the door.

She links her arm in mine as we walk.

"Oh! I almost forgot," Cait says, "are you available on Saturday evening? The charity I work with is revealing a project house they want to remodel to be a safe house of sorts. It will be for women transitioning out of dangerous or difficult situations."

"I remember you tell me about it."

"Yes. I intended to let you know once they started the bidding process for the rehab, but they'll be showing a preview at the dinner. With Ford tied up and unable to go, you might as well get a first look at it. If you're available, that is, and interested."

Her look is almost sheepish that she had almost forgotten to ask me.

"Sure, as much as I hate to admit it, my Saturday night is free," I laugh. "I'd love to go with you. What's the dress code?"

"It's just a dinner so not formal," she replies, "men in suits and women in pretty dresses, but more cocktail or business than super fancy. If you still have that coral red one, that would be perfect, and the color is beautiful on you."

Again, I laugh. "I'll keep that in mind. I think it might be in my dry cleaning pile, but that gives me an idea of what to replace it with, if needed."

As we walk through the area Cait calls the lounge, I see the fortune teller machine in the corner. "What do you think of that?" I ask Cait, waving a hand at the machine.

She shrugs. "I don't know if it is for real or not, but I asked it for something, and it happened."

My eyebrows try to climb up to my hairline. "What did you ask for?"

She takes a deep breath but doesn't speak for a moment. "If I tell you, promise me you'll never to tell another soul." She looks around to ensure no one else is nearby.

"I promise," I lean in and say low.

"That first night when we came to orientation, I told it my deepest desire. I told it I wished my husband were dead. I didn't truly bear him any ill will, it's just that I'd been racking my brain to figure out how to end things without breaking our prenup and had been thinking that death would be the only way I'd ever get him to let go."

"Really? You said you wished he would die?"

She nods. "I got a card from the machine that said, '*The question you ponder, the answer you'll find, when the story you've started begins to unwind.*' I had just met Ford and begun speaking with him when things were just beginning to come to a head with Benjamin. A few weeks later, Ford and I were involved, and Benjamin snuck into the house through the garage and attacked me; it was like he was crazed. In self-defense, I grabbed a knife and stabbed him. Just as I had wished, my husband was dead. I never dreamed it would be by my hand, but he was dead nonetheless."

"Ho-ly shit," I reply.

She laughs.

"Sorry," I say.

She pats my arm, still chuckling. "It's fine. I'm not that strait-laced. You should hear Ford when he gets going. I cannot believe with certainty that there is a direct correlation between the wish and Benjamin's death, but it is an interesting coincidence. I'm not saying you should wish someone dead, but if there's something you want, it can't hurt."

She stops, giving me a chance to decide. I drop her arm and walk over to the machine. I take a deep breath, trying to get the words right in my head before speaking them out loud. I press the button and speak to the machine, "I wish I could find someone who could love me, even the broken parts."

The machine clicks and whirs before a card pokes out of a slot in the front. I pull it out and read the message. *The love of your life will appear in front of you unexpectedly.*

I return to Cait. "Well?" she asks.

"Is it like a birthday wish where you're not supposed to tell anyone?"

"I have no idea," she says.

"Well, maybe I shouldn't take chances. If it comes true, I'll tell you what it was."

"Deal. You're right, best not to take chances on jinxing it."

Chapter 3

Mr. Smith

"Mr. Smith, your table is ready," the attractive hostess says. I act surprised, as if she has pulled me out of some deep contemplation of life's mysteries. The smile I give her is tentative, signaling my insecurity about talking to someone so appealing.

With that heart-shaped face and its pouty pink lips, she is quite lovely. Her loveliness does nothing for me, though. She's too young and still too grounded in her boyish frame for my liking.

However, I can tell she's already learning the art of using her captivating face and fair form to her advantage. A small pout or a flirtatious glance and this little coquette can probably get anything she wants from any man with a heartbeat. Not from me, though.

My tastes are more refined than the imaginings of a nubile, barely legal, damsel fulfilling my every whim in return for whatever she desires. I've had those encounters, but they grow tiresome oh, so quickly.

As she weaves through the crowded hotel restaurant, I mark my surroundings and the other diners. To everyone watching,

I appear to be a bit unsure, even bumbling as I am shown to my table. I appear oblivious, but in reality, I am taking note of everyone in the room.

They're the ones oblivious to the prey among the sheep. If they knew who I really was, their looks of contempt and pity would turn to fear. A few of the weaker ones might even lose their bladders from terror if they knew the kind of man I am and what I've done.

I have been here many times and I know the placement of every chair and table, every door, every exit. Not a single person on the staff would be able to point me out, though. Particularly not in a police lineup. How could the timid, weak man I appear to be ever do something like harm a fly, much less another person?

I almost laugh out loud at that thought, but I don't. That would bring unwanted attention, and my invisibility shield would be shattered. The hostess stops by a two top table, and I turn to gauge the position.

"Might I have that table instead?"

I point to a different two top a couple of seats down. It would provide a much better view, but it's also on the end next to a wall which would mean fewer people to keep in my awareness. In addition, it's what most diners would label as a less-desirable seat, so she happily agrees.

I sit, pretend to study the menu for a moment, although I know exactly what I'll be ordering, then pull out a book. Here I am, a poor, lonely, middle-aged man dining alone with only a paperback book for company. I could be on business, or I could just be a loser. No one will guess who or what I truly am.

I am also not Mr. Smith, but what better name to use when you want to fade into the background, but Jim Smith? It is essential that I go unnoticed. However, bland, is my superpower, especially when I'm Mr. Smith.

I push my glasses up on my nose and pretend to read. I have eaten my mediocre meal, nursed my drink, and not read almost a chapter when she arrives. She's the lady in blue tonight and I should never have been concerned about missing her.

I set down my book and take out my phone as if I've just gotten an urgent message that needs my attention. In reality, I take a few photos of her. She truly is beautiful, but she will be even more beautiful by the time I'm done with her. Beauty will be replaced with never-ending perfection.

Her escort for the evening approaches her at the bar, but he isn't her usual sort. This one looks like he belongs behind a computer writing code for some tech company or categorizing beans as an accountant.

Her every mannerism says she's not interested. That's my cue. I know she won't be sneaking upstairs once her date has secured them a room for the night, as usual.

I get my server's attention and wave him over. Before I get up to leave, I hand him enough cash for my ticket and a generous, but not too generous, tip. A glance at my watch signals I might be late to make it to an urgent appointment.

In reality, it's my excuse for walking briskly, but not too briskly, toward the exit. Striking a balance that says you belong and are purposeful while not standing out is a well-developed skill of mine. I am an expert at it, if I do say so myself.

I slip into the driver's seat of my non-descript four-door sedan and wait. The slightly dirty black Toyota Camry with its license plate obscured with just enough mud to trick the eye is no match for my usual car.

I know white is the most popular car color in the US, but it also stands out at night. Therefore, I forego the opportunity to be one of the most, in order to be one of the many.

Just as I thought, her date is ended quickly, and she leaves the restaurant. She pulls out onto the street. I wait for her to pass along with a car right behind her and maneuver my vehicle onto the road. There's no need to rush because I know where she's going.

Not far behind, I watch as her taillights disappear around the corner into her neighborhood. I slow and allow her plenty of time to get to her house before I drive through, just in time to watch her garage door lower.

A couple of blocks over, I park my car. Once I've traded my sport coat for a dark warm-up jacket and my dress shoes for sneakers, I get out of the car and start back toward her house. I stride with purpose as if I am an upstanding member of the community out for an evening stroll.

It's the gloaming hour, that time when it's not quite light but not quite dark. By the time I cross the two intervening blocks, the darkness has started to spread. I act as if I'm enjoying the colors cast by Mother Nature on darkening blue velvet, but in reality, I'm embracing the dark as it infiltrates the world as it did my heart so long ago.

Chapter 4

Morgan

I cut off another piece of my steak, enjoying the meal. It's not the best I've had, but for a hotel restaurant, it's not bad. I am washing down the steak with a swallow of a truly excellent wine when something catches my eye. Or should I say someone?

There are several beautiful women in the restaurant, but none of them strikes my fancy. It has been a long while since anyone has, but the brunette winding her way to the bar is built just the way I like my women.

I'll never understand how men set aside a woman with curves for the twigs with big fake tits that seem to be so popular these days. Give me a real woman with real curves any day.

I keep tracking the woman, enjoying the view. Her vibrant blue dress screams, "Look at me!" so look at her, I do. When she turns to perch her luscious round ass on a stool at the bar, I'm surprised to discover that I know her. I know who she is, anyway.

The last time we met, she was involved with the loser she was working for. At the time, I was in a relationship, too, but it had been nothing serious.

Her situation, though, was complicated, according to her, so I didn't follow up with her. Based on the guy taking a seat across from her, her relationship status appears to be no longer complicated.

I watch them from across the room. It looks like a first date. Their body language is tentative, but he's leaning in toward her and she's sitting back in her seat. I doubt he gets a second date.

She finishes her drink and must be breaking the news to him if the look on his face is anything to go by. She slips off her stool and heads for the door. I watch as his face morphs from astonished disappointment to something else, something darker. I get up and leave some bills on the table and follow her out the door.

Once outside, I don't catch up to her. I step back around the corner and watch her as she walks down the street. Her date comes out just in time to see her get into her car and pull into traffic. He looks upset, but he walks the opposite direction up the street.

For a moment, I think about following her home. You know, just to make sure she is safe. However, that is just me trying to kid myself. I should have said something to her, reintroduced myself, but if I'd done that, I would have wanted more than just a hello.

Something had sparked in me when I'd seen her. I can't identify it. The response was too visceral, too primal to label. On the surface, my body wanted hers, but it was deeper than just lust, too.

I'll let her go. For now. I wonder if she was the reason someone had suggested I might discover something interesting in this restaurant tonight.

If fate or someone playing the role of fate has made sure I noticed her once, I want to see what else they might engineer. Regardless, what I thought was going to be a boring Friday night has turned out to be something else entirely.

The next night I wait at the bar for my scotch while pulling at my tie to loosen it a millimeter or two. Every time I come to one of these things, I tell myself that next time, I'll forego the tie, but I always end up putting it on again.

I don't hate suits. I'm just never as comfortable in them as I am in a t-shirt, jeans, and a pair of work boots. Give me a hard hat and a hammer over a pen and a necktie any day.

Beckett is standing next to me in line, yammering on about some upcoming project. He's the reason I come to these things. Although I have no great interest in charity, he does.

He serves on a couple of boards and drags me along more often than I care to admit. However, I have to say I've been pleasantly surprised by the amount of business our company has gotten through the connections we've made while attending these events.

"Well, hello red," Beckett says with a low whistle. He also likes the fact that the people attending these events are often wealthy and occasionally beautiful. Beck's sexuality is a bit more fluid than mine, and he tends to be attracted to someone based on factors beyond the equipment they're packing in their pants. He also doesn't need a woman to be a sugar mama or a man to be a sugar daddy, but he says he appreciates an even playing field.

I turn in the direction of his stare. A smile spreads across my face as Gabriella Carmichael crosses the room. Seeing her twice in as many days is making me a very happy man.

She's traded her blue dress for a red one that shows off every curve. I give into my baser self for a moment and imagine what she looks like without it. I feel my cock twitch and pull back on the reins before everyone in the room has clear evidence of my attraction.

She stops beside a woman who looks to be a little older than her, closer to my age. The woman brightens and gives Gabriella a hug.

"That's Gabriella Carmichael," I tell my brother. "Remind me who that is that she's talking to. I know I've met her before, but that's about it. We didn't get a chance to talk when we met." Beckett knows everyone at these things and usually everything about them.

"Caitlyn Foster, her family was in manufacturing until a little over twenty years ago. Her father sold the business after her mother died, then he passed away a few years later. Rumor is that she's valued in the nine-figure range. Cait killed her husband last year."

I remember meeting Cait previously, but it was a few years ago. I turn my head to see if he's joking about her killing her husband, but he is only taking a sip of his drink. Once he swallows, he elaborates.

"It was ruled self-defense. He was hopped up on something, I don't remember what, and attacked her. She stabbed him and he died." He shrugs as he pauses for another drink. "How do you know...what was it? Carmella?"

"Gabriella. Gabriella Carmichael," I correct. "I met her once, but I'm thinking I need to reacquaint myself."

"Met her once? So, there's no connection, right? Fair game?"

I look at him and narrow my eyes. Just the thought of my brother touching her makes me want to lay him out on the floor. "No. Not fair game. She's mine."

He raises an eyebrow at me, making me want to hit him all the more. I clench my fist, but instead of making a scene, I decide to make my move. I leave my brother standing with a shit-eating grin on his face and surrender to the magnetic pull of Gabriella Carmichael.

Chapter 5

Morgan

"Hello."

She turns at the sound of my voice. "Oh. Hello," she says. I'm not sure how to interpret the look on her face. Surprise? Definitely, but there's more swimming in the depths of her gorgeous brown eyes. After a pause she says, "It's been a while."

My lips tip up. "It has. Almost three years."

For a moment, I'm lost in those eyes. The other woman she met moves next to her, breaking the spell, and I watch Gabriella's cheeks turn pink.

Flustered, she says, "Forgive my manners. This is my friend, Caitlyn Foster. She's one of the board members. Cait, this is..."

I'm not sure if she remembers my name, so I hold out my hand, "Morgan Masters. It's very nice to see you again, Cait."

Cait beams at me as she shakes my hand. "I know we have met before, but it was some time ago. Masters...Are you any relation to Beckett Masters?"

"He is the significantly older, much less attractive Masters brother," my brat of a little brother says as he approaches.

"Beckett!" Cait exclaims as she greets him. He leans in and kisses her on the cheek. "It's so good to see you. Have you met Ella?"

Beckett smiles and takes Gabriella's hand in his. I feel my blood pressure rise.

"I have not." He kisses the back of her hand. I know he's doing it to yank my chain, but I'm back to wanting to punch him and wipe that smug smile off his face. "It's a pleasure to meet you, Ella. How do you know my ugly old brother?"

She pulls her hand from his. *Good girl.*

"Actually, if it weren't for your brother, I wouldn't be where I am today." Her comment surprises me.

"Oh?" Beckett asks, a sly grin spreading. "Do tell."

She looks up at me and then away as if she can't bring herself to hold my gaze. Is she shy? That's not an impression I'd had the last time we met.

"Well, when we met, I was working for someone, and it was a situation that was quickly becoming in tolerable. He said some things to me that day," she says to Beckett.

She takes a breath as if to steel herself and looks back up at me. "Those words from you were the spark that led to a lot of change for me. I quit that job the next day and went out on my own. Three years later, I have my own business." She puts her hand on my arm and it feels warm and right. "I can't ever thank you enough."

I smile softly. "I knew you had it in you. You just needed a little push."

She drops her eyes and lets out a huff. "I'm glad someone did, because I didn't."

"I think they're ready to start the dinner," Cait says, touching Gabriella's arm.

"Come sit at our table," Beckett says, tucking Cait's hand into the crook of his elbow. "You and I need to catch up."

"I guess we're sitting with you," Gabriella smiles up at me.

Maybe I won't punch my brother after all. I motion for her to precede me and put my hand on the small of her back as we move through the crowd.

Beckett and I sit at the table with the women between us. Four other people sit at the table. They're all colleagues or employees who regularly attend these types of events, so I introduce them to Gabriella.

The dinner is served, but it's the typical the dry chicken meal that doesn't appeal to me. I'll get something to eat afterward. I watch Gabriella from the corner of my eye and based upon her reaction as she chews her first bite, she's not impressed either. Maybe I'll be able to convince her to have dinner with me.

Beckett leans toward the middle of our group as he pushes his untouched plate away. "I say we head over to Red Prime when this is over and get some proper food. Cait, Ella, you all game? Morgan's treat."

I can't help the snort that escapes me. Beckett is redeeming himself from being punched again.

Cait looks at Gabriella. "I don't know why we even bother to serve food at these things; no one eats it. What do you think, Ella? You up for dinner after?"

She looks over at me and licks her lips. I can't help but notice and raise an eyebrow, wondering if the enticement is intentional. I guess she likes what she sees because she turns back to Cait with a nod and a smile.

"Sure, I'm game."

"Good," I offer my approval.

"We could sneak out now," Beckett says.

"No!" Cait replies. "I want Ella to see the project house."

Gabriella perks up at that. "Oh, yeah! I almost forgot that you mentioned a house when you asked me to come."

As if hearing his cue, the Chairperson for the organization takes the stage and starts the presentation. As soon as the first photo of the house is brought up on screen, Gabriella is rapt. She leans forward in her chair and sucks in a deep breath.

I could swear I hear her whisper, "Hello beautiful."

A smile tilts my lips and I notice Cait watching Gabriella, too, with a big grin on her face. I continue to watch Gabriella, fascinated by her reaction to a possible project. She is entranced and I can almost see the wheels in her brain spinning with all the possibilities.

When the presentation is over, some people start to move around again while others stay seated at tables. "I say we make our escape now," says Beckett, and I couldn't agree more.

We're in the elevator when Cait's phone rings. She pulls it out of her bag and looks at the caller ID. "Sorry, but it's Ford. I'd better take it." She accepts the call and puts the phone to her ear. Because of the enclosed space, we get to hear her side of the conversation.

"Hi Honey."

"I'm in the elevator leaving the hotel."

"You know it wasn't."

"Oh, I was headed to have dinner with the Masters brothers and Ella."

Beckett leans over and says loud enough to carry through the phone. "Come with us, Ford, Morgan's buying."

Cait laughs and looks at me. I give her an affirmative nod. If Cait goes to dinner somewhere else with her boyfriend, Gabriella would likely go with them, and I want her with me. I still need to get reacquainted.

Ford arrives at the restaurant a few minutes after we do. Cait introduces him. "Ford, you know Beckett and Ella. This is Beckett's brother Morgan Masters."

I shake the other man's hand. "Morgan, I'm Ford Pickering. Nice to meet you."

"Same," I nod. He has a good handshake.

"You and your brother run Masters Construction, right?" Ford asks.

"We have a younger brother, Kellen, who's involved, too, but yes, that's our company. Beckett's the talker, so he's the sales and marketing guy. Kellen has a knack for numbers, so he's the finance guy. I oversee all the general operations and construction teams. What is it you do?"

"I'm a Homicide Detective with OKCPD."

I nod. It seems I remember catching a bit of conversation about that between Beckett and Cait. I need to start paying more attention at those charity dinners.

"Party of five?" the hostess calls behind me.

At the table, I make sure I'm sitting next to Gabriella.

"Ford, are you working on that serial killer case?" Beckett asks. For someone who likes to talk, sometimes I'm amazed at his lack of tact.

"Beck..." I start.

Ford waves a hand. "It's all right. Yeah, I am, but that's all I can say about it. That's also why I won't be having anything other than iced tea to drink because I may get called back in. I'm waiting for some test results to come in."

"Nothing, huh? Not one single nugget of information?" Beckett pushes good naturedly.

"Nope," Ford shakes his head with an amicable smile.

The server arrives and takes our orders.

"So, what did you think of the house?" Cait asks Gabriella once we settle again.

"It has the potential to be truly beautiful. Just from the pictures, I have so many ideas. However, I don't think I'll be able to put in a bid."

"Oh, no, why not?" Cait asks with concern.

"The design part would be no problem, but my construction team has projects stacked up for months. However, even if they didn't, I don't think they'd be able to handle something so large and requiring such a high level of craftsmanship. Queen Annes are beautiful, but all that beauty comes from the frilly details and that takes an artistry beyond just framing and drywall."

She shrugs, but I can tell how disappointed she is.

A crazy idea sparks and before I have too much time to talk myself out of it, I ask, "What if you partnered with us?" The question earns me a look from Beckett. I return his look.

"Brenda's out on maternity leave and it's looking like she might not return," I remind him. "We have some junior designers, but no one close to her ability. Without her, we'd have to contract it out. Why let some contract person we barely know have the accolade of the project? I think a collaboration between Gabriella's company and ours would be a better approach."

"Makes sense to me," Beckett says with a shrug.

If it doesn't have to do with making a deal, Beckett doesn't much care. Then there's Kellen who cares about every little thing with me stuck between them, trying to balance it all. As much as I enjoy having a successful company, there are a lot of days when I wish I could go back to just pounding nails.

"What do you think, Ella?" Cait asks.

Gabriella is looking at me, a confused look on her face. "It seems as if you're making a big presumption with that statement, like it's a given that your company will be awarded the project. Besides, how do you even know my designs would be any good?"

"I've seen your designs, remember? The work you did on the Sanderson project was excellent, and I can't imagine you've gotten worse over the past three years."

"Oh, yes. I forgot about that," she says as she looks down.

"Sanderson? When did we do a Sanderson project?" Beckett asks.

"Three years ago," I tell him. I'm watching Gabriella, but she's still looking at her lap.

Our food gets delivered, breaking the moment and the conversation lightens. I lean over to Gabriella and whisper conspiratorially.

"To help you decide, if you want to get an in-person look at the place, I can arrange that. I went out there with the structural engineer to inspect the house before the purchase was completed. I know the code to the key lock on the door." Unable to help myself, I linger, inhaling the scent of her perfume.

She looks up at me, her eyes round and full of excitement, and whispers back. "Really? You won't get in trouble?"

"Sure. I don't want to push you, but maybe an up-close look will help you decide. Plus, Beckett is on the Board, so it gives me a little leeway." I say with a wink.

She smirks. "Trying to seduce me with coffered ceilings and wood paneling, eh?"

There she is. That fire and spark that I saw in her three years ago seemed to be missing all evening except when she was engrossed in the presentation showing pictures of the house. I grin back.

"Something like that. Is it working?"

The smile she gives me lights up her entire face, and I have to check myself to keep from leaning over and kissing her. "Maybe," she teases and bumps my shoulder. I'm glad she's finally starting to relax.

"Well, if house porn is your thing, I've got plenty." I waggle my eyebrows at her, and she laughs.

Chapter 6

Gabriella

I walk around the outside of the house, taking pictures of the exterior while waiting for Morgan to arrive. At first, I wasn't sure I had the right location. The driveway was long, and I couldn't see the house from the road, but when I topped a small knoll and saw the grand damme sprawling against a rise, I gasped at the picturesque setting.

Why someone would build a house like this out in the country is beyond me. The sprawl of the metro area will overtake it eventually, but this area in the rolling hills east of Edmond and past Arcadia would have been quite remote when the house was constructed. However remote, the site is lovely despite the obvious neglect over the past few years.

I think about the presentation the night before and to say the pictures did not do her justice is an understatement. Last night was fun. Not the first part. I hate those kinds of events with a bunch of well to do people. I never know how to act. Once we went to dinner, I felt much more comfortable. The smaller group was easier, fewer people to keep track of.

I am not the dirt-poor little girl I used to be, but growing up had been an ongoing exercise in figuring things out on my own.

Feeling completely comfortable in social situations is something I never quite mastered.

Even with my peers, I feel awkward and unsure. Although I've learned to fake being confident on the outside while inside, I'm a nervous wreck.

In a group of people my mother would have called my betters, I feel like I've been dropped into a culture where I didn't know the language or the customs. I'm still amazed every day that Cait wants to be my friend because we are from two very different worlds.

"There you are."

I jump, startled, my hand flying up to my chest to make sure my heart doesn't burst through. "Oh! I was lost in thought and didn't hear you drive up."

Morgan's lips quirk. "House porn?"

I grin back at him. I can't help it. This less-serious, playful guy is much less intimidating. "Something like that."

I look him up and down. We're dressed similarly in jeans, brown work boots and red t-shirts. The only difference is mine has long sleeves.

I chuckle. "I guess we both got the dress code memo."

The ink on his arms is on display. I'd forgotten about noticing it when we met the first time. I'm itching to get a better look at it, but pull my eyes away.

His gaze on me is back to being intense, the laser beams in full force. I stop myself from taking a step back. My confident and teasing demeanor has morphed to shy and intimidated in five seconds flat.

Although I struggle in groups, since I figured out the power of boobs and a pretty smile, I have been pretty self-assured when dealing with men one on one...at least until we get into the bedroom. Morgan Masters completely throws me off my game, especially when he's looking at me like he is now.

I hate that I have to use my assets with men. It would be nice if we could just interact person to person with the respect that any living creature is due, but that just isn't reality. Men on the construction side of my business continually try to bully me or treat me as if I'm stupid or an easy lay, so I don't feel bad about using a smile to disarm someone occasionally.

"I guess we did," he says. "Do you need more time outside, or are you ready to go in?"

"I think I've captured every square inch of the exterior already, so let's go inside."

Morgan unlocks the door and lets me go in first. I take a few steps in and stop. All the photos in the presentation were muted and now I know why. The interior looks as if someone had decided to turn the place into a bed-and-breakfast styled after a technicolor bordello.

"Oh my God, honey, what did they do to you?"

Morgan steps in behind me. "Huh? Are you calling me honey?"

His tone is teasing, but my cheeks warm. Houses, especially old ones like this one, are like people to me.

They're alive, breathing, and have their own personalities and histories. Sometimes I talk to them, but usually I'm alone. It was love at first sight and I forgot Morgan was here.

"No sorry, I was calling the house honey. You said a structural engineer has already gone through the place, right?"

"Yes. She has a clean bill of health. Most of the refurbishing will be cosmetic, but there is some water damage in one of the bathrooms upstairs, so be careful up there because the floor is weak in a few places."

"Got it. Do you have basic floor plans with measurements already?"

"Yes. I'll email those to you."

"Thank you. That saves me some time. Just so you know," I wave my cell phone in the air, "I'm going to be recording."

"You just do what you do, and I'll tag along in case you have questions."

"Perfect," I tell him, but my attention is all for the house.

Once I restart the recorder on my phone, I begin talking about what I'm seeing as I take pictures. I get lost in it. This is the part I love most, the envisioning of the possibilities, seeing how a house can be the best version of itself.

Because the house has already been refit from its original purpose as a private home into a bed-and-breakfast, there are already plenty of bedrooms and bathrooms.

I can see the original parlor being remade into a multi-purpose room that could be used for anything from a classroom to a conference room. The office wouldn't take much to make it a secure space for the leadership and staff.

I keep moving from room to room, taking my time to investigate all the nooks and crannies. Morgan's presence is always there in the periphery, but true to his word, he lets me amble around as I please. I see the damage that he mentioned and when I start testing boards before putting my full weight on them, I feel him move closer.

The house has the potential to be a dream, a fairytale, and that's what I want to make it. I want it to be a magical place for the women who need to come here. There's no way my crew could carry out the plans that are taking form in my mind.

If I want this project, I'll have to do it with Morgan's construction team. Or one of them, anyway. From the sound of it, he has enough people working for them to have several crews out on jobs for Masters Construction.

I should have taken the time between last night and this morning to look up information about their company. Besides being nice to look at when their laser beam eyes aren't focused on me, the brothers must be pretty good at the whole construction thing. That's the area where I am lacking the most in my business.

I love the design side of the business. However, I have no great love of construction other than enjoying seeing it done well. I only have my own crew because I grew tired of fighting with the owners of the companies I'd try to hire for my projects.

They all tried to treat me like I was some dumb woman and either tried to fuck me or fuck me over. Usually, if I didn't let them do the former, which I never did, they'd try to do the latter.

I'm looking up at the ceiling along the upper landing when my boot catches on an uneven floorboard. My hand reaches out to grab the railing that overlooks the first floor, but the dry wood cracks loudly.

My balance falters and I start to tumble toward the open air. The next thing I know, my back is against the wall on the other side of the landing, with Morgan's hands on my upper arms. Both of us are breathing hard.

The laser beam eyes are back, and they're topped by a scowling brow. "Umm...there might be some dry rot..."

His lips crash down on mine before I can finish what I had intended to be a joke. His hands let go of my arms. I'm sure I'll have bruises.

However, considering if he hadn't grabbed me, I'd likely be a bloody splatter on the wood floors below, I'm okay with a few marks. His kiss started hard and forceful driven by adrenaline, but it turns softer, sweeter. He wraps his arms around me and pulls me even closer.

He breaks the kiss and, with a hand to the back of my head, tucks it against his chest. His heart is pounding. I reach up a shaking hand and lay my palm flat against a hard pec.

"Are you okay?" I ask.

"Yeah." His answer rumbles through his chest. "You just gave me a scare."

"You and me both. I promise it wasn't intentional."

He doesn't seem to want to let me go and, considering I'm still shaking a little, I'm totally okay with that. After a few moments, he takes a deep breath and loosens his hold.

"You okay?" he asks.

I smooth down my shirt. "Yeah. Thanks for saving my life."

I'm still shaking but decide to make light of the situation.

"What is that old Chinese proverb about saving someone's life? If you save someone's life, their life belongs to you, or you're responsible for them?"

He gives me an odd look.

"I'm joking! One of my brothers took martial arts for about a minute but became obsessed with Bruce Lee and that old television show with...what's his name? He was in Kill Bill, too."

I think for a moment but am still drawing a blank.

"It will probably come to me in a dream and wake me up at 2 AM. Anyway, the guy in the show, Grasshopper, used that proverb in just about every other episode. At least that's how it seemed to me because he was continually saving someone from something with his mad kung fu skills."

"You have brothers?" he asks.

I hesitate. Better to stick to the bare truth than dump my family drama onto someone I barely know. "I do. I have two older brothers and a younger half-sister, but we're not close."

"I see."

Thankfully, he doesn't push, so I don't elaborate. "I think I've gotten all the information I need to get started on the design work."

Chapter 7

Gabriella

"Good. I heard your stomach start growling about a half hour ago. How about I take you to a late lunch? You know, since either you owe me your life or I'm responsible for you now." His mouth quirks up on one side.

"Considering you spent a boatload of money on dinner last night, trooped all the way out here this morning and saved my life, why don't you let *me* take *you* to lunch?"

"Sure, but I'm driving and we're having chicken."

I laugh. "All right then."

I climb into his truck surprised to find it to be super clean, like he just took it to the detailer clean. Most construction guys' work trucks I've been in have been a mess of dirt and tools and unidentifiable paraphernalia.

He navigates down the long drive and pulls a remote out of one of the cup holders to close the gate. I'm relieved because I was a little concerned about leaving my car there even if it can't be seen from the road.

Instead of turning back toward the metro area, he turns east, toward the next small town down the road. "Oh, chicken...and

Luther. I've heard about that place but never been," I say, a little excited. I love trying out new food places.

"Yep. Best damn chicken you'll ever have. Beckett still claims that Eischen's is better, but I like the Shack. You can be the deciding vote."

"I've never been to Eishen's either," I admit.

He looks over at me. "What?"

I shrug. Because I work so much, I don't go out to eat a lot. The restaurants around my office, I know well. The rest of the metro, not so much.

"Damn woman, your fried food knowledge is seriously lacking. We're going to have to do something about that."

I chuckle. "I guess so."

We're quiet for a few moments when I remember my thought from last night.

"Last night, it seemed you were pretty confident that your company will win the bid. Why is that?"

"We're bidding to do the construction for the cost of materials."

I suck in a breath. That's not at all what I expected to hear. "Wow. That's very generous."

He shrugs. "We'll use the donated labor costs as a tax writeoff. This is the perfect size project to do it with. If you decide to partner with us, you could still bid whatever you wanted for the design portion, and we'll present it as a collaborative bid. Even if you charge your normal fees, I don't foresee anyone else doing a no labor cost bid."

"I can see why you're so confident, then. I doubt anyone else could match you, either."

"Tell me about your business."

I shrug. "It's a lot like Frank's was. I tried to just do the design side of things, but dealing with the construction companies was exhausting."

He nods. "Yeah, there are a lot of construction guys that give us all a bad name."

"You're right," I say with a chuckle. "I can't tell you how many times I've had to move a man's hand off my ass. If I had a dollar for every time I turned them down for a date just to get told I'm a stuck-up bitch, I'd be rich."

The steering wheel creaks. When I look over, his knuckles are white and I wonder what he's thinking. He doesn't give me a chance to answer.

"But now you have your own crew, right?" he asks.

"Sort of. I love the design side of things and hate the construction part, but I do have a small crew of guys with solid fundamental skills, but that's all I can afford so far. Recently, I brought in a guy that I thought I could develop into a construction manager. Later, I found out he started telling everyone we were partners in more ways than one and cutting side deals using my guys while pocketing the money."

"Asshole," Morgan says.

"I agree, but apparently I was the bitch because I 'broke up' with him and cut him out of the company," I reply, bouncing my fingers in the air to emphasize broke up.

Morgan pulls into a gas station. I look skeptically out the window. Other than the giant metal chicken outside, there's nothing to signify that it's a restaurant. I finally notice a menu board next to a sliding window.

"Is this it?" I ask.

He laughs at me. "Come on, woman, where's your sense of adventure?"

"If I die of food poisoning, I'm going to haunt you forever."

We get out of his truck, and he holds open a door to the side of the window that I hadn't noticed. On the other side of the door is a dark, dirt floor enclosed area with tables.

We keep walking to discover farther in that the space opens up to a larger room with rows of long tables. Garage style doors are raised to reveal that beyond are even more tables scattered in an open area laced with twinkle lights that must come on at night. To one side of the open area is a raised platform where a guy is playing music.

I let Morgan take the lead as he goes to a counter on the far side of the dining area. "What do you want to drink?" he asks me.

I move up to the bar to peruse their selection. He smirks down at me. "Want me to get you a step stool?"

The playful side of him is beautiful and I decide to be playful back. I guess there's nothing like a potentially fatal accident to lighten things up. I bump my shoulder against his.

"Hush!" Once I make up my mind, I put my hand on his arm. "I'd like a Blue Moon and a glass of water, please."

"Are there any particular sides you prefer?"

"Sides?"

He points to the menu in front of him on the counter and I lean in to read it. He puts his arm around me and pulls me closer so I can get a better look. "What are we having?" I ask.

"I figured I'd get us a whole chicken and two sides; that'll be more than enough for both of us. I like the wedges, but we can get whatever you like. They don't have anything I won't eat."

"That sounds good. Either okra or onion rings for the other, whichever you like better."

He turns his attention to the gal at the register. "Make the second side the rings and give us a side of okra so she can try it. She'll have a Blue Moon and I'll have a Bud and a shot of Jameson."

"Shot?" I perk up.

He grins down at me. "Want one?"

"Yes, please, and thank you!"

"Got it," the gal says.

He leans down and puts his mouth close to my ear. It sends a shiver through me when he speaks. "There are cups and water over there. If you'll get us both a cup of water and pick us out a table, I'll bring the beers and shots."

I nod. "Sure!"

He gives me a squeeze and lets me go. It surprises me how comfortable I am with him. Instead of watching everything I say and do, it's relaxed and easy. Even his touches don't bother me.

I pick a table in the back close to the raised roll-up door but still under the shade of the roof. Morgan comes to the table with two beers, two shots, and a number on a pole. I watch him as he crosses the room.

He's broad and solidly built but has a grace and purpose of movement about him like his every step is placed exactly where he wants it. I also notice that he's paying attention to everything and everyone.

He sits at the end of the table, not right next to me and not across from me. He sits back in his chair and takes a drink of his beer.

I swirl the shot of whisky in the plastic cup. He picks his up and asks, "What are we toasting?"

"Here's to Delores and her future beauty," I say, raising my cup.

"Delores?"

"The house. I've named her Delores because she's an old school beauty."

He nods and says, "To Delores," as he touches his cup with mine and we both take our shots.

When we get back to the house, the sun is setting and draping the skies in glorious color. I get out of the truck and lean against my car, watching the display as Morgan goes and checks to make sure the house it locked up again. He checked it before he left, but I have to admit I would check it again, too.

The conversation at lunch had been easy around bites of outstanding fried food, and we ended up staying longer than it seemed. I realized too late that he ended up buying our meal again, distracting me by having me get water and a table. I really wasn't upset, but did rib him about it.

He insisted that because he invited me, he paid. I asked him whether I'd pay if I invited him somewhere, but the answer was still that he paid. He had me laughing more than I'd laughed in a long time.

He returns and leans on the car next to me. The lowering sun is bringing a chill with it, causing me to shiver. He puts his arm around me, and I lean into him, taking the warmth he offers. Neither of us speaks.

I have no anxiety with him, particularly when his blue laser beams are focused elsewhere or dancing with laughter. He's just a regular guy, very comfortable in his skin. I really like that he's not afraid to get his hands dirty but can put on a suit and rub elbows with socialites.

He has an air of being in charge without having to posture and throw it in your face. I barely know him, but even standing here in the middle of a field with no one in sight, I feel safe with him.

When the dark overtakes the day, I sigh, feeling sated and content.

"Gabriella," he says, "I'd like to take you out on a date."

"I thought you just did." I elbow him lightly in the side, and I know he can hear the smile in my voice.

He chuckles. "I guess I did. Does that mean I get a goodnight kiss?"

I turn and face him, putting my hands on his waist and can't help but tease a little. "I suppose. It will be a terrible hardship, but how can I refuse after you fed me excellent food twice in two days?"

He has a broad smile as he lowers his mouth to mine.

Chapter 8

Gabriella

I sigh with relief as my last appointment leaves. Hailey, my receptionist, comes in. "So, what do you think?" she asks.

"I don't know. A couple of them seemed okay, but I didn't really feel like I gelled with any of them, and that one guy was ridiculous."

I have been interviewing potential web designers all morning and into the afternoon. My company's website is something I created three years ago, but my technical skills are limited.

It looks dated and only has minimal functionality. Now that we have more consistently positive cash flow, I want to have it updated to be a better reflection of my company.

The problem is that I have a vision in my head and just need someone to carry out the technical application of what I want. Most of the people I spoke with today seemed resistant to working with me and wanted to create something on their own with only general input from me. I don't think my expectations are out of line, so I'll have to keep looking.

One candidate didn't bother to bring in a portfolio or any examples of his work but kept telling me, "I can do whatever you need." When it became clear that he was wasting my time, I started to wrap up the meeting.

He decided to turn his comment from statement to innuendo and eventually said he was really into MILFs. I kicked his ass out and was completely flabbergasted when he hit on Hailey, too, on his way to the door.

"Ew. He was so creepy. I hope you sanitized the chair after he left."

She knows me so well and it makes me laugh. I had, indeed, wiped down the chair with disinfectant when he had left.

Ding!

Hailey goes to see who came in. It sounds like a delivery, so I click into my email to catch up. It must be the UPS guy. Hailey has a crush on him, and I think he must have one on her too based upon the amount of time it takes him to deliver packages.

Ding!

Hailey comes back into my office holding a vase full of flowers. The flowers are bright and colorful and varied and more me than any bouquet of roses could ever be. My eyes go round. "What's that?"

"You tell me," she says with a big shit-eating grin on her face. She sets the vase on the corner of my desk, then hands me the accompanying card.

I open the card and pull out a photo taken up close of the details of beautiful, hand hewn, timber frame joinery. When I turn it over, there's a note in strong, block lettering.

Some house porn for your collection. I enjoyed yesterday. -MM

I bite my lower lip, trying to quell the huge smile trying to spread. I hand Hailey the photo.

She reads the note and fans herself as she adds raised eyebrows and wide eyes to her shit-eating grin. "Oh. My. God. What happened yesterday?"

I give her the highlights version of looking at the house and having lunch after.

"He sounds hot. Is he hot? Tell me he's hot."

I pull up a browser and go to the Masters Construction website and navigate to the company's leadership page. Once I click on the link to Morgan's bio, I turn the screen and show it to her.

She fans herself harder. "Wow. Hot is an understatement. Does he have a brother?"

I click back to the previous page. "He does. He has two, in fact."

Ding!

I pull out the business card Morgan gave me yesterday. With a flurry of nervous butterflies in my stomach, I pick up my phone. I take a breath and dial before I talk myself out of it.

"Hello." The sound of his voice sends shivers down my spine.

"Thank you for the flowers."

"Well, hey there. You're welcome. How's your day going?"

"Terrible," I tease. "I have been interviewing techie people all day and we just don't speak the same language."

He chuckles.

I lower my voice and let it go husky. "I really appreciate the house porn, though. It made my day."

"Porn over flowers, got it."

It's my turn to chuckle. "How's your day been?"

"I can't remember. Everything before about sixty seconds ago has faded away."

"Smooth talker."

"I do my best. What are you up to tonight?"

I sit back in my chair. "Client meeting. A couple has bought one of the older homes in Heritage Hills that hasn't been remodeled in the last twenty years and wants to do a walkthrough with me. Unfortunately, the husband can't be there until 5:30."

"That's too bad," he says. "I was going to have you come over for dinner. I got the last season of *Restored* last week and thought we could stream an episode or two."

I laugh. "I love that show. It's not as good as *This Old House*, but I like his work."

"Ah, a fan of the classics."

"I am. Watching that show on PBS is the whole reason I got into restoring houses."

"All right then. I've got someone with a problem they can't solve on their own, so I'd better get back to work, but I'm serious about taking you out again and I'd prefer sooner than later."

"I don't have anything going on tomorrow night."

"Now, that sounds promising." His voice fades and I hear him call to someone, "Okay, okay, I'm coming!" He comes back to me. "I'm sorry, I've gotta go. I'll talk to you later and we'll make plans, okay?"

"Perfect. Now get back to work."

"Yes, ma'am," he says and disconnects.

For the rest of the day, I can't stop smiling.

I pull up to the Yarborough's house and am surprised to see a familiar truck parked out front. Although I'm confused, I'm not going to read too much into it. I'm let into the house by Mrs. Yarborough, Anita, who leads me into a room where two men are talking.

Morgan is leaning against the fireplace mantle; he looks up when I walk in and raises one eyebrow. I do the same in return, making his lips twitch up.

"Morgan," Anita says, "this is Ms. Carmichael, our designer."

"Yes, Anita, Gabriella and I are acquainted," Morgan replies.

"Oh, well then," Anita says, a bit flustered. "Ms. Carmichael, this is my husband, Joe."

I cross the room and shake hands with Mr. Yarborough. "It's nice to meet you and please, call me Ella."

"Sorry to spring Morgan on you," Joe says, "but when you told me about the backlog for your construction team, I called Morgan. We've known each other for a long time, so I thought he might squeeze us in sooner with one of his crews."

"I see," I reply. "That's not an issue. I am amenable to working with other construction companies." I am actually happy to work with someone like Morgan, particularly since my margins on the build side for me are quite meager compared to the design side.

"Where do we begin?" Anita asks.

"If you'll just show me around to the areas you want to remodel and let me know any thoughts you might have, we'll start there," I smile at Anita. "Do you mind if I take pictures?"

She gives permission, then leads us through the house to the kitchen. As we're walking down the hallway, Morgan steps up next to me. He leans down and whispers, "He called me as I was leaving the office. I had no idea this was where you were going to be, but I can't say I'm disappointed to see you again."

"Good to know," I reply, trying not to smile too much. "I was wondering if you were stalking me or something."

"Nah. I can, though, if you like that sort of thing."

I bark out a laugh, causing Anita to look over her shoulder. "Sorry," I say.

A little over an hour later, Morgan and I walk out to our cars. He takes my notebook from me and puts it on the passenger seat of my car, then closes the door. He turns his back and leans on it, pulling me close. "You up for dinner, or do you need to get home?"

"Why are you always trying to feed me?" I tease, cocking my head to look up at him.

"Well, I enjoy your company and spending time together over a meal seems like a good way to entice you to hang out with me."

He drapes his hands around my waist and stretches out his legs so we're closer to being face to face instead of face to pecs.

He looks at my blouse and rubs the silk between his fingers. "I really like this outfit."

"You don't need food to entice me," I say before I can talk myself out of it. My pulse is hammering ninety miles a minute and I'm sweating despite the cool night air, but this man makes me want to be bold. I want him and I want him to know it, but he scares me, too.

He scares me because he's so great and he seems to like me, but if this goes to the next step, he's going to see how messed up I really am. Once that happens, he'll make some excuse and I'll never see him again.

He kisses me slow and deep. I wrap my arms around his neck and return his kiss, pouring everything I am into it. I think that maybe if I can make the parts outside the bedroom good enough, maybe that will be enough.

He breaks the kiss, breathing hard. "My place is just a few blocks away. We can leave your car here or you can follow me."

Chapter 9

Gabriella

We're riding up the elevator to his apartment and I'm so nervous I think I might pee myself. As usual, when I'm nervous, I start to chatter. "You built this building?"

He has his arm around me, holding me close to his side. As if he can sense my unease, he squeezes me lightly.

"Yes. It was the first project where I was the lead. My father had been holding onto the land for a while and I thought it would do well for privately owned apartments. It was nice because from the beginning, I intended the top floor to be mine, so I built it the way I wanted it."

"That *is* nice." Before I can make another inane comment, the elevator stops, and we get out into a small vestibule.

Oh my God. Keep cool, Gabs. Remember, you're going to fake it. Just relax and pay attention so you know what you need to do.

You don't even know that things are going to go to sex. Maybe you can just make out. Yeah. Just make out. Keep it easy. Keep it casual.

He unlocks the door and lets me in and my palms are sweating so much I have to resist the urge to wipe them on my thighs. I walk across the room to look out the wall of windows facing downtown, dropping my purse on the sofa on the way. He follows and drops his keys into a bowl on a table by the door.

"This is a great view," I say.

He steps up behind me and puts his hands on my hips. "It would be better if the building was taller. But like I said, first project. Live and learn."

I laugh as he had intended. He kisses the top of my head. "Gabriella, nothing will happen here tonight that you don't want. I'm in no hurry; I just want to spend time with you."

I lean back against him, feeling my nerves start to settle. "Thank you. I know that, but I appreciate the reassurance."

"I'm hungry," he announces. "Are you hungry?"

I laugh again as he lets go and moves to the kitchen. He opens the refrigerator and pulls out a container that goes into the microwave. I follow him and perch on a stool to watch him work.

The microwave beeps. He removes the container, and a heavenly aroma fills the room, causing my stomach to rumble in appreciation. "That smells good."

"I wish I could take credit, but it's my mom's lasagna. She sent a dish of the stuff to the office today and I dropped it off on the way to Joe's house. She says she misses cooking for her boys, so she's always sending food to the office. The employees love her."

"She sounds wonderful."

"She is, but I'm more than a little biased." He pulls out two forks and hands me one, placing the dish on the counter between us. "Do you want something to drink? Beer? Wine? I think Kellen left some..." He trails off as he digs in the fridge again. "Yeah, there it is." He pulls out a bottle of Blue Moon.

I clap. "Perfect!" He knocks it open against the kitchen counter edge and hands it to me, then opens some kind of stout for himself.

I take a bite of the food and groan with pleasure. "That is amazing."

We talk while we eat and drink, mostly about his family. I'm asking questions to sate my curiosity. His family is so far removed from my experience that I really am fascinated. He asks about my family, but after I give a basic answer, I steer the conversation back to him and his.

Once our stomachs are sated with food and drink, he clears the dishes away and comes around the counter. He leans down and kisses me. When he pulls back, I feel intoxicated, not just from the beer, either.

It's him. I have never been able to imagine what it might feel like to swoon, but that's what it feels like with him. I feel swoony. A giggle bubbles in my throat because I feel so light. I stretch up and slip my arms around his neck, pulling him back down to kiss me some more.

He picks me up and sits me on the island's countertop. His hand strokes up my leg, taking advantage of the split in my skirt. He looks down when he reaches my bare thigh without the skirt getting in the way.

"I really like this outfit."

I smile against his mouth as he takes up where he left off. His hands move from my hips up my sides, one rising to cup my breast. I am just starting to warm up when it begins. Everything around me dims.

No, no, no, no, no! Not now! Not with him.

Morgan starts to fade away, and the Preacher takes his place. All the heat and arousal from the fire Morgan was stoking in me fades away, replaced by the wet wool of numbness. I try to stay focused, but my senses are dulled. Inside, I start to panic.

Come on Gabs! Fake it! Don't blow this! Move, make some noise.

Morgan stops and pulls back. "What just happened?"

I plaster a smile on my face. "What? Nothing! I'm fine!" I try to pull him back to me.

He narrows his eyes. "Gabriella. If there's one thing I hate in this world, it's being fucking lied to."

I look down and away.

"What happened?" He presses. "If I did something wrong, I need you to tell me."

"It's not you," I breathe.

"Then what is it?"

I shake my head, unable to meet his eyes.

"I don't want to tell you." My voice is barely a whisper.

"Why not?"

I swallow. "Because then you'll know how messed up I am, and you won't want me." I shift on the slick stone. "It's okay. I'll go."

He puts his hand on my hip to stop me. "Look at me."

I don't.

His other hand grips my chin and turns my face toward him. "Look at me," he growls. The bite of his voice and his grip on my chin reminds me of being choked, and I feel the familiar craving for punishment start to seep into my blood.

I look at him.

Chapter 10

Gabriella

"Do you want to stop?"

I shake my head.

"Tell me what happened. It felt like you were right there with me, then something happened, and you weren't there anymore."

I start to look down again, but another growl from him has my eyes snapping back up.

"I'm sorry."

"Just tell me, baby."

I lick my lips and swallow. I feel completely dry and worn out, as if I might blow away if he let go.

"When I was younger, my mother worked for a man who built houses and was also a preacher. He was married with children, but that didn't stop him from having an affair with my mother, so he was around all the time."

I can't hold his gaze any longer. With my eyes focused on my hands in my lap, I go on.

"When he would say goodbye, he would position his body between me and my mother so she wouldn't see, and he would..."

I swallow. "He would fondle my chest and kiss me, pushing his tongue into my mouth. It went on for years."

I pause again and take a breath. "Ever since then, whenever someone stands over me and kisses me and touches me on my breasts, the preacher's ghost takes their place and I go numb, unable to feel anything."

"I'll ask again. Do you want to stop?"

I shake my head vehemently, feeling tears prickle. "No! I want you more than I have wanted anyone, ever. I wish I could get over it. For fuck's sake, it's been decades."

He flinches at that. "Exactly how old were you?"

I try to look away again, but his hand returns to grip my jaw harder this time, preventing me.

"It started when I was nine. That and a lot more went on with him until I was twelve and he moved to another state."

He wraps me in his arms and pulls me to his chest. "Oh baby, I'm so sorry that happened to you."

"The only thing that has helped in the past is having someone like Frank. He would say things and do things that would help me feel. It was all bad feelings, but feeling bad is better than not feeling at all."

"What do you mean?"

"Frank would choke me and say bad things, like telling me how stupid I am and how useless I am."

He growls again. "That will not happen with me and if I'd known it was going on with him then, I would have kicked his ass."

I sigh. "Like I said, I'm messed up."

"So, what do you want to do?"

I shrug.

"Will you let me try something?"

I nod. "I would love you to try something."

He kisses me, and I close my eyes and kiss him back. He pulls away. "Open your eyes, Gabriella. Who are you with?"

His voice is hard. Commanding.

"I'm with you."

He kisses me again. I keep my eyes open, locked on his intense blue gaze. The fire begins to stoke again.

The hand on my chin shifts down to my throat and squeezes. Not hard, but enough to let me know who's in charge. His other hand moves back to my breast.

My eyes drift closed but pop open when he tweaks my hard nipple through my shirt and bra. I gasp as a thrill surges through me.

I reach down and hike my skirt a little so I can spread my legs wider. Reaching around, my hands cup his ass and I pull him closer. He cups my ass in return and drags me even closer.

I can feel his hardness pressing into my sensitive flesh. I'm feeling more aroused than I've felt in a very long time, possibly ever.

Focused on Morgan's face, I keep my eyes open to remind me who I am with, but it's such ingrained behavior that my lids drift shut. Each time, the ghosts try to reappear along with the numbness.

When it happens, Morgan does something to shock me back into the now, a pinch, a hard squeeze, a sharp smack to my hip or thigh just hard enough to get my attention. I don't know that this is the best form of therapy for trauma, but for me, it's working. It's working better than all the hundreds of hours I've actually spent in therapy and it actually exorcising my ghosts...well, one of them anyway.

My blouse comes off, then he works me out of my skirt. He leans back to look at me and cocks his head.

"What?" I ask, looking down at my lacy lavender underwear, wondering what he's looking at. I've always loved the way the color looks against my brown skin, but I'm not sure what to make of his stare.

"I really like this outfit, but I'm liking the view even more with you out of it."

I laugh, spreading my legs and letting him look his fill. It's obvious from the bulge in his pants that he likes what he sees.

When I hit puberty, I went from string bean to curvy, seemingly overnight. My curves have never made me self-conscious, though. I like the soft roundness of my hips and breasts.

I sit up and take off my bra, giving him a show as he watches hungrily. When I start to push down my panties, he stops me, pushing my hands out of the way. He takes over, taking off my last bit of clothing to bare me completely.

He pushes my knees open wider and sucks in a deep breath. His eyes lock with mine. "Baby, you are so beautiful."

I smile shyly.

He moves back to me, taking his shirt off. Strong arms pull me to his chest. I lean up to meet his mouth with mine, dragging my hard nipples across the coarse hair on his chest as my fingers go to work on the fly of his jeans, but he again moves my hands out of the way, taking charge of the situation.

He trails kisses across my jaw and down my throat to my breasts and begins to explore with hands and mouth. His hands are powerful, the callouses on his palms rough on my skin, leaving gooseflesh in their wake.

I gasp as he grazes one nipple with his teeth before sucking it hard into his mouth. He pulls away, takes my mouth forcefully with his, then turns his attention to the other breast. The nip of his teeth draws a moan from me.

I reach between my legs. My clit is aching to be touched. He pulls my hand away before I have a chance to stroke even once.

He looks at me sternly. "You keep your hands where I put them until I give you permission to do otherwise."

His command makes me quiver with arousal.

"Do you understand?" he asks.

I lick my lips and nod.

He raises an eyebrow.

"Yes, I understand," I say, feeling a little breathless.

Having sexual attention forced upon me when I was too young to understand what was going on destroyed my innocence. However, having Morgan take control with my permission, knowing that if I asked him to stop, he would, is incredibly empowering.

I don't have to be meek and take what I can get. He's a man who can wrestle my ghosts to the ground and redirect my submission from something driven by trauma to something driven by desire and mutual pleasure.

"Good girl."

He nips my nipple again, making me cry out but I it's not from the pain, it's the surge of pleasure that flows through me.

Morgan cups my ass in his hands and pulls me to the edge of the counter. I have to lean back on my elbows to keep my balance. He kneels before me, pushing my legs wide. "So beautiful," he says.

Still watching intently, he pushes one rough finger into my slit, sinking it deep. He looks up at me, his eyes an inferno of blue flame. A second finger joins the first as he holds my gaze. I throw my head back and moan.

He moves his fingers with long strokes, making slurping noises because I am so soaked. Along the inside of my thigh, he plants kisses, first one, then the other. He is touching me everywhere but where I most want to be touched.

"Morgan, please." I rasp.

"What is it, baby?" he croons as he continues to kiss my thighs, my pubic bone, and right in the crook of my hip, which is driving me absolutely crazy.

"Please," I gasp. "I need...ooooh!"

His tongue strokes across my clitoris. The wave of pleasure it sends through me leaves me shaking. Morgan is stirring up things in me I've never felt before. I am aroused far beyond anything I've ever experienced before.

Maybe tomorrow I'll examine that more closely, but for now I'm just going to enjoy having what I've never had before.

"Is that what you want?" he purrs.

"Yes!"

He returns to tasting me as his fingers continue to stroke. I feel my blood starting to sizzle as the pressure builds. His mouth is absolute magic, sucking and licking and flicking and stroking.

"Oh, God Morgan. Mor..." I gasp. "Mor...ohgod! Oh, God!" The pressure explodes, my whole body clenching as wildfire ignites in my veins and I cry out his name.

I collapse back onto the island, unable to hold myself up under the onslaught of the waves of pleasure. He's moving, but I can't focus to see what he's doing.

My heart is pounding, and I am completely limp. He could roll me off the counter and I'd crash to the floor, powerless to resist.

He strokes my sensitive sex with the head of his cock, causing me to flinch. "Gabriella, I'm going to fuck you now. Is that what you want?"

I nod.

He tweaks a nipple.

My eyes fly open to look at him, and I rise to my elbows. He is holding his cock in his fist, rubbing it up and down my slit. He pushes the head in, making me moan.

"Is this what you want, baby?"

I nod again. His face goes stern, and he raises an eyebrow.

"Yes," I say.

"Yes, what?"

I pause for a moment, recalling his first question. "Yes, I want you to fuck me."

The smile he gives me is breathtaking as he pushes into me with one hard thrust, burying himself to the hilt. I cry out, part pleasure, part pain. His thickness has me stretched tight, and he gives me a moment for my body to adjust.

I sit up and take his mouth with mine. I love that I can taste myself on his lips and from his reaction, he's into it, too. He begins to move, pulling his thick cock out and slamming it back in.

Each time, it's a new shock, a new spark of heat. He picks up speed, the friction driving the heat higher and higher. The sound of our bodies slapping fills the apartment along with my moans, creating a symphony of pleasure.

I'm racing toward the edge like a runaway train, my heart pounding out a rhythm in time to the music of our lovemaking. My nails dig into his shoulders as he pistons his body into mine.

"Morgan! Oh God, Morgan!"

"Not yet, baby, not yet," he growls.

"I can't...I...I can't..." Instead of staving off my impending crash into the abyss, the grit in his voice sends me swan diving over the edge, unintelligible sounds pouring out of me. I fall back again, unable to hold myself up any longer.

My body clenches around him like a vise in orgasm, pulling him over the edge with me. "Jeezus," he says as he empties himself.

He leans over on top of me, his head coming to rest between my breasts. Both of us are breathing raggedly. I catch my breath and start to stroke his hair as he continues to gasp, his heavy body covering mine.

After several moments, he turns his head and kisses me between my breasts. He straightens and as he's pulling out of me, he says, "Christ, woman, are you trying to kill me?"

I laugh, sitting up. "Me? Seems like you were the one responsible."

He pulls off the condom I hadn't even noticed before. I'm glad someone was thinking clearly enough to take precautions. I'm on birth control, but nothing is foolproof. He drops the condom in the trash, then starts to walk away.

"Stay there," he says. "I'll be right back."

A snarky comment about not being a dog comes to mind, but I let it float away, choosing instead to enjoy the lingering sizzles of pleasure fueled endorphins as I watch his gorgeous ass flex while he walks away.

He returns, holding a damp washcloth. I hold out my hand to take it from him, but he just looks at me and pushes my legs apart. He cleans me gently but thoroughly. I've never had someone take care of me like that. It's kind of weird, but I like it.

When he's satisfied with his work, he stands and pulls me into his arms, kissing me deeply and thoroughly. He breaks the kiss and leans his forehead against mine. "Can you stay?"

I think for a moment. Should I stay? There's no reason to go home, but staying is...intimate. Even when I used the hotel for liaisons, I didn't stay all night, but he wants me to. After a few moment's thought, I realize I want to.

In just a short time, this man has dealt with one of my ghosts without kicking me out the door or acting like I'm some kind of freak. He's managing to bring my body back to life after so many years of nothingness.

I haven't orgasmed so intensely ever. Previously, what I thought were orgasms were like a couple of raindrops compared to the tsunami of sensation Morgan stirred in me, not once, but twice in one encounter.

I nod my head. "I'd like that."

His shoulders relax as if he was prepared for me to say no. He picks me up and carries me to his bedroom, eliciting a squeak of surprise from me. When he drops me onto his bed, I laugh as I bounce before settling. He's so intense sometimes that this playfulness is surprising.

Chapter 11

Mr. Smith

For the first time since I started the game with her as the playing piece and me as the master of her fate, I am guessing at where she is. Who am I kidding? I don't guess.

However, she didn't go home last night, and her car wasn't at her office when I passed by. That normally means she's at the hotel having some tryst with the flavor du jour. They're usually so predictable. She's usually extremely predictable. Usually.

Instead of driving all the way there just to prove myself right, I pull up the tracking app I have for her phone. Implementing that little piece of technology is always one of the first things I do once I gain access to their home.

The advent of facial unlocking on so many newer phones makes it incredibly easy to gain access to someone's entire digital world these days. It used to be a bit tricky to maneuver a finger into position and press it to the phone to unlock it.

For a time, I enjoyed the challenge of trying to figure out their unlock codes from the marks on their screens left by the oil of their fingers. However, it was very time consuming and now that I don't have that obstacle to overcome; I prefer it.

All I have to do is wait for them to be deep asleep, dim the display, hold it up in front of their face, and viola! Access! I can install anything I like and take my time getting to know them by scrolling through their pictures and reading their texts.

There's an incredible amount of information that can be gleaned from social media, but so many people keep everything on their phones. Their contacts, their appointments, even an astounding amount of personal information.

If I were an identity thief, I could make a killing. Get it? A killer making a killing?

I apologize. Sometimes I'm prone to fits of whimsy in my musings, but it passes soon enough. Back to business... Where was I? Oh, technology.

Uninstalling the app is the last thing I do before I leave them, staged in their ultimate perfection. Leaving such a luscious tid-bit for the police to find just wouldn't do. However, their efforts thus far have been so inept that I doubt they would have found it, anyway.

I have to double-check the readout showing on my screen. She is not at her usual hotel. She is somewhere in midtown. I turn my car around and head toward the location of the blue dot on my screen.

I drive by the building she's in. It looks like upscale apart-ments. My little Gabby has changed the game, bringing in a new player, and all that whimsy of a moment ago is usurped by blazing fury. I drive around the block, my fingers squeezing so tight the steering wheel squeaks.

Once I find a space, I pull in and park. My temper gets the better of me and I pound the steering wheel of the car.

"Fucking cunt!" I yell to no one. "Do you think you can get away from me? No! You cannot! You are mine and one day very soon, you're going to learn. I'm going to wrap my hands around that scrawny neck of yours and choke the life out of you! Fuck, fuck, FUCK!"

With that out of my system, I smooth my hair into place, straighten my jacket, and get out. There's a homeless person sleeping on a bus stop bench nearby. He keeps a cautious eye on me as I emerge from the vehicle.

Not turning his way, I avert my face so he can't get a good look at me. I stroll by the building, then turn the corner to view the structure from every side. All the windows are dark, but at three in the morning, that's to be expected.

There's a parking garage under the building. Unfortunately, it is gated and I can see the red glow of a security camera a few feet inside the entry so there's no going inside to see if her car's in there.

I contemplate which apartment she might be in. There are seven floors, with at least two apartments on each floor. Approximately fourteen apartments. Fourteen potential places, more or less, where she might be sleeping right now.

Or fucking someone right now. I don't care if she has sex with other men. The last man is always me, and that is the feast my ego requires. Everyone else is inconsequential.

She never goes home with the men she ruts with. She always does it at the hotel and even then, she does not stay the night. She does *not* stay the night!

Is this a man's apartment, or perhaps it is a friend? I will find out everything I can about this building tomorrow. With luck, I'll be able to get a list of tenants. If it is a man, this is an extreme deviation from her usual behavior.

This is not good. This is no time for her to become unpredictable. Not when I'm so close to adding her to my collection. What if it is a man? That is a risk I have never had to factor for.

However, it does add an element of challenge that has become so lacking of late. Perhaps her sudden unpredictability is a blessing in disguise. If a third player is set upon the board, the game changes. That change might be good.

The game has been feeling stale. It has all become so easy and the police's attempts at discovering my identity have been laughable at best. They don't have the first clue about who I am, they only know that I exist.

I would expect them to know that much simply because of the number of bodies I've left for them to find. It was all I could do to keep from laughing when they found the last one. They were running around like chickens scratching the ground, trying to dig up even a speck of evidence. God help the people of Oklahoma City if these people are the finest that the police force can deliver.

I sigh. There is nothing to be gained from lingering, so I may as well go home to the Missus. She will be wondering where

I've gotten off to. Wondering, but she won't question. She never questions where I've been or what I've done.

I taught her that lesson years ago.

Chapter 12

Gabriella

I wake up and panic for a moment when I find myself in unfamiliar surroundings. That panic intensifies when I find myself alone in an unfamiliar bed. Where am I and how did I get here?

I sit up and look around. The night before starts to come back to me. Morgan. I'm in Morgan's apartment. When I move to get out of bed, the ache between my legs reminds me that having sex on the kitchen counter had just been the beginning.

He is insatiable. However, once he slayed that ghost and flipped the switch on my ability to feel, I'd become pretty insatiable myself. The clock on the nightstand catches my eye.

I have just enough time to get home, shower, and change for the new day. Now I just need to find my clothes so I don't have to leave the building naked.

The apartment is quiet. I wonder if Morgan has already left for the day. I make my way to the bathroom to relieve myself and see a sticky note on the mirror.

Gone for a run. Stay put. -MM

I shake my head.

Give a man an inch and he takes a mile.

That brings a smile to my face because it brings to mind all the inches he gave me last night and early this morning. I find my blouse on one of the stools by the kitchen island. My skirt is draped over the back of the sofa.

I can't find my panties and bra anywhere. Giving up, I decide that going commando is going to have to do until I can get home and put on a fresh outfit. I'm tucking my blouse in when Morgan comes through the door.

God, he looks good. He's all sweaty and muscley and hot. I want to walk right up to him and rub all over until he's ready to give me some more inches.

No. No, I need to go to work. There's no time to play because once he gets me started, I'm not going to want to stop.

He looks me up and down, his eyes stalling on my breasts. I look down to see my dark areolas showing through the sheer fabric of the blouse. "No," he says and walks to the bedroom.

"Morgan, I have to go home to shower and change, and my underwear has mysteriously disappeared. It's better than going out naked," I call after him.

He comes back into the room with a shirt in his hand and pulls it over my head. It's one of his t-shirts, so it swallows me, hanging down to my thighs. I put my arms through the armholes and look down at myself.

Well, at least my tits aren't on display anymore.

"Okay. That's better," he says.

I smile and shake my head. "You went for a run? Do you do that every morning?"

He goes to the fridge and takes out a bottle of water. "Most." He opens the bottle and turns it up, drinking down the entire bottle without stopping.

When he's finished, he comes over to me and wraps me in his arms. "You sure you don't have time to take a quick shower with me?"

"As much as I would love to shower with you, I know that with both of us naked again and all that soapy hot water, quick would not be in the cards. Unfortunately, I have a meeting first thing this morning."

"Damn. Being a responsible adult sucks sometimes."

I laugh and stretch up on my toes to kiss him. "Yes, it does. All right, cariño, I'd better run." I kiss him again.

"I suppose," he grumbles.

He lets me go, but as soon as my back is turned, he swats me on the ass. I squeak. "Brute!"

"Yep. Now get out of here before I go all caveman and drag you into the shower."

"I'll talk to you later," I promise as I hurry out the door.

That evening, Hailey is gone for the day and I'm alone in the office working on drawings. I love these times when I can kick my shoes off, turn on some music, and surrender to the flow of it. I do my best work when I can immerse myself in the possibilities of what a house can be and make those possibilities into plans with my imagination and an excellent set of pencils.

I rub the back of my neck and look over the work I've done. A glance at the clock shows me it's later than I thought. I'm thinking I should call it a night when there's a knock at the front door.

I'm a little cautious about going out and letting someone know I'm here alone. Perhaps I should pretend like no one is here. My phone buzzes on my desk.

The caller ID says it's Morgan, so I pick up. "Hey."

"Woman, stop making me stand outside. Come answer the door."

I look around the corner to see him standing there with his phone to his ear so I move forward and unlock the door.

"Hey, baby," he says, wrapping his arms around me and kissing me when he comes into the office.

"Hi. How was your day?"

"Long."

"I just finished a set of drawings and was about to call it a night."

"Good. Have you eaten?"

"Um..." I think for a minute and realize I haven't had anything since that morning. "No. I had some breakfast after my early meeting, but nothing since. I started working on drawings, so I guess I forgot. No wonder I'm hungry."

He smacks my ass. "No wonder, huh? If I had the energy, I'd turn you over my knee, but I'm starving. Let's go get something to eat."

"Can we just grab something on the way to...um...your place?"

"We can go to yours, if you want."

I shrug. "Yours is closer. If you'll call something in, you can go on. I'll close up here and swing by to pick the food up on the way to your house."

This morning, I took the time to pack a bag in case I saw him and, by some luck of fate, we ended up back at his place again. I wasn't assuming. I was just hopeful.

"I'll call food in, but I'll also wait for you. What sounds good?"

"I would love a burger. Tuckers or Braum's, both are between here and there and either is great for me. Cheeseburger with mayo, please."

"A burger sounds fantastic." He pulls out his phone. While he's talking, he wanders around and stops at my drafting board, flipping through the drawings I'd been working on.

He puts his phone away and keeps examining the drawings while I shut down my computer. "These are fantastic. They're for Joe and Anita?"

"Yes. I wanted to get them out of the way before I start on Delores." I'm pleased that he likes my work.

"You're very talented."

"Thank you." I feel my face heat in reaction to his praise. It feels good. "Okay, I'm ready," I say, standing with my purse and keys in hand.

We walk out. He's right on top of me as I lock up the building, his hands on my hips, holding me against him, his lips nuzzling my neck. It tickles and makes me giggle. I turn the key and pull the door to ensure it's locked, then press my body back against his.

"If you keep this up, we're not going to make it to your house," I tell him breathlessly.

"Would that be so bad?"

"I think there are a few too many lights here."

"We can go back into the office. I'll be quick, I promise."

I turn in his arms and face him. "Gee, that sounds enticing," I say deadpan, but my smirk gives me away. I put my palm to his cheek, seeing the need in his eyes. "We can go back in…" I start to turn so I can unlock the door.

"No…no…" He shakes his head. "Let's just go to the house."

"You go on, I'll get the food and be there a couple of minutes behind."

He nods. "Okay." He kisses me and takes my hand, walking me to my car. "I'll see you in a few."

"Yes."

He waits until I'm in my car and pulling away before he goes to his truck to leave.

Chapter 13

Morgan

I watch Gabriella drive away. I know she's strong. Capable, too. But for some reason, I have an irrational need to keep her safe.

She's lived thirty some odd years on this planet and, if banishing last night's ghost is any indicator, she's been through some messed up shit. But she's still here, and she's thriving.

I know what it's like to deal with ghosts. I've had more than a few of my own.

Shit! I realize I forgot to give her the code to the gate, so I pull out my phone and text it to her. Motion in my periphery snags my attention.

It's just a car pulling out into the street going the same way as Gabriella did. I watch it drive by, then get in my truck and head home. With a hand on my jaw, I twist to pop my neck.

God, I'm tired.

I probably should have just gone home and left her alone tonight because I'm likely not going to be wonderful company. However, I had to see her. That first night when I saw her at the hotel bar, I was intrigued. Then, seeing her Saturday at the dinner, that intrigue sparked into something bigger.

There's no denying my initial physical attraction. She's just my type. I have to admit, the physical was in the forefront of my head when I offered to meet her at the project house. What did she call it? Delores, that's it, old school beauty.

Following her around the house that day, I was entranced. Watching the way she moves. Hearing her thoughts as she poured them out for the recorder.

It all stoked the spark of attraction into a flame of desire for more than just something physical. She's smart. She's funny. Her talent oozes out of her with effortless grace.

I've known her for less than a week and she's already getting under my skin. It's crazy, but it feels right, so I'm going with it. Trusting my gut saved my life more than once in the military and saved my ass in some tough situations since.

I hear the bell ring just as I'm getting out of the shower, so I wrap a towel around my waist and hurry to the door. If we keep this up, I'll need to get her a key. When I open the door, she looks me up and down. I lean on the doorjamb.

"See something you like?"

She bites her lip, trying to hide her smile. I lean over and kiss her. "Get in here, woman, I'm starving."

She goes into the kitchen with me following close behind, watching her ass. I almost run into her when she stops because I'm so focused on her assets.

She looks around at me. "Go dry off. I've got this."

"But..."

She turns and puts her hand on my chest. "You don't have to get dressed if you don't want to, but you're dripping all over the floor."

"Okay," I grumble.

The woman laughs at me. Laughs at me! I'm trying to be all sexy in just a towel and she's laughing. I stalk off so she can't see the grin on my face.

"Morgan, wake up."

I startle awake to find Gabriella standing over me. Reaching out, I pull her into my lap. The last thing I remember is settling down to watch television. I glance at the clock in the kitchen to see that over an hour has passed.

"Cariño, you fell asleep," she says, putting a palm to my cheek. "Let's get you to bed so you can rest."

"Are you staying?"

"Si, yes, I brought a bag."

"Good girl." I release her so she can get up and let her believe her hand pulling mine actually lifts me off the sofa.

She leads me to my bedroom. "Get in. I'll go turn off the lights and I'll be right back."

"Leave them," I say.

"No. Ambient glow is not conducive to quality rest."

I can't argue with that, so I get into bed. Just as I'm dozing off, I feel the bed move, signaling her return. I reach out and pull her close to me, but pause when I realize she's naked.

"If you're planning on jumping my bones, you'll have to do all the work."

"Sleeping in the nude is healthier for your body," she says matter-of-factly.

I mumble something even I don't understand, spooning my body to her back. I wrap an arm around her, cupping one of her breasts in my hand, and slide back into sleep.

My internal alarm clock goes off at 0500, just like it does every morning. It has been twenty years since I left the Marines, and I still can't sleep past five in the morning. I get out of bed, moving slowly so I don't wake Gabriella.

She's gorgeous. Her dark hair is strewn across the pillow. I would like nothing better than to crawl back into bed, wrap her hair in my fist and wake her up with my cock sliding into her pussy.

Instead, I decide to let her sleep.

I am getting dressed when I hear a quiet, "Hey," from the bed. I look over to see her watching me. She raises one hand and crooks a finger at me. "C'mere."

I lean over to kiss her. She has me sucking in a breath when she snakes a hand out and cups my balls through my shorts, my dick coming to attention with her touch. Her hand shifts to reach inside my shorts and wraps around my stiffening cock.

"Mmmm..." she says and sits up on the side of the bed. She pulls my shorts down. "I think I'd like to have some exercise this morning, too."

"Did you bring some running shhh..." She runs her tongue around the head of my cock, turning my snarky comment to a hiss. Then she gets serious about sucking me.

I pull her hair back and wrap my fist around it, urging her on. She gags as the head of my cock hits the back of her mouth, but it only seems to make her hungrier. She's licking and sucking and fucking me with her mouth so good that I can't hold back.

"Gabriella, I'm close," I rasp.

She takes a deep breath and pulls her mouth away. "On your back," she orders.

I do as she says, moving around her to lie on the bed. She pulls a condom out of the nightstand drawer, opens it, and rolls it down my length. Then she wastes no time climbing on top of me.

She impales her body on mine, sliding my cock deep inside. "God, you feel good," she says as she wiggles her hips to work me all the way in. It appears she wants to be in control, so I let her set the pace as she moves on top of me.

She grabs my hands off her hips. One is moved up to her breast and the other to her mouth. Her pink tongue darts out to wet the pad of my thumb, then she sucks it into her mouth.

I feel it pull all the way to my dick. Once it's wet with her saliva, she pushes it back down, wedging my thumb between our bodies. Understanding what she wants, I begin to stroke her swollen clit.

"Yes!" she cries. She's breathing hard now. "I'm. So. Close," she pants out.

"Me, too, Baby," I answer.

Her hand goes over mine on her breast and she squeezes hard, pinching the nipple. I follow her lead and pinch it harder.

"God yes! Like that! Yes!"

She's riding me hard now. Her head is tossed back as a cry pours out of her, something in Spanish that I can't make out.

Her body is squeezing mine so tight in her orgasm that I can't hold back any longer. I grab her hips and move her hard and fast along my length and with a few strokes, I'm coming like I've never come before.

She collapses on top of me, and I wrap her in my arms. We're both breathing hard, hearts pounding as we lay there chest to chest, our bodies still connected. I smooth her hair back from her face and kiss her forehead. "Good morning, Baby."

She chuckles. "Good morning."

Chapter 14

Gabriella

My focus is shot today and I'm not being very successful at drawing. I need to start on Delores, but I won't force it. A lesson I learned early on is that when the flow isn't there, it's better to move onto something else for a while.

"Hailey, is there any paperwork that needs to be done?"

She appears in my doorway. "No, sorry. It's all caught up. Feeling stuck?"

"Sometimes you're too efficient," I smile. "Yes, the flow is eluding me right now."

"You could go down to the furniture store and browse."

There is a consignment furniture store at the end of our little row of shops. Sometimes I go down there to see what's new. I've gotten several great deals on quality pieces from them.

"I shouldn't. Every time I go down there, I find something I can't live without and I'm out of space. Plus, I have three pieces in my garage that are on my list to refinish, but I haven't had time to mess with them. I've banned myself from buying anymore furniture until I make some room," I tell her.

"Why don't you go for a walk? The weather is beautiful today. It's almost lunchtime so you could walk over to Iron Star, it's close, or go north. It's a little farther, but there are lots of options just up the road."

"That's an excellent idea." I pull out a pair of flats I keep on hand for just such an occasion and grab my purse. "You know the drill if I'm not back by the time you need to go."

"I'll be here. I'm going to take my lunch at the end of the day. I have an appointment for an oil change this afternoon."

"Okay. Can I bring you anything back?"

"No, but thank you," Hailey says. "I brought something."

"I'll be back soon." "Take your time," she says and waves me out the door.

She was right. The weather today is absolutely beautiful with plenty of sunshine but not too much heat. By the time I return from lunch, I feel relaxed, refreshed and clear-headed, ready to get back to work.

"You got a delivery while you were out. I put it on your desk," Hailey says when I return.

On my desk is a padded manila envelope. There's no re-turn address, no postage, just my name and business address. I frown.

I pick up the envelope. It's heavy. "Did UPS or Fed-ex deliver this?" I ask Hailey.

"Nope. A courier dropped it off."

"Huh. That's odd."

I pull the envelope open and pull out a book. The cover reads *The Elements of Style: A Practical Encyclopedia of Interior Architectural Details from 1485 to the Present.* As I flip through it, a white card falls out of the pages. I pick it up and read the note.

I thought I'd send you some house porn to tide you over until I see you again. Miss you already.–MM

Hailey comes to my office door. "So, what was it?" She sees what I'm holding. "A book? Someone sent you a book?"

"Someone sent me the perfect book," I reply, grinning like a loon. I show her the card and the cover of the book.

"This guy is good," she says.

"That is the understatement of the century."

Tonight will be the first night Morgan and I won't spend together in almost a week. It's strange that in such a short time we've gotten so close. I'm meeting Caitlynn for our regular Thursday dinner date at the Society. Morgan is going to be visiting job sites in Tulsa all day today and tomorrow, so he won't be home until late tomorrow.

I was surprised to learn just how far-reaching their projects are. They are working all over the state on projects of all kinds, large, small, commercial, residential.

They seem to have their fingers in every aspect of construction. I can't imagine overseeing that volume of work, but Morgan seems to handle it all with aplomb.

I go back to my office and start leafing through Morgan's gift. It's fascinating. A few minutes later, Hailey pops into my doorway. "I'm off to my appointment."

"What?"

"My appointment. Remember, I told you I was leaving early."

I glance at the clock on my wall. "Oh, yes, sorry."

"Have you spent all afternoon looking at that book?"

"I...um...I guess I have," I laugh. "Yes, yes, go on, get to your appointment."

She laughs at me and heads out the door.

I pull out my phone and text Morgan.

Me: *You're making a junkie out of me! I frittered away my entire afternoon looking at your gift. It's wonderful. Thank you.*

Morgan: *Woman, you were already a junkie. I just took advantage of an opportunity to become your supplier. Gotta get you addicted to me somehow.*

Me: *It's working.*

Morgan: *Call me when you get home tonight.*

I look at my drafting table, knowing I should be working on the drawings for Delores. However, I know I'm a lost cause for the day so I decide to close up.

I'll go home and get my workout gear and go to the Society early for some exercise. I haven't been to the gym all week because I've been with Morgan getting a different kind of exercise.

By the time I get home, I'm completely done in. I hit the gym hard, trying to distract myself. Then I had been hoping for a quiet dinner with Cait, but for once, our entire group of five showed up. I spent the evening on mostly surface chatter, which is so exhausting for me.

We all joined La Société Belladone, The Belladonna Society, or just the Society as we like to call it, at the same time and went through orientation together. We committed to having a regular dinner together on Thursday nights each week. Each of us shows up whenever we can, but most of the time it's just Cait and me.

At first, I was unsure about laying out the kind of cash it took to join, but I decided it would be an excellent opportunity and wrote it off as a business expense. It has turned out to be a smart move. I have more than made back the cost of membership with projects gained from other members in the six months since joining.

I like the other women in our orientation group. We're just not as familiar as Cait and we don't have a lot of common ground to draw upon. Once I spend more time with them, I'll feel more relaxed. It's silly, I know, but I just can't seem to get past the thought that people are judging me.

I'm most comfortable with Cait, of course. Then Demi is a close second. Demeter Lawson seems to have come up in a less than well-to-do family as I did, but she inherited money from somewhere. She's a little younger than me and has a psychology practice.

After Demi, is Serena Chilton who is a law professor at the University of Oklahoma. She has joined us a few times. While I know a little about her, she tends to be circumspect in our conversations.

The last member of our quint is Alicia Pham, an anesthesiologist resident at Integris. I'm very intimidated by Serena and Alicia simply because of the level of intelligence that was required for them to have the roles they do. I never finished college and while I know a lot about houses, I don't hold a candle to them when it comes to general smarts.

I'm always extra tense when they are at dinner. It's all in my head, I know. They've done nothing to make me feel like they look down on me.

When I walk through my door, it feels strange to be in my house alone for the night. Other than stopping by to pack a bag or change clothes, I haven't been here in almost a week.

It's quiet. And empty. I drop my gym bag on the washer, then go to my room and collapse on the bed.

I lay there, staring at the ceiling, and wonder what Morgan is doing right now. Remembering that he wanted me to call, I heft myself up and go back to the table by the front door, where I put my purse to retrieve my phone.

I dial his number, then double-check the front door to be sure I locked it.

"Hey baby," he answers.

"Hey. I made it home safe and sound."

"I would expect nothing less."

I go to the back door and make sure it's locked. "What are you doing?"

"Wishing you were here."

"Yeah, same here. Listen to us," I laugh. "We make it seem like it will be weeks before we see each other again. It will just be until tomorrow." I go back to my bedroom and sit on the side of the bed.

"I'll still be lonely tonight without you," he says.

"Are you in a hotel?"

"No, we keep a condo here because one of us is in Tulsa so often."

"That's nice that you can stay in familiar surroundings."

"What are you doing?"

"I'm about to get ready for bed and settle in with some house porn." I look over at the nightstand where I left Morgan's book. It's not there. "That's odd."

"What's odd?"

"I brought the book you gave me home and could swear that I put it on the nightstand because I knew I'd want to look at it some more once I settled in for the night."

"It's not there?"

"No, I..." I look around the room and spot it sitting on the corner of my dresser. "There it is. It's on the dresser. I swear I'm losing my mind lately. Putting it on the nightstand must have only been a thought that I didn't carry out."

"Are your doors locked?""Yes," I say with a little laugh. "I just checked them."

"Windows?"

"I haven't checked them. I'm sure they're fine."

"Check them. Now." His voice is commanding and I can't fight the instinct to obey.

"Morgan..."

Softening his tone, he says, "Do it. If for no other reason than to make me feel better."

"Okay." I start going through the house checking the windows, giving him a play-by-play as I do. "There. I've checked them all and they're all locked."

"Maybe you should go stay at my place."

"Morgan..."

"I'm serious. If you want to go to my place, I'll call Beck and have him let you in."

"Morgan, that's unnecessary. I'm exhausted, so I'm probably just misremembering. I'll be fine, I promise. I've lived in this house for years and never had any problems."

He's quiet. I can almost hear the wheels turning in his mind. He sighs finally.

"All right. Speaking of Beckett, he reminded me we have a dinner Saturday night with the Homebuilders Association. It's a fancy thing where they bring in several chefs and have live music and stuff. It's one of the few of these things that I actually enjoy. If you're available, I'd love it if you would come with me."

"I can do that."

"I still want to see you tomorrow, though."

A smile splits my face. "I can do that, too."

"Good girl," he says. I can hear the smile in his voice, too.

Every time he says that, it gives me a little thrill. I enjoy pleasing him as much as he seems to enjoy pleasing me.

"I know you're tired," he says. "Get some rest and I'll see you tomorrow. Good night, baby."

"Good night cariño."

Chapter 15

Mr. Smith

These women are so incredibly, irreparably stupid. They think that just because their doors and windows are locked, that means that no one can get in. I broke in the first time while she was sleeping.

Ever since then, there has been no need to break in because I had a copy of her key. Seriously, how foolish is it to drop your keys into a dish right by the front door?

Not only that, but to have keys labeled with little tags letting me know which one is for her house. It's almost as if she wants me to murder her.

Maybe she does. From what I gleaned from Dwayne after I got him drunk, my little Latina pawn has had a less than nurturing childhood supplemented by significant sexual abuse.

Something like that could spur a woman to do foolish things that might bring her harm. Maybe she's too weak to commit suicide and would love for someone like me to come along and take care of it for her.

Don't worry about poor little Dwayne. I didn't hurt him, just got him drunk and high enough that he spilled everything he knew about her. With the last pill I gave him, his memory of me would be all but obliterated. Hazy at best, but mostly obliterated.

There will be no identifying me in a police lineup for Dwayne.

Now, where was I? Oh yes, the idiocy of women. Women also think that locked doors and windows mean that there's no way anyone is already on the inside as I am. Little do they know that I'm here, tucked away in the closet in her second bedroom, listening to every word she says.

On one visit to her home, I carved out a little niche for myself among the boxes and suitcases. Even if she were to open the door to look inside, she wouldn't easily see me. Just to be safe, though, besides this hiding place, I've created two others so that I can maximize my ability to hear her conversations and see what she's doing.

I listen to her move around the house while she's talking on her phone to Morgan Masters. Yes, I have discovered with whom she has been spending her nights. At first, I thought it might be a problem, but as my father used to tell me, problems are merely challenges waiting to be overcome.

When she began to check her windows, she put her phone on speaker so she didn't have to hold it to her ear. That makes it all the easier for me to hear everything.

From the sound of their conversation, their relationship has progressed quickly in a short amount of time. My initial research into him was cursory, but perhaps I need to dig a little deeper.

He seems more concerned about her misplaced book than she did. Women have been taught since birth to second guess themselves, which makes this part of the game particularly fun. I'll move their things and they always chalk it up to a faulty memory, blaming themselves.

The shower comes on in her bathroom. I'll have to decide whether I want to hang out for a while longer or make my exit now. I stop by her bedroom door. She's put the book back on her nightstand.

I choose to leave, if for nothing else, to get some supper, lest my growling stomach give me away. However, I will play with her one more time before I go. I take the book and put it on the corner of the dresser again before I go out the back door, locking it behind me.

I sit outside long enough for her to finish her shower. It's clear the moment she sees the book has been moved again. The lights start coming on one by one as she moves through the house. This time she's checking not only the doors and the windows but looking in all the rooms and in her closets, too.

She's probably still oblivious. Women are such dullards. They will make sure all their blinds are drawn at night only to parade around their houses half naked with their blinds open in the morning because they think no one will be watching then.

I'm laughing to myself when a car pulls to the curb in front of her house. The driver parks and looks as if he's settling in for the night. It's marked with a security emblem on the door. Her new boy toy must have called them. He is definitely a challenge to be overcome.

I guess I'll have to go home to the Missus after I get something to eat. It has been a while since I let her out of her box and played with her. I suppose that will have to do for the evening's entertainment.

As I make my way through town, a thought occurs to me. Although I'm not a homebuilder, I have ties to that industry through my business. I wonder if I could wrangle an invitation to the event this weekend.

A big fat donation would probably garner one. How fun would it be to mingle in the same room with my prey? The prospect makes me giddy and stiffens my cock.

I'll even spring for a new dress for the missus to wear. Something long sleeved that will cover her bruises. It wouldn't do for those to be on display.

To be extra nice tonight and get her excited about going, not only will I let her out of the box, but I'll just fuck her with none of the extras I love so much. I know. I'll put her in a black wig and a red dress and have her lay oh, so still. She's good at that.

It will be like a preview to fucking Gabriella once I've choked the life out of her. The thought is so exhilarating that I almost come in my pants.

Chapter 16

Gabriella

I check myself in the mirror one more time. Tonight I'm wearing a new dress I bought for the occasion and I want to make sure there are no issues with moving in it. I sit and stand and bend and even squat to make sure that I'll be able to do whatever I need to do. It would be horrible to get to the event only to spend hours being uncomfortable.

I have been eyeing it in the dress shop for a few weeks now and decided to bite the bullet. The beautiful berry color is fantastic for me and the style is nice enough to be worn to a variety of events without being over the top fancy. It's a bonus that my most comfortable pumps will go well with it and it matches my favorite lipstick.

Morgan stayed the night with me last night. I could tell he didn't rest well. He kept prowling around the house, checking doors and windows. If I'm honest, I hadn't slept well the night before when I was here alone, either, and was doing much the same thing until I noticed a car parked out front.

At first, I panicked when I saw the car was inhabited, but then I noticed the logo on the door. Morgan sent someone to watch over me in his absence. Although it was total overkill, I slept a little better after that, but not much. I might have mistaken where I placed that book once, but not twice.

The thought of someone being in my house creeped me out. I might have ghosts in my psyche, but in the five years I've lived here, I have never experienced any in my house. If there are any, I wouldn't have thought they'd take so long to make an appearance.

Morgan left this morning to go into the office today to do some paperwork related to his site visits in Tulsa. By the time he got out of bed after thoroughly letting me know how much he missed me the night before twice last night and once again this morning, the sun was up, and the birds were singing. He said he'd go home to get ready, then pick me up for the event. He also told me firmly to pack a bag and plan on staying at his house tonight.

My doorbell rings. I check through the peephole to make sure it's Morgan. It is. "Who is it?" I call in a singsong voice.

"It's the big bad wolf. Let me in or I'll huff, and I'll puff..."

I open the door and stand back for him to enter, chuckling at his playfulness. He stands there staring at me, slack jawed, all playfulness gone. He shakes himself and comes in, shutting the door, taking me by the hand and striding toward my bedroom.

"Morgan, what are you doing?"

"I just need a few minutes. Fifteen, tops."

I set my feet. "Morgan, no! We cannot have sex first. I spent a long time on this hair and makeup, and it will get messed up."

"I just need you out of that dress, so I don't wrinkle it. I promise I won't mess with your hair or makeup either."

"Morgan..."

"Dammit, woman, it's your fault for wearing something like that. It's made to rile a man up and now that you've riled me, I need you to unrile me."

"Okay..." That's all I got out before he moved behind me and unzipped my dress. He helped me out of it and draped it over the back of a chair. Then, true to his word, he bent me over the back of the sofa and pounded the hell out of me until we both found release without mussing my hair or makeup.

With some minor clean-up, we are both dressed again and ready to go. We will be a few minutes later than originally intended, but nothing that will be terribly noticeable. Before we go out the door, he leans down and kisses my cheek and squeezes my ass at the same time.

"Thank you, baby. I would have been walking around with a hard on all night if you hadn't let me do that."

"It's a terrible hardship keeping you satisfied, but I'll manage somehow," I grin up at him.

"You look beautiful. Do you have your bag?"

I point to it by the door. "Good girl. We should probably take your car. It will be easier for you than climbing in and out of my truck."

I take my keys out of my clutch and hand them to him. He stalks through the house and checks the back door, then follows me out the front, locking it behind us. He helps me into my car, then puts my bag in the back before going around to slide into the driver's seat.

"Damn, you're short," he teases while moving the seat back.

"Hey," I say, getting his attention. "You look pretty beautiful yourself."

He takes my hand in his across the console and pulls it to his lips so he can kiss the back. "Thank you, baby," he says and turns onto the street.

"Will Beckett be there tonight?" I ask.

"Yes. Beckett, Kellen, and our parents, too. Mom likes this event, so she always makes Dad bring her."

"What?"

"What what?" He asks, confused.

"Your whole family will be there? I'm going to meet your whole family?"

"Yes. Is that a problem?"

I feel like I'm going to hyperventilate. "Um...I..." I look down at my dress with its low-cut bodice. It's too much; I should have worn something different.

His mother's going to think I'm some kind of slut. But then, I really am, aren't I? I mean, I barely knew the man, her son, before jumping in bed with him and now I've been sleeping at his house practically every night for a week. Not to mention that I let her son bend me over my sofa just a few minutes ago. Her son.

Oh God. This is a disaster.

I've never met a man's parents. I've never been in the kind of relationship where the meeting of parents was even a consideration. Morgan's parents are probably like him, good and nice. And high quality. They'd have to be to have raised two sons, like Morgan and Beckett.

Ohshit, ohshit, ohshit. I can't do this. They will know that I'm trash and hate me.

I can feel him looking over at me while trying to keep an eye on the road, too.

"Maybe you should take me home," I finally manage to say.

He squeezes my hand. "No, I want you to go to this event with me, and I want you to meet my family."

I stare out the window. I can feel myself starting to shake. He exits the highway and pulls into the first parking lot we come to.

"Hey, look at me," he says gently. When I don't, his voice grows firm. "Gabriella, look at me."

I look at him and his face gentles.

"Baby, you have nothing to be nervous about. My family wants to meet you, especially my mother."

I shake my head. "I...uh...I've never...How does she even know about me? Thes kinds of things always make me feel so awkward. I'll talk too much, and they'll think I'm an idiot or I won't say enough, and they'll think I'm stuck up. Everything will be a mess and I'll make a fool of myself and they'll hate me." I can feel myself breathing harder and tears prickle in my eyes.

"Take a deep breath, baby. There, that's it. Take another. Look at me. You have nothing to be afraid of, Honey. I'll be right there with you. If you really don't want to go, I'll take you home, but I would like you to go with me and I would like you to meet my family. My Mom is gonna love you."

I am terrified, but I know if I don't go, it will change how he feels about me. Maybe he won't want me anymore. My breathing has calmed, but I'm still shaking.

"I tell you what," he says, "let's go for thirty minutes, just long enough for you to meet my family and, if after thirty minutes you still want to go home, I'll take you. How does that sound?"

I take a deep breath and let it out. I nod. "Okay, I can do that."

A huge smile spreads across his face. "Good girl." He gets us back on the road and within minutes, we're walking into the venue. I have a death grip on his hand, but he acts like it's nothing.

I see a bar in the corner and pull on his arm. He leans down to me. "What is it, baby?"

A vision of me sloshed and out-of-control flutters through my mind.

"Don't let me drink too much."

"I won't," he replies before kissing me on the temple and continuing into the room.

I see Beckett across the room, with a redhead standing next to him. Next to her is a younger man who resembles the Masters brothers. That must be Kellen. He has a tall blonde on his arm. There is an older couple between the brothers. Their parents.

Their father is tall and broad like Morgan. He has a head full of silver hair and the same piercing blue eyes.

Their mother is petite, about the same height as me, and slightly plump. If her hair were white, she'd remind me of Mrs. Claus. She looks up as she's talking to Beckett and smiles when she sees Morgan.

Morgan gives my hand a squeeze before letting it go. He leans over to hug and kiss his mother on the cheek, then shake his father's hand. He puts his hand on the small of my back and presents me to his parents.

"Mom and Dad, I'd like you to meet Gabriella Carmichael. Gabriella, these are my parents, Rebecca and Declan."

"I'm very pleased to meet you," I say, holding out my hand to his mother.

She waves a hand and pulls me into a hug. "We're so happy to meet you, dear."

When she releases me, the impression of Santa Claus' significant other is reinforced by the mischief I see dancing in her eyes.

Morgan's father shakes my hand, smiling at his wife's antics. "It's good to meet you, Gabriella."

Next, I'm introduced to Kellen and his date, a woman named Belinda. Kellen is very stoic compared to his brothers and, other than the fact that Belinda is standing next to him, he doesn't seem particularly interested in her. I greet Beckett since we've met before and he introduces me to his date, a woman named Candy.

"I'm going to the bar to get us something to drink," Morgan announces. "Does anyone need anything?"

He takes a step, my hand in his, but his mother puts her arm in mine. "Leave Gabriella here with me, Morgan. I'll take good care of her, and we need to get better acquainted."

He looks at me and I give him a small nod. I might as well get this over with. I'll put my foot in my mouth, his mother will tell him I'm no good for him, and I'll never see him again.

"Morgan is right," she starts, "you are lovely. He tells me you're quite intelligent and talented, too. He says you do design work. Is that interior design? He didn't elaborate. You know how men are. Why use ten words when they can get away with two?" She chuckles as she says that last.

"No, Mrs. Masters, not interior design, although I do refinish furniture as a hobby. I do construction design mostly for home remodel projects."

"Please, call me Rebecca. How exactly does that work?"

"Well, for instance, one of my most recent clients bought a house in Heritage Hills which was last renovated over twenty years ago and is in dire need of an update. I met with them and did a walkthrough of the house with them so they can tell me what they want to update and how extensive they want the remodel to be."

I pause, trying not to talk too much. When she doesn't say anything, I go on.

"Based on our meeting, I create drawings to show them how things will look once the remodel is done all the way to the technical construction documents that can be taken to any contractor and used to complete the build."

"So you do the design work, but not the construction?" she asks.

"I have a small construction crew, but most of the time people have a construction crew on line to do the work. For instance, the Heritage Hills project, the owners know Morgan, so Masters Construction will be doing the build out. I also often take on more of a consultative role and offer options for them to take their ideas to the next level and or capitalize on getting the most bang for the buck on their budget."

"Well, it seems my son is correct on all three counts, smart, beautiful, and talented."

I blush and duck my head. "I don't know about all that, but thank you."

"Come dear, let's you and I go see what kinds of food they're cooking up for us."

She leads me away, her arm still in mine, so I'm powerless to say no. I cast a glance toward the bar and see that Morgan is still in line.

"Don't worry about him. He will come find us," Rebecca says.

The event is set up with a central room and several other smaller rooms around the outside. Each of the smaller rooms is a kitchen with a different chef. They each have a tasting menu of food with the offerings spanning a variety of cuisines.

Rebecca seems to want to just make the rounds to see what's available before deciding which ones she wants to try. I appreciate that because that's what I would have done, too. I like to see what's available before I choose.

She knows a lot of the attendees. We're stopped every few minutes by someone who wants to say hello. She introduces me to all of them, but there are so many that I'll never remember their names.

We're moving into the third kitchen when Morgan catches up to us and hands me a drink. "Mom, are you trying to steal my girlfriend?"

I startle at that but manage to hold it inside. Girlfriend? We haven't talked about what this thing is between us, but I learned a long time ago not to make assumptions. I'd be falling in love when the guy I thought was my boyfriend was apparently just having fun. Perhaps a conversation needed to happen sooner rather than later.

"I might be," she replies. "I got tired of waiting for you boys to get in gear. I can tell that Gabriella is just as hungry as I am, so I thought we'd get the lay of the land before deciding whom we're going to grace with our appetites."

She winks at me and puts her free hand in the crook of Morgan's elbow so she has us on each side of her.

Morgan isn't as circumspect when it comes to the food. We're just browsing, but he's tasting something at every kitchen.

"We'll let him be the guinea pig," Rebecca says as Morgan is tasting something from the BBQ kitchen. "He can let us know what's good and what's not."

"I like your plan," I reply with a grin.

"Although don't trust him when he tells you something isn't spicy. That boy has a cast iron stomach."

"Well, my Spanish heritage has insulated me, so I can take quite a bit of spice myself," I tell her.

"Spanish?" she asks.

"Yes. My mother's family is from Spain. They immigrated to America three generations ago."

"Are your parents still living?"

I hesitate. "My father is not. He was killed in a car accident when my mother was pregnant with me. As for my mother, I'm not sure. I...I don't have any contact with my family."

I know that might be a misstep to tell her I'm estranged from my family. Her family seems to be tightly knit, and she might not like that I'm essentially an orphan. An orphan by choice, but an orphan living alone in the world, nonetheless.

Her only response is to pat my hand. Morgan returns and she puts her hand in his arm again. To see her actions, you'd think she is frail and unable to move under her own steam, but she's as hardy as they come.

Morgan is in his early forties, so she's probably at least in her sixties. However, sixty today isn't like sixty was twenty or thirty years ago.

We finally make it through all the kitchens. "Let's go find our table and we'll send the boys to gather what we want," she tells me.

We find the others exactly where we left them. Kellen's date looks put out with him, and he still seems completely disinterested in her. She seems plenty interested in her phone, but not much else. Beckett is talking with his date and his father and from the looks of it, he's telling quite a story because both of them are laughing at him.

Mr. Masters looks up and sees his wife. His eyes are so full of love and adoration for her that it makes my eyes misty. I wonder if someone will ever look at me that way after over forty years of marriage.

Chapter 17

Gabriella

"Gabriella and I have scoped it all out and Morgan has already taste tested all but a few of the menus." She then tells her husband and sons what she wants and tells me to give Morgan my order.

Morgan is also grinning adoringly at his mother. The love among the family is quite evident. I wonder what it would be like to be in a family who loved each other with such devotion.

The group takes off with their marching orders, except for Belinda. She goes with Rebecca and me to lay claim to a table for the group. When we sit, I notice that the placard in the centerpiece designates the table as sponsored by Masters Construction. Of course, it is.

"Aren't you going to eat, dear?" Rebecca asks Belinda.

"No," is her only response.

Rebecca continues to try to engage Belinda in our conversation, but she doesn't seem to want to talk and cares more about what's on her phone screen than anything. Her answers are short and only give the requested information.

Belinda works for one of the large oil and gas companies in town as a Landman. That's about all the information she contributes, but Rebecca, bless her heart, keeps trying.

Thankfully, the rest of the family returns and lays plates of food out in front of us. Morgan has also brought me another drink. He slouches in the chair next to me, relaxed and happy. His hand cups my knee and gives it a squeeze. "You doing okay?" he asks quietly.

I nod and put my hand over his, squeezing back. "Yes. I'm okay."

"Good." He leans over and kisses my temple, then pulls a plate over to me. "I know you didn't ask for this, but you've gotta try it. Delicious."

"Thank you, but I'm not a fan of shellfish."

"Allergic?"

I shake my head. "No, I just don't care for it."

"Then try the sauce. The sauce is what makes it."

"That's usually the case with shellfish, which is why I don't care for it."

"Ahh," he says. "I gotcha."

With the return of the boys, as Rebecca calls them, the conversation at the table becomes loud and animated. Unlike Kellen's date, Beckett's date Candy is a lot like him, gregarious and funny. She also seems to know the family well but I'm not sure if she's his girlfriend or just a frequent plus one.

Once we've all eaten, Beckett and Candy head over to the small dance floor. He's an excellent dancer. "Do you dance?" I ask Morgan.

"No, sorry, baby."

"Don't you let him fib to you," Rebecca interjects. "I had all my boys take lessons when they were younger."

"And that's exactly where I learned that I'm not made for anything faster than a slow dance. Don't you remember the instructor asking you to let me quit? I think her toes were permanently bruised," he reminds her.

"Oh yes!" she laughs. "I had forgotten about that!"

"The next slow song, I'm your man. I can sway like nobody's business," he tells me. He reaches down and pulls my chair closer to his, then puts his arm around me. I snuggle against him, and his arm tightens around me.

Out of the corner of my eye, I can see Rebecca watching our interaction, and I wonder what she's thinking. Morgan, Kellen, and their father are talking business, mostly discussing one of the projects in Tulsa that Morgan had visited.

Beckett and Candy return. Candy is breathing hard from exertion, but Beckett looks like he could go on dancing forever. He goes to fetch a fresh drink for her, then returns to his seat beside her.

A couple of songs later, he asks her if she's ready to go again, but she shakes her head no and says she wants to rest a bit longer. "Gabriella would like to dance," Rebecca says. "Take her, since your brother won't."

I look at Morgan to make sure he's okay with it. "Sure, go ahead," he says with a smile, then says to his brother, "Beckett, behave yourself."

"Never," he replies with a devilish grin. "Come on, Gabs, let's go."

Before I can stop myself, I snap, "Don't call me that." Realizing what I've done, my face flushes. "I'm sorry. Please, forgive me." I can't keep the shame from my face. "That nickname has some terrible memories attached to it. Please either call me Gabriella or Ella, if you don't mind."

Beckett takes my hand in his and kisses the back of it. "Think nothing of it, Ella. Please accept my apology. No offense was meant." His look turns wicked again. "Now let's go dance."

I'm so grateful for the grace he's given me that it makes my eyes prickle with tears. The odd thing about Morgan flipping my sensation switch is that he seems to have also put my emotions into overdrive. I've never been so mushy and weepy. I don't risk speaking again, so I just nod.

"Excellent!" He laughs and ushers me out to the floor.

We dance through several songs, laughing and chatting. When the music slows, I feel Morgan's presence at my elbow. Like a sunflower, I turn to face him, my sun. "I got tired of waiting, so I bribed them to play a few slow ones." He takes my arm. "Get lost," he tells Beckett.

Beckett, good natured as ever, hands me over and bows. "Thank you for the dance, Ella."

Morgan wraps his arms around me and tucks my cheek to his chest before kissing the top of my head. I slide my arms around his waist and let my body meld to his. We sway through three songs before the tempo speeds up again.

"Do you want dessert? I'm thinking I need some dessert," he says.

"Sure," I reply and let him lead me back toward the kitchens.

Hours later, we're finally riding up the elevator to his apartment. I was so worn out from dancing and socializing that I'd fallen asleep in the car almost before we were out of the parking lot. Although I am awake now, I'm swaying on my feet so much that Morgan keeps an arm tight around me to make sure I don't slump to the floor. If I hit the floor, chances are I would just go right back to sleep and not get up until morning.

He gets me to the bedroom and unzips my dress. It slides to the floor. He sits me on the edge of the bed. I try to be helpful by pushing off my shoes, but I can't get my legs to work.

"Be still, baby. I've got you," he tells me and pulls off one shoe and then the other. I fall back on the bed as he hooks his fingers in my panties and pulls them down my hips.

A memory from one of my nightmares slams into the forefront of my brain and, with a surge of adrenaline, I'm crab-walking up the length of the bed. With my back against the headboard, I pull my knees up, hugging them tight, and I'm breathing like a bellows. I'm so disoriented that I can't see.

Someone is talking so loudly. It finally registers it's me saying "No no no no no..." over and over. There's another voice, quieter, calmer.

"It's just me, baby. It's okay. It's just me, Morgan."

I hear him and realize what's happened and I break. "Sorry, I'm so sorry," I sob.

He's on his knees in front of me. He reaches out and gathers me in his arms, pulling me into his lap. I let go of my knees and wrap my arms around him. I can't stop apologizing.

He holds me and smooths my hair. "Hush. It's okay. You're safe. I've got you."

After what seems like an eternity, I'm just as emotionally drained as I was physically drained when we arrived at the apartment. "I'm sorry."

"Hush. We'll talk about it tomorrow."

I nod against his chest and move to get up. His arms tighten on me. "I want to take my makeup off and brush my teeth."

He kisses the top of my head and lets me go.

While I tend to my ablutions, he takes a shower. I finish undressing myself and get into bed. In a few minutes, he climbs in behind me, spooning against my back. His scent wraps around me, comforting me, making me feel safe.

I lie there. I know he's still awake as I am. Sleep is probably going to elude me tonight. I roll it over in my mind for several minutes, then decide to tell him my darkest secrets, the things I've never told anyone.

"I was born into a family that didn't want me."

His arm tightens around me. "Baby, go to sleep. We can talk tomorrow."

"Neither of us are sleeping and some things are best spoken in the dark. I want you to understand what you're getting into with me so you can run before it's too late."

He only growls in response.

I pour out my history in short, concise sentences, my voice wooden. "The Preacher was one of my ghosts, but he's not the worst. My mother married my father at seventeen. She was a senior in high school, and he was a senior in college. He had already been offered a teaching position, and he wanted them to get married so she could go with him right after graduation."

I take a moment to organize my thoughts and decide how much background to tell him.

I tell him about my mom's early married life and losing her first child, a daughter. Her second was a son, born with a heart defect. After that, she had two more sons.

She found out she was pregnant with me just a few weeks before my father was killed in a car accident. While heavy with child, she moved across two states with three small boys, one of whom was very ill.

He died in surgery a few months later, then I was born soon after. Although I was just a baby, I became the representation of their despair. My brothers, in their minds, had a happy family until I came along.

My mother shut down emotionally and went about trying to earn a living. When I was seven, we moved to a small town, and became latch-key kids. I learned early about figuring out what people's expectations were and living within them.

I worked hard not to make trouble, not to create problems. That's why I never spoke up when the preacher started molesting me.

My brothers Peter and Joseph were two and a half and four years older than me, and we spent a lot of time alone together. When they hit puberty, they developed the same curiosities that most boys do.

However, they had their own personal play toy right under their own roof. They used me to satisfy their curiosities because, after all, I wasn't really their sister, just some girl that ruined their lives.

Over and over, they told me with words and actions that I was some sort of foreigner that had somehow infiltrated their family. I was just a shadow lurking in the corners. I didn't matter. I wasn't real.

Now comes the hard part of the story, so I bury my face against his chest, needing the connection with him. I'd better take it while I can because it could be taken away at any moment.

With a deep breath, I say, "The memory that was triggered tonight is one where they laid me back on the edge of the bed like you did. They covered my face and took off all my clothes, then explored between my legs. I remember clearly them using their fingers, but in my nightmares, my oldest brother, Joseph, also has sex with me. I was twelve at the time."

"Twelve," he echoes.

"Yes," I confirm. "Usually, when their ghosts come back, I can banish them by changing my position or something like that, but I guess because I was half asleep and unable to take control, it hit me hard."

He doesn't say anything and goes quiet for a long time. Finally he says, "Go to sleep Gabriella."

Okay. That's it; I've done it. I've finally shown him enough of my crazy that he's reached the tipping point and has decided it's too much to handle.

I lay there staring into the darkened room, trying to be still. After what seems an eternity, his breathing deepens, and I can tell he's asleep.

I let myself cry then, quietly shedding tears over losing the best chance at love I've ever had. Although I have started to develop real, deep feelings for Morgan, I know in my heart of hearts that he deserves someone so much better than me. He deserves someone that he can love freely without worrying if something he does is going to trigger her craziness.

Sometime in the early morning hours, I finally fall asleep.

Chapter 18

Morgan

I'm still furious the next morning when I go for a run. I meant to run my normal three-mile loop, but it's not enough to work out my anger. When I reach the end of my path, I go again, running the loop twice. Last night when she told me everything, I was so fucking pissed off that, for the first time in my life, I wanted to hunt someone down and kill them.

I did tours in Afghanistan and Sudan when I was in the Marines and killed in the name of country and following orders. I didn't want to do it and every day I prayed it would be a casualty free day. But I wanted to kill her brothers last night. I was so torqued up that I couldn't talk, not even to reassure her.

I'm glad she cut them out of her life, including her mother. It's difficult for me to believe that her mother was oblivious to everything that was going on under her nose. Call me an asshole for making the leap that her mother was complicit, but I'll carry that burden gladly. In my book, she's guilty until proven innocent.

Once I got Gabriella past her original freak out about meeting my family, everything went so well. She was relaxed and having fun. So much fun that she completely forgot about being nervous and afraid.

My mother is completely enamored with her. She didn't have to say anything; I could read it all over her face. This is the first time since I was a kid that I've brought a woman around to meet my family and Mom is eager for grandbabies.

I don't know that Gabriella and I will get there. We haven't gotten to a point of even talking about those kinds of things, but so far, she's it for me. She punches all my buttons and ticks every box for what I'm looking for.

Yeah, she has some issues, but who doesn't? Considering the shit she's been through, I'm surprised she's as pulled together as she is. If I can help her banish those ghosts, I'll be glad to do it. She's worth it; I know that in my bones.

When I finally make it back, she's still in bed. I'm not surprised. When I leaned down to kiss her before I went for my run, I put my hand down on her pillowcase. It was wet from where she'd apparently been crying. For it to still be that damp, she cried a lot. Who knows how long she stayed awake?

I jump in the shower and dry off quickly, then slide back into bed behind her. She tenses when I pull her close, but once I wrap my arms around her, she relaxes back against me. I kiss her shoulder and smooth her hair off her face with one hand. She presses her face against my hand.

"Hey," she says sleepily.

"Go back to sleep, baby; I didn't mean to wake you."

"Hmm mmm." She presses her hips back against my cock, which started to harden as soon as it came in contact with her skin once I got back into bed.

I move my hand down between her legs, slipping a finger between her folds. She's wet. I stroke her clit as she presses back against me again with a whimper. My girl is needy this morning, and I intend to take care of her and make sure she knows she's all mine.

I slide an arm under and around her, cupping her breast, molding and reshaping it. She's grinding her pussy against my fingers, letting out little grunts and moans. We stay there for a while, me stoking her fire. She lurches forward suddenly, grabbing a condom out of the drawer, tears it open, and hands it over her shoulder to me.

I have to let go of her pussy to put it on, but she replaces my hand with hers, rubbing at her drenched cunt. Just a slight shift of position and I slide into her from behind. She arches her back to accommodate my length and presses her hips against me.

I return my hand between her legs, holding her tight, making love to her slow and easy as I worry her clit. Rocking our bodies, I lay kisses along her shoulder and neck. Between kisses, I whisper to her, telling her how beautiful she is, how desirable she is, how much her body inflames me.

She tries to get me to speed up, to give it to her hard, but I want this slow burn. I want this prolonged intimacy. I want to drive into her that I want this closeness where we are one rather than just a quick fuck.

Her body begins to clench around me, which brings on the buildup of pressure at the base of my spine. I tell her to give herself to me, all of herself, and assure her she can trust me with all of who she is. I tell her I want all of her just as I want her to have all of me.

She cries out in orgasm, the spasms of her pleasure taking me over the edge with her. I lean over and kiss her cheek, tasting salt. She's crying again, so I hold her tight and tell her that everything is going to be all right as long as we're together.

We stay there for a while. She eventually pulls away and gets out of bed. "Sorry," she says, "bathroom."

She left the door open, so I follow her in to dispose of the condom. I like that she's not overly shy about the mundane things. I dated a girl once that threw a fit if she thought I was going to walk in on her peeing.

"Do you have anything you need to do today?" I ask.

She shakes her head. "Not really. I could work on Delores, but there's still some time before she's due."

"Nope, no working. You and I are going to hang out and be lazy today," I tell her.

She gives me a skeptical look. "I don't think you have a lazy bone in your body."

After a shower, breakfast, grocery store run, and retrieving my truck, I show her just how lazy I can be. We snuggle up on the couch and watch some house porn, talk, cook, eat some more, watch some sports, and do a whole lot of making out.

When evening falls, we're so relaxed that I ask her to tell me about the situations that trigger her so we might start working on them. I tell her about having to deal with my own ghosts from my time in the service because I can't really ask her to bare her soul to me if I'm not willing to reciprocate. She's telling me things she's never told anyone before, so I do the same.

I take her to bed and make love to her thoroughly so she will have no doubts as to whether or not I still want her after learning her secrets. We both fall deep asleep soon after, wrapped in each other's arms.

Chapter 19

Gabriella

Hailey has class on Monday mornings, so I'm usually alone for a few hours. The quiet allows me to start working on drawings for Delores. I realize that there may be an issue with one wall I want to remove, so I decide to do two sets of drawings in case there's a problem. I figure Morgan will let me know when he reviews my work.

Ding!

I put down my pencils and go to see who's come in. When I step around the corner, I'm surprised to see Rebecca Masters standing there.

"Rebecca! What a pleasant surprise!"

She opens her arms and I walk into them for a hug. I know she'll never let me get away with a handshake.

"I was just in the area and thought I'd stop by," she says. "Are you here alone?"

"My Assistant has class on Monday mornings so I'm only alone for a short time. Please, come in," I wave her around the corner to my office. "Can I get you anything? Coffee? Water?"

"No, no, I'm just fine. I mostly wanted to stop by to extend an invitation." She follows me into my office, and I see that she's taking in everything from the art on the walls to the furniture. She lingers at my drafting table, looking at my work.

"Invitation?"

"What is this?" she asks.

"That's a project house for a charity. I believe Beckett sits on the Board of Directors. My friend Caitlyn Foster does as well. The bid I'm working on will be a collaboration between Masters Construction and my design company to refurbish the house and not only modernize it, but make it usable for women in transition."

"Your drawings are beautiful," she says as she flips through the pages. "Did you go to school for architecture or drafting?"

"Thank you. No, I started college intending to get an art degree, but only went a few semesters before dropping out. I got a job as a receptionist at the company I was working for when I first met Morgan. My boss there learned I had some artistic ability and began to teach me how to do the artistic renderings. I grasped that quickly, so he taught me the technical aspects as well. Before long, he had pretty much handed all of that over to me."

I let her look her fill. She goes through each page several times, then turns away. "I apologize. What you do is fascinating to me. I don't have a creative bone in my body and am a bit jealous of those who do."

I smile at her.

"Anyway," she says, "back to the invitation. I know you told me you don't have contact with your family."

I nod. "That's right."

"This Sunday is Mother's Day, and I would like to invite you to come to my house for lunch with the family. I know it can be difficult when someone doesn't have a mother or father and those familial holidays come around and I, well, I suppose it might be a silly request, but I felt compelled to make it."

"It's not silly at all," I whisper. "I'm honored by your invitation."

"So, you'll come?"

I nod my head. "Yes, I'd be happy to come."

"Excellent! Now that that's settled, I'll let you get back to work. Morgan will have all the details for Sunday."

"I look forward to it. Thank you for the invitation and I'll see you Sunday."

She hugs me again and breezes out the door. I return to my work, feeling all warm and fuzzy, a big goofy grin plastered on my face. I'm just getting back into the flow when the front door dings again. A man is standing in the reception area, looking confused.

"May I help you?" He's completely nondescript, average height, average build, brown hair, brown eyes, and his face is so undistinguished that he could fade into a crowd with no one taking notice.

His clothes are slightly rumpled, and he's wearing round frame glasses ala Harry Potter. He looks like an absent-minded professor.

"I'm sorry. I think I must have taken a wrong turn. I'm looking for something called the Purple Penguin. My wife ordered some things that I need to pick up."

I smile, taking in his wedding ring. Absent-minded professor, indeed. "You're close. It's two doors down that way," I tell him, pointing in the right direction.

"Oh, so sorry," he says, looking abashed.

"It's all right. Happy to help."

He turns and pushes through the door, turning to give me a little wave. "Thank you, Gabriella." That last bit was spoken as he walked through the door and was turned away from me, so it took me a moment to realize what he'd said.

What? Wait, how did he know my name?

Once it sinks in, I rush to the door and look out. I look in the direction of the store he mentioned, then the other way toward the intersection. He's gone.

That's weird. Did I imagine him saying my name? I rack my brain trying to figure out if we've met before, but I cannot place him.

I'm still looking when Hailey comes around the corner. She smiles and waves as she approaches. "What's up?" she asks.

I shake my head, deciding I'm probably just overreacting. "Nothing. Some guy came into the office. He was lost, so I pointed him in the right direction."

"Oh. That's odd. All the businesses have their names right there on the door."

"I know, but there's always gotta be that one…" I say, forcing a smile. "How was class?"

That sets Hailey off, chattering about what she's learning in her classes as we go into the office. I go back to work on the Delores drawings, but that guy keeps popping back into my head.

The more I think about it, the more it creeps me out. My brain is in overdrive drawing connections between the stranger and what happened at my house last week, no matter how much I tell myself to calm down and quit being ridiculous.

I usually stay and work for several hours after Hailey leaves, but I leave with her at the end of the day. Thinking of going home makes me queasy, and that makes me angry. I've always loved my house. It has been my sanctuary, and now I'm afraid to be there alone.

I want to go to Morgan's and lock myself in behind several restricted access doors and an elevator that doesn't let just anyone up to the top floor. I can't do that, though, because I don't have a key to any of those doors.

Maybe Cait would want to do dinner. I could go to the Society and workout, then do dinner by myself. Neither of those options makes me super excited, so I call the person I really want.

"Hey, baby. What's up?" Morgan answers.

"I'm done with work for the day and was thinking about fixing dinner, so I wanted to see what your plans are for the evening."

"My plans are eating whatever you're fixing."

That makes me smile. "How late will you be coming over?"

"I can be done in about thirty minutes. So, are we staying at your place tonight?"

"Either that, or I can swing my place to refresh my bag, then go get groceries and meet you at your place when you get off."

He pauses. "Why don't you go pick up groceries and meet me at my place? After dinner, we'll go to your house so you can pack enough stuff for several nights. You're staying there all the time, so you might as well get enough things so you don't have to run back and forth every day."

I get it. He doesn't want me spending time alone at my house. I can't blame him because I'm starting to feel the same way.

Should I tell him what happened at the office today? If I do, he may post security outside my door there, too. Would that be such a bad thing?

I have no idea if the man from this morning is the same one that broke into my house, if anyone really did break in. There's still a chance that I was just being forgetful. Maybe he looked up the location and looked up the surrounding businesses. My first name is easily found on our website.

I'm not willing to sound an alarm just yet. My gut says do it, but my head says I'm overreacting. I've given Morgan enough shit to deal with, so I will keep my mouth shut for now.

Chapter 20

Gabriella

I thought I'd be nervous, but I'm actually feeling excited as we pull up to Morgan's parents' house. They live north of Edmond in a sprawling home that reminds me of an English cottage because of its stone and roughhewn wood touches.

However, it's mostly the gardens that are coming to life with explosions of color that make me think of a cottage. I've never been to England, but I have lots of pictures of cottages and their architecture in my house porn collection.

"Are we the first ones here?" I ask when I don't see any other cars in the drive.

"Yes," Morgan replies.

"Why?"

He shrugs. "When it comes to my Mom, I mostly do as I'm told. She said she wanted you to be here early so she could spend some time with you."

"What?"

"I told you, she's crazy about you. Maybe she wants some girl time before the house is full of testosterone. I'm sure she tires of being surrounded by a bunch of loud, obnoxious men all the time."

"That's probably true," I tease.

He leads me to the front of the house and walks in without knocking or ringing the bell. "Knock, knock!" he calls.

"Morgan?" Rebecca calls in return.

"Yes, and I have Gabriella with me."

We are walking through the entry when something catches my eye, causing me to stop. "That's one of mine," I say.

Morgan cocks his head. "One of your what?"

I run my fingertips across the top of the small chest in the foyer. It was a beautiful little piece that was the perfect canvas for me to replicate a William and Mary floral design I saw in a photograph. I had almost kept it instead of selling it because I loved it so much.

"One of my pieces. Remember, I told you I refinish furniture as a hobby? This is one of mine."

"What is that, dear?" Rebecca says, coming late to the conversation.

I look up and smile. "Nothing!" I say brightly.

"This chest you bought a few years ago and haven't been able to stop ranting about how you wish you knew the artist because you'd buy a million more of their pieces," Morgan says, pointing at the chest then at me. "Well, now you know the artist."

"What?" Rebecca says.

My face heats.

Realization dawns on her face. "Gabriella, you painted this?"

I nod. "Repaired, stripped, refinished, and painted. I struggled with selling her because I loved her so much."

She comes over to me and puts her hands on my cheeks. "Well, I am certainly glad you did because I love her, too!" She hugs me with a laugh. "Come to the kitchen and keep me company while I finish lunch."

"You're cooking your own Mother's Day meal?" I ask.

"Absolutely," she says with a wave of her hand, "you never know what you're going to get from a restaurant."

I look over at Morgan and grin because I've said that same thing to him more than once. He rolls his eyes at me as he grins back.

"Morgan, your father is out in the den watching golf or something equally boring on the television. Why don't you go keep him company while I steal Gabriella to hang out with me in the kitchen?"

"Yes, ma'am," he says. He gives me a light kiss on the lips before going off somewhere deeper in the house.

"Come, come," Rebecca says as she goes in the opposite direction.

The kitchen smells like heaven. "Is there anything I can do to help?" I ask.

"Do you cook?"

"I'm no chef, but I haven't poisoned Morgan yet, so I guess I do all right."

She chuckles as she pulls open a drawer and hands me an apron. "Put this on so you don't mess up that pretty dress." She then puts me to work.

As we work, we chat. After a lot of innocuous conversation, she gets to the topic I knew she most wanted to discuss.

"So, how long have you and Morgan known each other?" she asks.

"We first met three years ago, but hadn't seen each other again until two weeks ago."

"Here, trade with me. I'll take over there if you'll make the Brussels sprouts. They're one of Morgan's favorites. The recipe is right there on the counter. From what he says, you've been spending a lot of time together."

My neck gets hot. "Yes, we have."

"That's just like him," she says with a knowing smile.

"What is?"

"When Morgan was a boy, he wanted a bike. He mowed yards and raked leaves until he was big enough to do some of the safer menial jobs on construction sites with his father. He was in the bike shop several times a week, looking at the inventory. It was rare that he would take a test drive, though. Even when he had enough money to buy any bike in the shop he wanted, he abstained. We offered to take him to other bike shops, but he said when the right one came along, he'd know it. Sure enough, a few months later, a fresh supply of inventory came into the shop and Morgan found his perfect bike and laid out his money for it that very instant. He rode that bike until the wheels fell off."

She pauses to grab a cucumber out of the refrigerator. "It's the same with anything he's ever wanted. His senior year, he announced he wanted to go into the military with no warning at all. While I can't say I was in favor of it at the time, I don't know if he'd be able to handle the position he's in now without having had that experience. The last time I met someone he was dating was the girl he took to the senior prom."

I don't know what to say to that and thankfully I'm saved from responding by Beckett breezing into the kitchen, followed by Kellen. "Happy Mother's Day, Mom." He kisses her on the cheek, then turns his attention to me.

"Ella, so good to see you again! You look beautiful, as always." He comes over to where I continue working and kisses my cheek, too.

"Must I keep telling you to stay away from my girl?" Morgan asks from the doorway.

Beckett puts his arm around me and gives his older brother a cheeky grin. "Maybe at least one more time," he says.

Kellen says hello to their mother with a kiss on the cheek as well and gives me a nod. "Gabriella."

"Pleasure to see you again, Kellen," I tell him.

Morgan comes to me and pushes his brother away. He stands behind me and wraps his arms around my waist. "What's the ETA, Mom? I'm starving."

"You boys are always starving," she retorts. "We should be ready in about fifteen minutes. Why don't you all make sure the table is set and open some wine to breathe?"

"I'll get the wine," says Beckett, "you two set the table."

Morgan kisses my cheek. "Copy," he says and goes to do his mother's bidding. I look up to see his mother smiling at me.

It's so strange to share a meal with a family that actually likes each other; not just likes, but loves. They're loud and laughing. Everyone is included. Everyone takes part. Even Kellen becomes slightly more animated in the glow of his family's fellowship. I am basking in the glow right along with them.

When everyone has eaten their fill, I help clear the table, along with Morgan, Beckett, and Kellen. Rebecca orchestrates as leftovers are stored, dishes are rinsed, and the dishwasher is filled. Morgan starts coffee percolating while Beckett uncovers a cake and Kellen takes down dessert plates and coffee cups.

"I'll be right back," Morgan says.

We're moving back into the dining room when he returns with the gift I brought for Rebecca, having apparently gone out to his truck to get it. He sets it in front of her place at the table. It's the only gift.

Rebecca comes into the room carrying the cake plate. "Ooh, a present! I love presents!"

"It's from Gabriella," Morgan tells her.

I feel my face heat. "I thought it was tradition to get gifts for parents on their day."

"Oh, it is, dear, but when I was up to my eyeballs in scarves, robes, and slippers, I told them to stop. Here, Morgan, take this so I can open my present!"

She hands the cake off to her son and starts unwrapping her gift. When she pulls the box out of the shredded paper, she puts a hand over her mouth, her eyes bright. "Did you do this?"

I nod.

It's a wooden box that I painted with a folk-art scene depicting a fox with a sly smile playing hide and seek with a clever rabbit among a grove of trees. On the top is a smiling moon watching them play.

She turns it around in her hands, looking at every side, a smile playing on her lips. Her husband Declan is watching her, smiling too. He looks over at me and gives me a wink and a nod, letting me know I've done well.

She sets the box down, gets out of her chair and comes around to me. "It is beautiful, dear. Thank you so much; I will treasure it always." She's misty eyed, which makes me misty eyed when she hugs me and kisses my cheek.

Beckett has picked up the box and is looking at it. "Put that down before you break it!" Her voice is sharp, but there's no real heat in it.

"I'm not going to break it," he says back with a grin. "This is beautiful, Ella. You painted this?"

"Yes."

"We also found out today that the chest in the foyer Mom's been raving about for years is one of Gabriella's, too," Morgan tells him.

"Well, I'll be damned," Beckett says.

Rebecca swats him with her napkin. He just grins wider.

Feeling uncomfortable with the scrutiny, I excuse myself from the table to go find a restroom. When I come out, I find Morgan leaning on the wall opposite the door. He backs me up back into the bathroom and closes the door behind us.

"I haven't had my hands on you in hours and I'm having withdrawals," he tells me as he boosts me up on the counter.

He cups my ass in his hands and pulls me to him, his broad body between my legs. I stretch up and put my arms around his neck, guiding his mouth to mine.

He breaks the kiss and puts his forehead to mine. "I have half a mind to take you to my old bedroom and have my way with you."

"Only half a mind?" I tease.

"If I thought I could get away with it, I would, but my mother has a sixth sense and would have perfect timing to walk in right in the middle of things. That thought is holding sway over the other half of my mind." He kisses me again. "You are incredible, you know that, right?"

I smile and look down. He lightly grips my jaw in one big hand and turns my face up. "Look at me, Gabriella," he says firmly.

I look at him.

He holds my eyes and repeats. "You are incredible."

"Thank you, cariño."

He kisses me again, then helps me off the counter. "We'd better get back out there before she comes looking for us."

Sure enough, when we step into the hall, Rebecca is coming our way. "I was wondering what happened to the two of you."

"I wanted to make out with my girlfriend for a minute, that's all," Morgan tells her.

"Nothing wrong with that, dear," she tells him. "We're holding dessert for you, though."

"We can't have that," he says, his eyes dancing with mirth.

After dessert, the family settles in the den. Morgan pulls me onto his lap in an overstuffed, oversized armchair. I curl up in his arms and watch, taking part here and there.

I've never had anything like this, so I love just sitting back and taking it all in. Morgan strokes my back and the rumble of his voice in his chest against my ear lulls me. Between that and my full belly, I soon find myself feeling relaxed and sleepy.

It seems I'm not the only one feeling that way. The conversation has died down. I look over to see Declan dozing in his recliner. Beckett and Rebecca are sitting on the sofa, chatting softly with Morgan commenting occasionally. I have no idea where Kellen has gotten off to.

Kellen reappears as if my thought of him conjured his presence. "I need to go," he says.

"Oh, so soon?" Rebecca asks.

"Yeah," he says, not offering an explanation. Rebecca starts to rise. "Don't get up, Mom." He leans down and kisses her cheek. "I'll call you next week."

He shakes Beckett's hand, then Morgan's, giving me a nod. Declan is sleeping through it all, so he pats his father on the shoulder with a small smile. Kellen waves to us all and heads toward the front door.

"Something is going on with that boy," Rebecca says, her gaze lingering on the front door.

"Woman trouble," says Beckett.

"I was wondering what was up with them last weekend," Morgan adds. "They barely spoke to each other all night."

"I worry about him. He's going to be a tough one," Rebecca says. "That boy has a poet's heart ruled over by an accountant's brain and it's going to take someone special to crack him open."

"Do you worry about me?" Beckett asks unabashedly.

"Absolutely not," she replies, patting his hand. "I doubt you ever decide to settle down for long. You're too restless."

"True," Beckett agrees. "Don't worry Mom, you'll eventually get your grandbabies even if I have to go adopt one for you."

She pats his cheek. "As much as I would love to have a grandchild to spoil rotten, I only want them when one of you is ready for them. My biggest hope is for you to be happy. That trumps everything else."

We only stay a little longer. It's apparent that Rebecca's energy is waning after the busy morning. When we get up to go, she walks us to the front door, hugging me, kissing my cheek, and thanking me again for the box. She hugs and kisses her sons before bidding us all goodbye.

As we're driving back to Morgan's apartment, I decide it's time to ask some questions. I don't have the courage to ask the question I most want to ask, so I start off with something else.

"Considering your Mom's comment to Beckett, I'm curious. Do you want children?"

He shrugs. "I've always thought I'd have kids someday, but I'm almost forty-three. I don't worry about stuff too much because I figure if it's meant to happen, it will happen. That's not to say that if I was with someone that wanted kids and there were issues with fertility for one or the other of us I wouldn't get all the medical help we could or consider adopting. What about you? Do you want kids?"

"I don't know. On one hand, my childhood was so messed up that I worry about being a parent. I never had any good examples of competent parenting, much less great parenting, so I wonder if I'd only end up messing my kids up because I don't know what I'm doing. I have always been very careful because the thought of being a single parent scares the pants off me. On the other hand, I think I'd like having children. At least they would be loved with everything I have because I never had that growing up. But I think it would depend on who the father would be and how he would be with them. I'm thirty-four, so I don't have a lot of childbearing years left."

We ride in silence for a few minutes. "Am I your girlfriend?" I blurt out before I can stop myself. "I mean, I'm not seeing anyone else, and I don't want to," I add quickly, "but we haven't talked about it, and you've called me your girlfriend a couple of times now to your family."

"You're right, we haven't talked about it. I don't juggle. When I'm seeing someone, I'm only seeing them. I'm not like Beckett who juggles partners so much I have a hard time keeping their names straight. Don't get me wrong, there's nothing bad about that; he's very up front with his partners and to me that's the key, but it's not my thing. Although, I'm usually up front, too, because I don't want to lead anyone on when I'm just having fun. I thought you and I were going to be that way when I first saw you at that dinner. However, even though we've only been together a short time, I have feelings for you and to me, that's the point where my mind shifted you over to being my girlfriend. I'm well beyond just having fun and I'm a little blindsided by it. I think I haven't brought it up just because I was afraid of scaring you off if you were just in it to have fun."

I'm quiet for a minute, processing what he's said. He has feelings for me. I feel something inside me relax because I care more about him than is warranted by the two weeks we've been together, too. "Soooo...I can call you my boyfriend?"

"Do you want me to be your boyfriend?"

"I guess so," I tease.

"Guess so? Maybe I need to do some convincing when we get home," he slides his hand up my thigh under my dress. "Maybe I should start now."

"Maybe," I say, but I can't help the grin spreading across my face.

Chapter 21

Gabriella

I lock the door behind me when I get to work. If someone wants to come in, they can knock. I don't want a repeat of last week when that guy waltzed into the office when I was alone.

Feeling secure in my surroundings leads to a very productive morning. I've gotten most of the drawings completed for Delores and will probably be able to finish up this afternoon. I love the feeling of getting things done.

By the time Hailey arrives, I'm famished. I missed breakfast this morning because Morgan was in a very frisky mood, and I simply cannot resist him when he is like that.

"I'm going to go grab some lunch," I tell her.

I pull out my keys but decide to walk instead. I'll have to put up with smelling like smoked meat for the rest of the day, but my tastebuds are set for Iron Star's corn pudding and it's only a little over a block away.

It's early so I'm one of the first ones there. I ask the server for a booth in the corner against the far wall. She suggests a two-top table in the middle of the room. When I assure her I will only be there long enough to eat, and she will be able to turn the table quickly, so she gives in.

I recognize that I'm developing a heightened level of paranoia. I argued with myself all the way to the restaurant about eating in or ordering to go and taking my lunch back to the office.

A little paranoia is okay, I told myself, but too much is crippling. Thus the compromise of eating in the restaurant, but taking a booth where I can monitor everyone who comes in.

I place my order and take out my phone. I text Morgan just to say hello. It takes a few minutes for him to reply, and when he does, his message is a photo of some intricate crown molding. I smile at him, sending me more house porn. The man knows me.

My plate of food arrives, so I take a picture and send it to him. My phone buzzes with his reply.

Morgan: *Dammit, woman, you're making my mouth water and I'm stuck at this site.*

I feel just a teensy bit guilty because he might not have gotten anything for breakfast either.

Me: *I can bring you some. I've had a productive morning so I can slip out for a bit.*

Morgan: *Nah, I'm fine. I had a late breakfast because someone distracted me this morning.*

I am grinning at my phone now. God, I love how this man is with me. The restaurant is filling with a lunch crowd, so I focus on keeping my word to the hostess. I look around at the other patrons as I eat.

Most tables have groups seated at them, but there are several single diners at the bar. I don't see anyone who looks like the disheveled, absent-minded professor of the week before.

See, there was no need to be paranoid.

I pay my bill and take my leftovers feeling much lighter as I walk back to the office.

It's nearing the end of the day and I am putting the finishing touches on the drawings for Delores when the doorbell goes off.

"Oh Ella," Hailey croons.

I go out to the lobby to see a bouquet of red roses on her desk and a delivery person's back as they leave the building.

Roses. That's odd.

I pull the card to read it, noticing that the florist is the one just a couple of blocks north of here. I wonder why Morgan would go there and not come by here to at least say hello. The message makes me feel faint. The card flutters to the ground as I back against the wall.

Hailey picks it up and reads, "I hope you enjoyed your lunch. I enjoyed watching you eat, but don't you know no one should put Baby in the corner?" She frowns. "That's weird. Why would Morgan write that?"

"He didn't," I tell her. I can't stop shaking.

"Ella! What's wrong?"

My heart is pounding, and I can't catch my breath enough to answer her.

"I'll call Morgan," she says, and picks up the phone.

"No!" I exclaim and take the phone from her.

"You tell me what's going on right now or I'm calling him, and you won't stop me."

I take a breath. "Someone's been stalking me."

"What? Why didn't you tell me? And why don't you want Morgan to know?"

"I...I just. I didn't think it would affect you and didn't want you to worry. Morgan knows part of it, but, well, it's complicated."

"Complicated, huh? That's a bunch of hogwash! Tell me what's happened."

I tell her about the things that happened at home and the guy coming in the week before. She is scowling at me by the time I'm done.

"You don't need to be here by yourself anymore," she says.

"You neither!" I say.

"I'm not the one being stalked. You are," she retorts.

"Yeah, but I don't know that he won't do something to you if he can't get to me. Morgan has me locked down when I'm not at work."

"So, do you want something to happen?" she asks.

My breathing was calming, but her question sends me back into hyper-drive.

"No! I want him to go away, but I don't know how to make that happen."

"Have you called the police?" she asks.

"About what? A bunch of stuff I can't prove and an unsigned card on some flowers?"

"Okay. If either of us is here alone, we'll keep the door locked and only let in the UPS or Fed-ex folks or clients who have appointments. You have site visits tomorrow, so I'll start with the whole door locking thing tomorrow." She pauses. "Are you going to tell Morgan?"

I shake my head. The last thing he needs is for me to dump more crazy on him. "I don't know. I don't want him to worry any more than he already does."

"I still think you need to tell him."

I nod, but don't commit. I'm distracted, replaying my time in the restaurant. Every single person there was scrutinized as I tested for some spark of recognition. There was none.

But did I really look at everyone? I have to admit to myself that I focused mostly on those at the bar and the single diners at tables. Could he have been there with a group? Maybe he worked there.

No, that didn't make sense. Would a restaurant worker be allowed to leave in the middle of lunch rush to go purchase flowers? It would have taken time for the florist to prepare the arrangement and work the delivery into their schedule.

Was he wearing some kind of disguise? Or maybe the absent-minded professor act was a disguise. I'm going to drive myself crazy with this. Well, crazier, anyway.

Hailey takes the flowers out the back door and throws them into the big dumpster for our complex. It's satisfying to see them arc over the lip and to hear the vase crash into pieces inside.

She comes in and locks the back door. "Come on. Let's lock up and head home."

I stop by the grocery store on the way home. I'll need to start making a little extra for supper so that I can take some for lunch the next day.

Tomorrow will be easier because I'll be able to just drive through somewhere and grab something between site visits. Little by little, my fear is eating away at my life, making me a prisoner and I hate it, but I don't know what else to do.

Morgan gave me a set of keys to his apartment, so I don't have to wait for him any longer. It seems so weird that after a few weeks, we are essentially living together. When I told Hailey that he had me on lockdown, it wasn't a euphemism. I drive to and from work alone, but if I'm not in the office or commuting, he is with me.

I wrestle with the idea of telling him about today all the way home. If I tell him about today, I will have to tell him about last Monday. He's going to be mad.

Maybe I'll get a spanking. That thought cheers me up, but I still get stuff to make something for supper that I know he really, really likes hoping that will soften him up.

"It smells great in here, baby." Morgan says when he comes into the kitchen after showering.

He comes up behind me as I stir, slipping his arms around my waist and nuzzling my neck. A shiver tickles down my spine when he kisses me right below my ear, then he releases me. He crosses to the refrigerator and pulls out a beer.

"How was your day?" he asks.

I'm nervous about telling him, so I don't want to put it off. Might as well rip that band-aid off and get it over with. "Well, I have something to tell you."

He pushes himself up on the island to sit and watch me. "Lay it on me."

I keep my back to him and focus on cooking. "So, last Monday something weird happened..."

"Last Monday, as in a week ago?" I can hear the growl in his voice.

"Will you hush and let me tell you?"

He doesn't reply. I turn to look at him and he's taking a drink of his beer. He swallows and says, "I'm hushing!"

I scowl at him, and he winks.

I tell him about the man coming into the office and knowing my first name. Then I tell him about the flowers today. I also tell him about our plan for when we're alone in the office and that I plan on taking my lunch from now on.

When I finally stop, he says, "Roses, huh? I'll bet you knew as soon as you saw them that they weren't from me."

"Yes," I agree.

"So, when are we calling the police?"

I shrug. "I have no idea of who it might be, and what am I going to tell them? Someone sent me flowers? Gee, that's such a threat. They'll probably just say I have a secret admirer or something."

"You should get a report on their books even if you don't know who it is."

"I'll think about it."

"Okay."

I look at him again.

"What?"

"I thought you'd be mad at me," I tell him.

"Nope. You have a plan on how you want to handle it, and I don't think that you're taking any extreme risks."

I don't know what he sees on my face, but he laughs.

"What?" I ask.

"You act like you're disappointed that I'm not mad."

"I was kind of hoping for a spanking," I grumble.

"Oh, I'll be happy to warm that ass up. You just wait."

Chapter 22

Mr. Smith

I have never felt the urge to toy with someone the way I do with Gabriella. Oh, I have played with them, but never for such a prolonged period of time. I have to say that she has brought something out in my psyche which wasn't there before.

They say that anticipation makes the pleasure more intense. Whomever they are, I hope they're right. I do love my work, my true work, so to have an even greater payoff, a more intense experience would be delicious, indeed.

I have a keen understanding of delayed gratification. I proclaim the benefits of the concept all day, every day, in my dull, gray vocation. However, I know, despite my proclamations, that sometimes the end result is not as gratifying as one would hope. I certainly hope Gabriella does not disappoint.

It has never taken this long for me to collect one of my prizes. When she became involved with this current man, I thought seriously about moving on, but I just couldn't.

Whatever it is in the twisted wiring of my brain that drives me to rid the world of whores refuses to let her go. She may be in a relationship at the moment, but a whore is a whore is a whore and she will return to her true nature soon.

Losing access to her at her house has driven me to become more creative. I have been forced to seek her out at her place of business, which requires more care, more planning. I have also had to adjust my schedule to be available to observe her so that I might find an opening, an opportunity.

This has become supremely more frustrating, but I keep telling myself that soon she will bear the brunt of that frustration. Very soon. When I met her and shook her hand ad the homebuilder's event, she had no clue and the mantra of "Very soon" was ringing in my ears.

Today is proving to be most fortuitous. She is in the office alone, as she usually is on Monday mornings, but I don't dare visit her in person as I did last week. That was risky, but, as usual, she doubts herself. Women are so predictable.

I am watching from across the street. When her assistant arrives and Gabriella leaves the office on foot, I decide to follow. I can watch from the corner to see where she goes, so when she steps into the restaurant, the temptation is too great.

I wait to ensure she's dining in and to allow a few other diners to enter before I follow. My appearance is nothing like it was a week ago, nor even how I looked at the event, having donned a new affectation for today's observation session.

I take a position at the bar where I can watch Gabriella with ease. I chat up the server working in this area. To the casual observer, I never look Gabriella's way.

She has taken a position in the corner which makes me think of a certain movie. She spends some time on her phone, probably texting that brute she's been staying with. When her food arrives, she eats quickly, casting furtive glances around the room.

She leaves and I know she's going back to her office, so I don't rush with my meal. As I am engaged in gastronomical delights, an idea sparks. I pay the bill in cash, leaving a healthy, but not outlandish tip for the server before leaving.

I walk a circuitous route just a few blocks to the north to the florist. The order for a dozen red roses pleases the clerk and an additional fee for a rush delivery pleases her even more.

It incenses me, although I don't show it. The bitch is extorting an additional forty dollars from me for a delivery that's only three blocks away.

Thankfully, I have enough cash to cover the fee and extortion payment. I try to carry plenty on these observation days in case I have an unexpected need or brilliant idea, such as today's machinations.

I return to my observation point and wait. The end of the day is fast approaching, and I am tempted to go back to that florist and beat her to death with one of her own vases. My hand is on the door handle when I see the delivery van enter the parking lot.

I hold my breath as the scene plays out. I wish I had a camera in the room to film it. Initially, I think the look on her face when she reads the card is priceless, but then when she drops it to the floor and hits her back to the wall! The way it excites me has my cock as hard as steel and ready to explode.

Several minutes go by as I wait to see what happens next. The assistant picks up the vase and goes to the back, where I can't see. When she returns empty-handed, I know what has happened.

The flowers I sent have been flung into the dumpster. I should be angry, but instead, I'm giddy that I was able to create such an impact without laying a finger on her.

I stop by the grocery on the way home. My sniveling significant other was being clingy and annoying when I was trying to leave this morning, so I had to put her in her place. It places an extra burden on me to pick up her slack for things like grocery shopping, but a man has to do what a man has to do.

As I round the end of one aisle, I see the display of flowers and a new idea sparks. These aren't as fine as the flowers I sent from the florist, but they'll do. I add a bundle of red roses to my basket and go to check out.

I wish I could be there in the morning to see Gabriella's reaction again, but alas, I need to put in an appearance at work. That place of tedious inanity that, as much as I despise it, funds my ability to fulfill my true calling.

Through monitoring her phone, I will keep an eye on her movements so that I can pounce as soon as an opportunity presents to collect her.

Chapter 23

Gabriella

*Y*ou idiot; I can't believe you forgot to bring the drawings home!

I am racing to the office to pick up the drawings for Delores. I meant to bring them home last night, but I was so flustered by the flowers that I completely forgot.

Morgan needs them to estimate the cost for the build out so that he can finalize our bid and get it submitted by the deadline. The committee is meeting early next week to review the submissions.

I get out of my car in a rush and look down to see something red on the pavement. It's so incongruous that I can't help but stare. It's a rose petal. My gaze lifts to take in the entry to my office and the sidewalk. Red rose petals are piled in front of the door.

I look around. It's very early and there are no other cars in the parking lot. I turn a full circle and see no one else except the occasional car driving by with early morning commuters on their way to work.

I reach back into the car and get my phone out of my purse, snapping pictures of the petals. As the slight breeze whispers by, the pile slowly shrinks, bits of flaming flower flesh being carried to points unknown.

They're everywhere, strewn across the parking lot with Mother Nature's wild abandon. Should I go in? Should I not? It will only take a minute to unlock the door, grab the drawings, and get back out. It is imperative that I get the drawings.

I close my car door and hit the lock button until it beeps, so I know it's sealed. In a sprint, I hurry to the front door, jamming my key in so hard I fear I might break it. Heaving breaths in an attempt to calm myself, I watch the window's reflections for anyone approaching.

Calm down, you idiot, this is what he wants.

Still, I don't linger inside. I get the drawings and I exit the office. Feeling calmer and more than a little pissed off, my steps are purposeful, steady. I'm alert, observing my surroundings. A childhood spent staying out of other people's ways, ingrained this ability for hyper-alertness.

I double-check the door is locked before getting in my car and driving away toward Masters Construction. I call when I'm just about a minute away. Morgan had to be on a conference call first thing, so Beckett is going to meet me at the door to take the drawings.

I see him standing there, all dapper in his expensive suit. He really is a handsome man. He's a little too perfectly put together and polished for my taste, but that doesn't change the fact that he's pretty to look at.

I pull up and roll down my window.

"Hey gorgeous! I like this butch look on you," he says, taking in my jeans, boots, and tee as he leans on his arms on the window.

I laugh. "You sure know how to flatter a girl. You look very nice yourself."

"I know," he says, which makes me laugh more.

I hand the drawings out the window to him, frustrated that my hand is still shaking enough that he might notice. He does.

"Are you okay?"

"Yeah, just rushing this morning and maybe a little too much coffee. I meant to give these to Morgan last night because I have a full day of site visits today. But silly me, I forgot them at the office."

"I see. Well, I won't keep you. Get to work, woman, as my ugly older brother would say."

I laugh again. "Thanks Beckett, have a great day!" I roll up the window and pull away as he raises his hand in a wave.

I pause before I exit the parking lot and send the pictures to Hailey so she's not surprised when she arrives and remind her to keep the door locked. Thankfully, she arrives and leaves when there will be plenty of foot traffic in the complex, which makes her an unlikely target. I still worry about her, though.

I send the pictures to Morgan, too. He doesn't respond right away, which doesn't surprise me. I'll probably hear from him after his call is over.

Setting this morning aside, I focus on work as I make my way from site to site. These visits are for me to check on the progress of each location and see if any adjustments need to be made in the plans. Often there are unexpected finds during demo that create a need for a slight, or sometimes extensive, change.

I'm just leaving the second site when Morgan calls. "Hi there," I answer.

"Can you talk?"

"Yes, I just got into the car to leave the site I'm at."

"Good. Are you ready to call the cops yet?"

That's my man, straight to the point.

I sigh. "Yes, I will go by a station and file a report."

"Good girl," he says.

"Did you get the drawings?"

"Yes, I haven't looked through them yet, though. I just got off my conference call and wanted to call you first. How are your site visits going?"

"They are going well. The first two build outs are moving along smoothly, but those are my guys and they've learned how I like things. I have two more this afternoon and then I'm done for the day."

I don't tell him I'm dreading one of those visits. The contractor is a pompous ass that resents me checking in no matter how much the homeowners want me to. He does good work, but besides being a condescending jerk, he likes to get handsy when no one is watching.

"Why don't we do dinner out tonight? You will have had a busy day and eating out once instead of slaving away over a stove after a busy day isn't going to kill you."

I smile. He's always taking care of me. "Okay. I'll touch base with you when I'm done, and we'll decide what we're doing."

"Perfect," he says. "I'll talk to you later, baby."

It's on the tip of my tongue to say "I love you", but thankfully, I stop myself. I'm surprised by the impulse but squelch it. "Have a good day, cariño," I say instead, and hang up.

Love? What the heck was that? I care a lot for Morgan, but love?

He is amazing and wonderful and takes care of me in ways I never dreamed of. He's gorgeous and strong and everything I never knew I wanted in a man. He's smart and powerful and has taken the time to help banish my ghosts, at least in part so far. I have no doubt that he will banish them completely over time.

As I work through all of this in my crazy, mixed-up head, I realize the truth. I love him. I love Morgan Masters. Holy fucking crap, I LOVE Morgan Masters! How can a month be enough time to fall in love?

It has been so long since I've felt this way and even then, what I felt before was a pale comparison to what I feel for him. How did this sneak up on me? I'm overwhelmed with tenderness and joy. It's so foreign for me to feel this way for anything other than a fleeting moment that I don't know what to do with myself.

Thankfully, I pull up to my next site and can go back to focusing on business. However, I don't even try to hide the huge goofy grin on my face.

I lose my smile at the last site I visit. Chris Sparks of CSS Construction is trying to explain to me why he had to deviate from my plans. Of course, he also took it upon himself to tell the homeowners that I had no clue what I was doing, and he had no choice.

I have already been paid, so I tell Mr. Homeowner that if he wants to accept the contractor's changes, that's up to him, but it is very much not what his wife wanted. Sparks then proceeds to pull me aside to have a talk with me after rolling his eyes at Mr. Homeowner and my blood starts to boil.

He positions himself between Mr. Homeowner and me and puts his hand on my shoulder. In the past, I would have been triggered with the preacher by this type of move, but thanks to Morgan, that no longer happens. I knock his hand off.

"Do not put your hands on me," I say directly.

He raises his hands palms out in a conciliatory gesture and looks over at Mr. Homeowner, who is watching. "Touchy, touchy."

This man is the epitome of why I hate dealing with contractors.

"If you change my plans and the homeowners approve it, I have no issue with that, but if I ever hear you besmirching my work to one of my clients again, I will sue you for slander."

He leans in and lowers his voice. "Besmirch, huh? That's a big word for a little girl like you. I'll say whatever I goddamn well please and if you can't take the heat, get the fuck out of my kitchen."

He raises an outstretched index finger to poke me in the chest. I knock his hand away before he can make contact.

"I said do not touch me or I will add sexual harassment to the suit. Listen here, you arrogant jerk, I have clients stacked up to work with me, and from what I hear, the same can't be said for you. My clients often ask me for contractor recommendations so you can bet your bottom dollar, which is very close to hand based on reports, that I will never recommend you. When it comes to letting our work speak for itself, I know whose says quality."

"Fuck you, you stupid cunt."

"Only little words from you, I see. I'll reach out with the homeowner's wife to ensure that she knows the deviation from the plans was instigated solely by you and I was not looped in on the changes so that I can have her sign a statement that I'm no longer responsible for upholding the satisfaction guaranty I offer. Do you offer guaranties, Chris?"

"Get off my job site," he says.

"Gladly," I throw back.

I say a quick goodbye to the homeowner and go to my car. I call Hailey and ask her to send out the statement to both Mr. Homeowner and his wife. It is sad when this kind of thing happens often enough that we have a standard form and message language in our files for it.

I am finished earlier than I expected. With Morgan's admonition that I need to file a police report, I pull up a mapping app on my phone to see where the nearest station is located.

Oklahoma City isn't like a lot of larger cities that seem to have a station on every corner there appears to be only five or six. I find the closest and head to it since it seems my house would be located in their scope of responsibility.

I'm sitting in the lobby waiting to speak with someone when I hear, "Ella?"

I look up to see Cait's boyfriend, Ford. "Oh, hi, Ford. Fancy meeting you here."

He smiles broadly. "What are you doing here?"

"I need to file a report about some trouble I've been having."

"Trouble?" His friendly smile turns to a look of concern.

"Yeah, I think someone's been in my house and there have been some incidents at work. I don't know if I should call it stalking or what, but Morgan wants me to file a report."

"It is always better to get something on record," he replies.

"That's what Morgan said. I just thought I was misremembering where I put things or blowing it out of proportion."

"Stalkers count on that. Let me see if I can scare someone up to take the report."

"Thanks Ford."

"You're welcome. Cait and I need to have you and Morgan over for dinner sometime."

"I'd like that." I tell him with a smile.

He turns and goes through the door into the belly of the building and I go back to waiting.

"Mrs. Carmichael?"

I'm pulled out of my thoughts by a middle-aged, uniformed officer whose nametag says Ingram. "It's Ms., but please call me Gabriella."

He leads me through the door that Ford used and takes me to a small room that has a glass front, so I'm assuming it's not an interrogation room.

"Have a seat," he directs me.

I sit and put my purse on the floor after pulling out my phone.

He places a form and a letter size notepad on the table, a pen in one hand poised in the air to begin taking notes. "Why don't you tell me what has been happening," he urges.

I tell him about things moving in my house and that it started a couple of months ago, including the incident with the book. Then I tell him about the man coming by my office and knowing my name without being told and the whole thing with the roses yesterday and this morning. He doesn't tell me I'm crazy or that I should be flattered to have a secret admirer, which is a relief.

He asks a series of follow-up questions. We talk about my locks and whether I've had them changed. The answer is no. He wants to know if there has been any recent activity at my home. I respond that I started staying at my boyfriend's which is more secure, and only go home to gather what's needed for a few days at a time, always with Morgan in tow.

When I think through the various incidents, I can see that the change to bothering me at work came when I stopped being accessible at home. I wonder if changing my locks would help, not that I want to go back to staying at my place without Morgan.

The officer suggests changing up my routine to which I reply that it's difficult to run a business when you're being unpredictable. He suggests getting a security system installed at my home. I will give that one serious thought.

It might be a good idea to install some cameras and an alarm. While I would rather spend my nights with Morgan, there are some things I can't do at his apartment, like work on the furniture pieces clogging up half my garage.

The officer wraps up the interview and says he'll type up the report and get it filed. I thank him and leave the station. There's still plenty of time, so I head toward Morgan's apartment so I can take a shower and primp a little before meeting my boyfriend for dinner.

Chapter 24

Gabriella

Morgan surprises me by joining me in the shower. "Hi cariño! What are you doing home so early?"

"I made an executive decision to leave early because I have to haul my ass to the panhandle tomorrow, which means it's going to be a helluva long day. One of our clients wants us to build a series of commercial buildings out there. I have no desire to do it, but the guy's a long-term client, so I said I'd go up there with him to see the location. If I could clone myself, it would be great, but I already have my hands full with stuff around here and the Tulsa metro."

"Awwww...pobrecito." I tell him and wrap my arms around his neck. He turns us and lets the water run over his head as he kisses me.

We make out with kisses and touches, but that's as far as it goes. I care for him this time, washing his hair and lathering his body. He stands there with his eyes closed, letting me take my time. Stress radiates from him. Tonight will be a good night to try out a little surprise I got for him on my way home.

As I'm toweling him off, I say, "How about we stay in tonight and just order a pizza or something? I don't think either of us is in the mood to get fully dressed again to go out and you were right earlier. I don't feel like cooking."

He sighs. "You read my mind. Hideaway?"

"Sure. I have no preference on the pizza, but I'd like a Just-a-beginner, too."

"Done. I'll call it in."

He goes into the other room to call, not bothering to put any clothes on. That is totally fine by me. I'd be fine with him walking around the apartment naked as a matter of practice. I comb out my hair, then go out to enjoy the view.

"When did you do this?" Morgan asks me when I take him to the second bedroom. We've eaten and watched television for a while, so I decided to make my move. "And why did you do this?"

"You'll see. For now, just sit."

He goes and sits on the side of the bed. I've stripped the bed down to the fitted sheet and left only one pillow. I light candles and turn off the lights. There in the glow, I pull off Morgan's shirt that I've been wearing to reveal the new teddy I got.

"Well, hello," he says, perking up.

"Strip," I command.

"Yes, ma'am." He quickly pulls off his shirt and shorts.

"Lie face down and get comfortable."

When he's settled, I straddle his hips and pull out the massage oil I purchased on the way home. Maybe it was a premonition, but when I saw it in the drugstore, I grabbed it on a whim. I had no idea I'd need it so soon.

I pour a dollop into one palm and warm it between my hands before starting to smooth it across his back. My hands smooth over the long muscles in his back, steadily increasing pressure. He groans.

I work his neck, shoulders, arms, upper and lower back, pulling more groans from him. His muscles loosen and he finally starts to relax. When it's been a while since he has made a noise, I lean over and see that he is asleep.

Carefully, I move off him and cover him with a sheet. To ensure I don't burn the building down, I blow out the candles and leave him to rest.

I turn off all the lights in the apartment except one lamp to read by and curl up on the couch with my book. The story isn't pulling me in like it usually does.

I look across the apartment to the city lights out the window. Never in a million years would I have thought I'd end up here. I am one lucky bitch.

When I wake in bed the next morning, I'm not sure how I got there. Morgan is gone. He had to leave early for his off-site meetings.

It's odd starting my day without him. Our mornings have become ritual with hugs, kisses, good mornings, and often, some morning delight. The apartment is so empty when he's not here.

I go to the kitchen for coffee and find a sticky note on the machine.

Good morning. Hugs and kisses, baby. Have a good day.–MM

He always knows how to make everything all right.

After a long day at work, I come home to a still-empty apartment. He messaged me and let me know he wouldn't be home until late. I didn't want to come home, but I promised I wouldn't stay at the office late alone, and Cait was having dinner with Ford. She invited me to come, but I know they get to spend so little time together that I didn't want to interfere when they were finally able to.

I clean up the mess in the massage room aka second bedroom, change the sheets and remake the bed. Thoughts of cooking something linger for a moment, but I end up eating a piece of leftover pizza instead.

I pull out my book, but it doesn't sound appealing either. Feeling at loose ends with nothing to occupy my mind, I brush my teeth and my hair and go to bed.

All my evenings used to be spent alone, and it never bothered me. However, when I was in my own space with my own things, it was easier. I would most often end up in the garage working on furniture.

I can't do that here and haven't since getting together with Morgan. If I'm going to keep staying here - which I want to, I want to be wherever Morgan is - I'll need to figure out a way to do furniture. It's a creative outlet I love.

I jump when my phone rings, but smile when I see it's Morgan. I hope he's calling to tell me he's on his way home.

"Hi handsome," I answer and sit on the sofa.

"Hey baby."

"Are you on your way home?" I ask hopefully.

"Unfortunately, no."

"Oh."

He sighs. "The guy drags me all over hell and half of fucking creation, showing me land he owns that he wants to build commercial assets on. Then, just about when I think we're done, he gets a call and tells me he's due to close on a building tomorrow morning and he wants me to stay and assess the refurb and build out. I tried to convince him I'd come back next week and look at it, but he insisted. I'm sorry."

"Cariño, there is no need for you to be sorry. I understand. My only complaint is that since my weirdo stalker isn't going away and I can't go home alone, being here without you and all of my things leaves me feeling at loose ends."

I don't want to complain. He's been so kind about bringing me into his home, but it's important to communicate what I'm feeling with him.

"I understand that. We'll figure something out, set you up with a high security studio or something." I can hear the smile in his voice.

I laugh, "Or something. Do you know when you'll be home tomorrow?"

"Not sure. I'm hoping to be home at my usual time, but I'm afraid to jinx myself."

"I have dinner with Cait at the Society tomorrow evening, so if you get tied up, don't worry about me."

"That's right. Thursdays with Cait at the No Boys Allowed Club."

"I can skip it if you want."

"Nope. As much as I miss you, Cait is important to you, and you should spend time with her."

"I miss you, too, cariño." I curl in on myself, feeling intimate.

"Hang on," he says. The sound of a door opening comes through the phone followed by voices. A man says something about dinner, and I know my call is about to end. He comes back on the line. "Baby..."

"I know. You have to go in search of food."

"You heard?"

"Yes. Have a good night, cariño. I'll see you tomorrow."

"I'll make it up to you when I get back. Think of me there with you when you go to bed."

"Always," I tell him.

The call disconnects and I'm back to searching for something to occupy me. Being sequestered with nothing to do is making me a little itchy. And cranky.

At least when Morgan is here, I can occupy myself with cooking and playing with him. This is the most time we've spent apart, and I don't like it.

Chapter 25

Gabriella

"Hi, Cait!" I join my friend in the dining room at the Belladonna Society. It's good to be doing something besides working and hanging out at Morgan's apartment.

"Ella! How are you?" Cait greets me with a hug.

"I am well, and you?"

"The same. Beckett tells me that your proposal was submitted to the foundation."

"That's good. Is the committee still set to meet next week?" I ask.

"Yes, they want to review all the proposals and decide by the end of the week. However, it will be difficult to beat the Carmichael-Masters proposal. I don't know of any other company that could do it for the cost of materials. It is very generous of you to donate the design work, too."

I shrug. "I decided to take a note from them and use the donation as a tax write-off."

"It sounds like you and Morgan have been spending a lot of time together."

"Yes, we have. We were together quite a bit, but then the stalker ramped up his activities, so I've been staying at Morgan's apartment since."

"What stalker?"

I tell her about everything that has happened. "At first, I thought I was just imagining things at home, but the incident with the book made me realize it wasn't just in my head. Ever since then, I've been staying at Morgan's. That's when the stuff started happening at work. I've filed a police report, so at least there's a record now."

"How is staying with Morgan going?"

"It's great. Really, really great until he's not there, as has been the case the past few days. When that happens, I realize just how much I rely on him. Not that I mind, but there are so many things I used to do that I haven't been able to. I mentioned it to him and when he gets back, we'll talk about it. We'll need to find a balance."

Talking about this stuff is uncomfortable for me. It feels like I'm airing our dirty laundry, although it's not all that dirty, but I segue the conversation, anyway. "Enough about me. Did you and Ford have a good dinner last night?"

"It was good. He has been so busy at work that it was nice to have him to myself for a whole evening."

Her comment makes me glad that I didn't ask to join them. "He's still working on the serial murders?"

"Yes," she nods. "They're very concerned because the killer has deviated from his pattern."

"Oh? How is that?"

"He's overdue."

"What?" I ask.

"Up to this point, there has been a very specific time period between killings. If he had held to that same pattern, there would have been another body found by now. Some of the team hope that means he's been stopped in some way such as being incarcerated for an unrelated offense or him being killed in a car accident. Ford is worried that it means he's evolving and changing things up so as not to be as predictable. That will make him harder to find and arrest."

I'm suddenly wondering about the stalker who has been targeting me. Things started happening not long after the last murder. "Did he say if any of the victims reported stalking prior to their death?"

She looks up sharply at me. "I don't know. I'll ask Ford about it."

"He was at the station when I filed a report. I even mentioned the stalking, and it didn't seem to be fazed by it."

"I am still going to ask him about it."

"How did we get back on the topic of me? How are things going with the house?"

"We've found the owners, but they don't live in the house full time. We don't know if they even live in the house part-time. Perhaps they rented it out for a while, but we don't know if there is anyone living there now. I have reached out to the owners but haven't had a response yet."

"Well, at least you're making progress," I say. "If anyone can make this happen, you can, but if there's any way I can help, don't hesitate to ask."

"I appreciate that," she replies.

We continue to chat for a while, but in the back of my mind, I can't stop thinking about how the man after me could possibly be not only a stalker, but a killer. A killer who has me in his sights as the next victim.

Is he overdue because he hasn't been able to get to me since I've been secured in Morgan's building? I suddenly want to go back to Morgan's apartment, lock myself inside, and never come out again.

If only I could figure out what the stalker wants. If he just wants to stalk, watch, and play mind games, that's not so bad, is it? I could at least go to my house when Morgan's away and do my usual things. Or even feel free to roam around in the world without supervision or a bodyguard. But most especially, without fear.

My entire life, I've only had myself to rely upon. From the time I was seven, when we moved to small town Oklahoma, I pretty much did things for myself. I would pull my little red stool up to the washer and dryer to work the knobs and wash the family's clothes.

My cooking skills weren't very developed, but I was an ace at making mac and cheese or ramen noodles for supper because that's usually all that was available to make. Often the cabinets were bare.

Besides keeping my room clean, I was in charge of the entire house, from dishes, to dusting, to dragging the giant Electrolux vacuum over the marigold yellow sculpted shag carpet.

I started working when I was fourteen to buy my school clothes. Other than a brief foray into living with a boyfriend at seventeen to get out of my family's house, I have lived on my own, paid my own bills, and stood on my own two feet. Being an independent woman sucks all kinds of donkey balls when all that independence is blown to hell by a stalker who might be trying to kill me.

After dinner, I go back to the apartment and am saddened to find it still empty. I take a shower and go to bed, worry taking away my ability to sleep. After an eternity, I finally get up and go sit on the sofa.

I turn on the television for the glow, but I'm not really paying attention to it. Locking myself in and never coming out again is much less appealing at times like this, but I have no idea what to do about it.

Chapter 26

Morgan

I walk into the apartment to find Gabriella on the sofa again. At first, I think she's fallen asleep again, but she turns to look at me.

"Hey, baby."

"Hey," she replies.

"Can't sleep?" I ask.

"No."

"Wanna talk about it?"

"No."

"Gabriella, you know you can talk to me about anything," I remind her.

She sighs and gets up from the sofa, coming to me and taking my hand. She pulls me toward the bedroom.

"You've had a long couple of days and just drove however many hundreds of miles. I'll talk to you, but not tonight. I need to sort it out in my head, and you need some rest."

I know she's right, but it bothers me that something is bothering her. Something that has her eyes clouded and sad. I just have to trust that she will tell me what's going on with her when she's ready.

Considering everything that's gone on with the asshole who has been stalking her, I wouldn't be surprised if it is getting to her. I want to keep her safe, but I don't know how to do that without locking her in the apartment and taking away her independence. Maybe some counter surveillance is warranted.

If I watch her somehow, maybe I can discover who else is watching her, too. The fact that the idea sounds great to my road addled brain probably means it's not.

For now, I'll keep my peace. I'm so tired that I would love to skip the shower, but I feel grungy and won't take that to bed with her. By the time I crawl between the sheets and settle behind her, I'm ready to drop.

I put my arm around her and pull her back against me, big spoon to her little spoon. Her eyes are closed, but I know she's not asleep. I don't know how to make it better, but I need to figure something out.

I'm up at the usual five o'clock the next morning and instead of a run, I get dressed and head to the office. I would much rather linger in bed with my girl and love her cares away, but after being away from the office for two days, there's a mountain of work to catch up on.

I know it won't fix what's wrong, but I leave her a love note on the coffeemaker. I'll put some thought toward making it up to her this weekend.

"Hey, baby, stop what you're doing," I tell her when I come in and find her pulling out ingredients to make dinner. She looks so tired.

"What? Why?"

"We're going out. Put on something comfortable." I go to the pantry closet and pull out a small ice chest. I put several beers in it and dump the ice bin from the freezer into it.

She's watching me with a frown on her face. "Why do I need to be comfortable? Are we going to an all you can eat buffet?"

"Nope. I'm thinking Mexican." I get the throw blanket she keeps on the sofa and put it on top of the ice chest.

"What?"

"Mexican for supper, woman. Are you going to change?"

"I'm so confused," she says.

I wrap her in my arms and kiss her.

"Just go with it, baby. I want to get you out of this apartment and go have some fun."

I pull her into the bedroom and start pulling off my clothes, replacing them with shorts and a t-shirt and running shoes.

She finally concedes and changes into a pair of shorts that have me checking out her legs. I shake my head to clear out the lustful thoughts infiltrating my mind. If I go there, we'll never get out of the house.

She slides into a pair of flip-flops and holds out her arms. "Okay, I'm ready."

I look her up and down from pink painted toenails to long bare legs to tank top. "Don't do that again or we won't get out of here."

"Where's your truck?" she asks.

"It's at the lot. We're driving this one tonight."

"Is there something wrong with yours?"

"Yep. It doesn't have a bench seat."

"You are so confusing," she says.

I open the passenger door for her.

"Yep, now get in the truck, woman."

Once she's settled, I close her in and put the ice chest on the floorboard behind her seat. She finally starts to relax on the way to the restaurant. Hiding her in the apartment has affected her more than I realized.

She needs this night out and I'm enjoying kidnapping her to go on an unknown adventure.

"Are we having Mexican or Tex-Mex?" she asks.

"You'll have to wait and see."

"Where are we going after supper?""

"You'll have to wait and see."

She scowls at me.

I grin at her.

She looks through the window once we park. "I've never been here," she says.

"You're going to love it," I assure her.

Good food and a healthy dose of margarita relaxes her even more. Her light and playfulness are coming back to life and pushing away the sadness I saw in her eyes last night.

I hated seeing it and would love to just take it away, but she's still processing and not ready to talk, so I have no idea what to do to help her. Back in the truck, I point the truck north.

"Where are we going?" she asks again.

"Guthrie," I reveal.

"What's in Guthrie?"

"You'll just have to wait and see."

She scowls again.

I grin again.

She rolls her eyes and turns away, but I can see her reflection in the window and she's smiling.

There's my girl.

When we pull in, she says, "You're kidding me."

"Nope."

"I didn't know any of these were still around."

"Ever been?"

"Yes, when I was little. There used to be a drive-in movie theater outside of Sapulpa that we went to a couple of times."

I pay for entry then drive through, selecting a space in the back. The truck is tall, and I don't want to block anyone's view. Plus, we might want to make out. I haven't had my hands on her in what seems like forever.

"Do you want snacks?" I ask her.

"Not right now. I'm stuffed. I may want something sweet later."

"I've got something sweet for you, baby." I waggle my eyebrows up and down and give her a cheesy grin.

She smiles back. "Is that so?"

I reach down and pull the lever under the seat and scoot it all the way back. "Yep. Want some candy, little girl?"

She undoes her seatbelt and scoots over next to me. "Yes," she says.

I lean down and kiss her soft lips, pulling her even closer. We're both a little breathless when we break the kiss.

I put my forehead to hers. "I've missed you."

She's gripping my t-shirt in her fist. "I've missed you, too."

I cup her jaw and turn her face back to mine, kissing her again. Pouring everything into it, letting her know I need her, letting her know that she's not alone. She kisses me back, sharing her own need and hunger.

Everything outside falls away. In this moment, it's just the two of us in a cab shaped cocoon. I can't get close enough to her. Right now, I wish we were home, in our bed with skin stretched against skin, nothing separating us.

I want to devour her and keep her with me always. Keep her safe. Never lose what's mine.

She shares the desperation. Her hands fisted in my clothes, in my hair. Her hands release their purchase to push my shirt up. She needs that skin-on-skin contact, too. Fingers tickle down my stomach to find my cock tenting my shorts.

In a deft move, she pulls at my waistband, freeing my shaft and taking it in her hand. She strokes me, the strokes of her tongue against mine matching in rhythm and ferocity.

She pulls her mouth away from mine, bending to take me in her mouth. My hand goes to the nape of her neck, encouraging her toward her destination.

She shivers and hesitates for a fleeting moment. If I hadn't been paying attention, I would have missed it. "Gabriella, what is it baby?"

She stops. Pauses. She's about to lie; I can feel the tension in her neck ratchet up exponentially.

"Nothing cariño. I'm fine." She starts to resume her intention, but I increase the pressure on her neck and pull her back. She keeps her eyes down.

I reach across and grip her chin to raise it. She looks at me, knowing that if she doesn't, I'll tell her to, and she won't be able to resist.

"Ghosts?" I ask.

She nods. "Yes."

"Tell me."

"We're supposed to be having fun and I'm ruining it." She pulls away from me and throws her hands up in frustration. "Gah! Why am I like this? Why can't I just be normal instead of so weak and useless?"

I can see her eyes are filling with tears and she's fighting them.

"Hey," I say gently. I pull her arm to move her close again, but she resists.

"Baby," I croon. "You're stressed out and overwhelmed with everything that's going on. I think that's pretty normal. It doesn't help that I've left you alone, locked up in my apartment for the past two days."

I don't give her a choice; I pull her back to me, take her in my arms, and onto my lap. She loses her control, and the tears fall.

"You are one of the strongest people I know, and that's saying a lot."

I cradle her, rocking as she cries quietly, releasing the stress she's built up. She feels so small and fragile curled up in my lap like this. I pull the hem of my t-shirt up and wipe her tears away as I kiss the top of her head.

She takes a deep, cleansing breath and lets it out. "My brother Peter was the worst. He was always at me. One of his favorite things to do was take me into the closet in his bedroom. He would close the door so that it was dark, and I couldn't see. He would pull down the waistband of his shorts, then put his hand on the back of my neck and push my face into his crotch. He would talk crudely to me, telling me what he wanted and how to do it."

She shivers with that last part.

"We'll get rid of that ghost, too." I say earnestly. "I really would like to kill your brothers, or at the very least, beat the shit out of them."

She laughs at that.

"I'm serious!" My voice is full of cold assurance.

"I know." She puts her palm to my chest and pats me.

We sit there like that just talking for a while. The first movie is a kid-friendly superhero film that doesn't really interest either of us. I ask her if she wants to leave, but she says no, she would like to see the second movie, so we stay.

I keep an eye on her as she goes to the restroom. My protective caveman wants to go with her just to make sure she's okay, but I won't smother her like that.

I've got to figure out a way to get some freedom and normalcy into her day without risking her safety. When she comes back, I go to the concession stand and buy a boatload of candy and popcorn.

We settle in for the second movie with our haul of junk food and a couple of beers from the cooler. By the time we're halfway through the movie, Gabriella is curled up next to me asleep with a half-eaten box of Junior Mints in her lap. I expected as much, considering the emotional release she had.

I think about letting her sleep but decide she will rest better in our bed than balled up on the front seat of the old truck. It takes some effort to move her so I can belt her in. She stirs, but goes back to sleep quickly. I gather up our trash and dispose of it, then start to make our way home.

Chapter 27

Gabriella

I join Morgan in the shower when he comes back from his run in the morning. If nothing else, my freak out last night at the movie released some of the tension that had me so bound up. I am feeling much better this morning.

"Mornin, baby," he says when he hears the door open. His eyes are closed as he shampoos his hair.

"Good morning, cariño." I kiss him in the middle of his chest to avoid his lathering. "Can we go to a farmer's market this morning?" I intend to spend as little time in this apartment as possible this weekend.

"Sure," he says. "Which one?"

"I like Edmond and Norman; they seem to have the most vendors with the most variety."

"Well, we went north yesterday. How about we go south today?"

"Okay."

We take a while to get out of the apartment because both of us had a keen need that was fulfilled by an extended session of shower stall sex. The physical release combined with the emotional release from last night has me feeling so light I think I could float.

I am like a kid in a candy store when we reach the market. If I didn't have a black thumb, I would have an enormous garden to grow fresh vegetables. However, sadly, my ability to grow plants is non-existent to the point that even cacti are in danger in my care.

"Just so you know what you're in for, I have to look at everything first and then I'll go back and purchase what I want," I tell Morgan.

I got into this habit early on. There were too many times when I'd go through buying whatever caught my eye, only to have to throw half of it out when it didn't get used up before it went bad.

It would be wonderful to live in a place where there are open-air markets where you can buy fresh items every day for whatever you plan to make that night. The highly treated, over refrigerated produce in grocery stores is a pale comparison.

"Got it," he says.

We wander the aisles commenting on various items. Morgan buys a couple of pretzels and eats one as we walk between the booths, stopping for a taste test from every vendor who offers one. We stop at a meat vendor to discuss the possibility of grilling and whether we should get chicken or steak. Morgan is voting for both.

"Gabriella?"

I turn to see Demi standing there holding a bag full of produce and the hand of a small boy. "Demi! Fancy seeing you here!" I hug her.

"I should say that to you. I thought you lived in the City," she replies.

"I do, we do. Demi, this is my boyfriend, Morgan Masters. Morgan this is Demeter Lawson, she is a member of the Society with Cait and I." I knew Demi had a child, but she only rarely talks about him.

Morgan shifts his load around to free up a hand to shake hers.

"It's nice to meet you," Morgan says.

"Hi, same" Demi says. She looks down at the boy. "This is my son, Henry."

Henry is fair with blue eyes like his mother, but his hair is dark, dark brown, almost black. "Hello," Henry says and holds out his hand. "It's nice to meet you."

I cock my head and look at him, surprised at such a grown-up mannerism. If memory serves, he's only six or seven years old, and that's how old he looks. Morgan shakes the boy's hand, swallowing it with his own.

I shake his hand. "It's very nice to meet you, too, Henry."

Demi smiles tenderly as she smooths his bangs over from where his wavy hair flopped across his forehead.

"Henry is quite precocious," she offers as an explanation of his behavior. "Anyway, I just wanted to say hello. I like to come out to the market early, before all the good stuff is gone. Grandma is fixing French toast, so I'd better get this guy back home for breakfast. It's nice to meet you, Morgan."

"Nice to meet you and Henry, too," Morgan replies.

"Nice to see you Demi and nice to meet you Henry," I echo.

"Goodbye," Henry says with a small wave.

We watch them walk away. "She doesn't look old enough to have a kid that age," Morgan says finally.

"She had him when she was getting her PhD. Sadly, her fiancé, Henry's father, was hit by a drunk driver one morning when he was out for a run when she was seven months pregnant," I tell him.

"That's rough."

"Yes, it is."

We make some other stops while we are out and it feels so good to be in the fresh air and sunshine. By the time we head back to the apartment with all our goodies, it doesn't feel like a burden at all.

After the farmer's market yesterday, I figured Morgan would want to stay home, but we're finishing breakfast when he says, "What do you think about going to your house today? I thought you might like to work on your furniture for a while."

"What?" I blink at him.

"Your furniture. I know you haven't been able to work on it since you started staying here since the creeper has gotten more aggressive and I thought you might be missing it."

I throw my arms around his neck and kiss him. "You are the best boyfriend in the world!"

"I know," he says with a sigh. "It's a terrible burden, but I'll manage somehow."

I get to spend the whole day working on furniture, which is a balm to my soul. I love the creative process, even the tedious parts. Morgan lounges on the couch watching television and occasionally checks in with me.

After lunch, we make love on that same couch before I return to the garage. By the end of the day, one piece is painted and one piece is repaired and ready for prep. I couldn't have asked for a more perfect weekend.

My Monday morning at the office has passed with no incidents. I'm feeling so positive that I tell Hailey it's okay to leave the front door unlocked.

Ding!

A familiar man's voice comes from the reception area, followed by a familiar dark head of hair poking around the corner. "Hey, baby," Morgan says.

I can't help the goofy grin that spreads across my face. "Hi, cariño! To what do I owe this pleasure?"

"I have some time available and thought I'd take my favorite person to lunch."

"Okay. Are we driving or walking?" I ask.

We walk the few blocks to the row of restaurants lining the trendy uptown area. Our lunch is relaxed and unhurried until Morgan's phone buzzes. He answers, and it's obvious that lunchtime is over. Still, we stroll without rushing back to my office, holding hands, and enjoying the bright day.

I expect him to jump into his truck and dash away, but he opens the office door for me and follows me to my office. "Don't you have to go?" I ask.

"I do, but I'm just needed. It's not an emergency. They can wait a few minutes while I get a proper goodbye."

"I see," I say and step close to him, stretching up on my toes for a kiss. He pulls me in and deepens the connection, the familiar heat stirring between us.

Ding!

"Where is that goddamn bitch?" a man blusters at Hailey. "Tell her to get her ass out here now!"

Morgan's actions are calm as he sets me away from him, but his face is thunderous. I hold up a hand to stop him and he raises an eyebrow. This is my place of business, so any trouble is mine to handle. He gets it and gives me a terse nod. He will stay out of it for now.

I step around the corner. As soon as he sees me, Christopher Sparks' mouth is off and running. "What the fuck is the meaning of this?"

He holds a piece of paper crumpled in his hand. I can see enough of it to make out that it's the notification we sent to the homeowner regarding his deviation from my plans and nullification of my guaranty.

"I told you Tuesday that I would be sending it because you had deviated from the plans accepted by the homeowners. If a contractor chooses to go off script and ignore the construction documents approved by the client, I give a warning, which I gave you two weeks ago. You ignored that warning and continued to do your own thing. The amount of work you had done when I was there Tuesday was a significant departure from the plans, so I told you I would be notifying the homeowners. I believe your response was 'Get the fuck off my job site.'"

"You bitch! Now they're threatening to sue me if the results don't turn out exactly like they expected."

I fold my arms and look at him deadpan. "If you had followed the plans, there wouldn't be an issue. The only time I make allowances for changes is if there is a problem that is discovered after demo or during the construction process that necessitates a change. There was no such issue discussed with me. It appears that most of the changes you made were designed to lower your output on materials and labor so that you could pad the amount going into your pocket."

"I hate working with bitches like you. Goddamn cunts...aaargh."

"Choose your next words very carefully, Sparks," Morgan says. He has the man by the collar up against the wall.

"Masters, what are you doing here?" Christopher sputters.

"It doesn't matter what I'm doing here. If you use one more slur when talking about Ms. Carmichael, I will make sure you never work in this industry again. I might do it anyway; your slipshod work already gives us all a bad name."

I put a hand on his arm. "It's okay, Morgan. Let him go."

Morgan looks at me, incredulous.

"He is not worth you getting an assault charge."

He narrows his eyes at me, then glares at Christopher. "You're a disgrace, Sparks," he says and lets go.

Sparks straightens his shirt while glaring at Morgan, then stalks toward the door. "You haven't heard the last of this you...Carmichael."

"Wow," Hailey says, "that was an intense one. Good thing he was here."

"What do you mean?" Morgan asks. "Does that happen often?"

I pick up the piece of paper from the floor where Christopher dropped it. "It happens often enough that we have a form letter," I tell him, handing him the paper.

"After a few hard lessons in the beginning, I started writing milestones into the contract and weekly site visits so I could monitor the contractors. They almost always try to cut corners to increase their profits. If they do, I offer one warning. If they continue, I notify the homeowner that my guaranty has been voided. I get paid before construction starts, so it keeps me from having to spin my wheels doing a lot of unpaid adjustments when the homeowner isn't satisfied with the end result. Most of the contractors cuss and bluster, but it's rare that one is as aggressive as he was."

"I had no idea it was that bad," Morgan says.

I shrug. "It's a big part of the reason why I hate the construction side so much. I simply don't understand why they can't just follow the plans and do the work that's expected of them."

"For the whole of the construction industry, I'm sorry. I've gotta go, baby, but if he comes back, let me know." He leans down and gives me a quick kiss then goes out the door.

Chapter 28

Gabriella

I look up to see Cait breeze into the office, a look of excitement on her face. I stand up to greet her. She's carrying a folder with a long roll of paper. Her excitement spreads to me. I know the committee was close to making a decision on the awarding of the house refurbishment project, so maybe this means good news.

"I thought we were meeting at the restaurant," I say.

She grins broadly at me. "We were, but I just couldn't wait." She hugs me. "It's decided. The Carmichael-Masters bid has been awarded the project."

"Oh Cait! That's fantastic news!"

She hands me the drawings, and I spread them open on my desk. My eyes linger on the *Approved* stamped in red just above my seal and company information. My gaze sweeps over the entire document. I pause.

I pull the page up to look at the following pages one by one, carefully at first, but as my anger grows, my caution goes out the window. My hand starts to shake, and I feel my face heat.

"These aren't my drawings."

"What? What do you mean? It's the set that was submitted with the bid."

"They've been changed."

My voice is low, but the cacophony in my head is deafening. This has to be a mistake. Surely Morgan would not have done this without talking to me. I knew the area that has been changed could have presented some problems, but I had contingency plans in place in case there were issues.

"Why would they have changed them without talking to you first?"

I shake my head, calming the boiling rage. I focus on keeping my voice even, as if it's no big deal.

Just fake it Gabby. After a lifetime of experience, you're good at that.

"That's the question of the hour," I answer, taking a deep breath. "Anyway, thank you for bringing this over. It is good news."

Good news for Masters Construction, that is. A cold dose of reality is what it is for me. However, that's not Cait's fault, and she doesn't deserve my ire, so I tamp it down and get myself under control. "Do you mind if I hold on to these, Cait?"

"No, it's your copy, so you can keep it."

"Thank you. Now, let's go to lunch; I'm starving!" I plaster a big smile on my face, doing my best to make it seem real.

When we settle at the restaurant, Cait asks, "Do you want to talk? I know you're upset."

I shake my head. "No. I am upset, but I need to take it up with Morgan. You don't deserve to get the brunt of the anger I'm feeling."

Through the rest of lunch, Cait is amazing. Instead of pushing, she drops the subject and doesn't bring up the project again. She launches into a detailed update on the situation with Ford's grandparent's house. Once they tracked down the owners of record I found, she and Ford had made an offer that was so high that Ford was appalled because of the state of the house.

The house has changed hands a few times since Ford's childhood and needs some serious repairs. However, because Cait and Ford are seeking them out, the owners see that as a reason to get greedy. I laugh as Cait lays out Ford's rant that ended with him threatening to go out and arrest the wife because of the way she'd acted toward Cait.

God, I love this woman. I can't ask for a better friend. There's a lot to be said for a friend who can understand when you need some space to assimilate things before you're ready to share. Because it's her, if I start to share what I feel, I'll likely turn into a big blubbering mess and if I do that, I won't be in any condition to confront Morgan.

She takes me back to the office and drops me off with a hug before I get out of the car. "Let me know if you need to talk after you see Morgan."

I nod. "I will; I promise. Thanks again for bringing everything by and going to lunch."

I close the car door and wave as she backs out. As soon as she's out of sight, I say goodbye to the nice act and let the anger stroll back through the door. I head back into the office and grab the packet Cait dropped by.

"Hailey, I'm going to be out the rest of the afternoon."

It would probably be more accurate to say I stomped in and out of the office, which is probably why Hailey is watching me with round eyes.

"Okay, bye," she says as I go.

I get in the car and dial Morgan's number.

"Hey baby," he answers.

"Where are you?"

"Why? What's up?"

"I need to see you."

"Is that so?" he asks, his voice going all soft and sexy as if he thinks I'm coming to find him because I want to fuck him.

The ego of these men! Okay, that's not fair. Two hours ago, before I had found out what he'd done, it would be just like me to call him for some afternoon delight, but that is not on the agenda for today.

"Yes," I keep my reply short, afraid I'll lose it if I say too much.

"Commercial build site at Hefner and Kelly."

Without saying goodbye, I disconnect the call. During the drive, I try to keep my anger reined in. I should give him a chance to explain, but I am pissed. Not just fucking mad. I'm mad and hurt but most of all, I feel stupid. When will I learn?

When I arrive, I'm thankful that the build is fairly far along and the concrete has already been poured. I hadn't thought to grab boots or flats before I left the office. Tromping around in the dirt in heels is not fun, but it's also a sure way to ruin your shoes. Considering I'm wearing my favorite fuchsia pumps, I'd probably have tried to go barefoot rather than risk them.

Morgan sees me pull up and comes out to meet me. I get out with the packet in hand and hold it out to him. "Well, you won the bid on Delores."

"Hey! That's great news!" He stretches out his hand to take the papers from me. "Wait, what do you mean I won the bid? Don't you mean *we* won the bid?"

"No. I mean exactly what I said. *You* won the bid. Those aren't my drawings."

"Of course they are," he says, clearly confused.

"Nope. They've been changed. Those are not the original drawings I gave you."

"Oh," he says, a bit more cautious. "Just one small part has been changed because it wasn't going to work the way you had it."

I start to shake, working hard to keep my voice even and not yell. Through gritted teeth, I say, "So, instead of treating me like a peer, a goddamn professional who may have realized there might have been an issue and drawn up contingency plans, you changed my drawings."

My face, really, my entire head, is on fire, about to explode, and my voice starts to rise. "Instead of having a mother fucking conversation with me, you decide you know what's best and whip out your eraser and change my work. You treat it as inconsequential and wipe away the details I worked hard on."

"Baby..." he croons.

I hold up a hand. "Do not baby me. You know, I thought you were different. I thought for once, I'd found someone who could see me as an equal, as a partner on this project."

"I did. I do!"

"Bullshit. If I were a man, you would have never taken such liberties. You're just like every other construction company head I've ever worked with. Just like Christopher Sparks. Every single goddamn time they try to fuck me and fuck me over. Well, congratulations, you were successful where no one else has been. You fucked me, so I guess I should have known that getting fucked over would be next! Well fuck you, Morgan!"

I'm yelling now. I can't stop. I throw the papers at him. It's a surreal moment, the drawings flying out like wings in the breeze drifting to the ground like a wounded bird as they fall to the ground. I turn and head back to my car.

"Gabriella, wait!" He grabs my arm to stop me. "Baby, let's talk about this."

"I have worked my ass off for the last three years trying to prove Frank wrong, but today, it is crystal clear just how right he was."

"I don't understand," Morgan says, trying to pull me into his arms. I don't let him.

"Frank used to tell me every day just how stupid I am. 'Gabby, you are just too fucking stupid to learn. You just keep going around the same mountain over and over, but like the stupid cunt you are, you never learn the lesson.' He was right. I don't learn."

"Gabriella…" his voice is soft. Tender. But I don't want to hear more of his lies.

I don't face him. Hot tears are now streaming down my face. I *hate* that I cry when I get really mad.

I want to be rock solid. I want to be strong. I want my voice to be steady and clear, but none of that is true.

"I thought you were different. I let you in. I told you things I've never told another soul in my entire life. I turned a light on my weaknesses and let you see the real me. I should have known better."

I jerk my arm out of his hand and run to my car as I dash the tears off my cheeks.

It really pisses me off that I couldn't keep from crying. I'm mad that I trusted someone when my whole life had shown me over and over how trusting someone, especially a man, is the pinnacle of idiocy.

My anger isn't really for him, because I'm really just mad at myself. He just did what people do, and Frank was right; I should have learned by now.

"Gabriella, don't go."

I ignore him as I get in the car and peel out of the lot. Before I get a block away, the car shows I'm getting a call from Morgan.

I reject it. Thirty seconds later, he calls again. I'm stopped at a light, so I pull my phone out and turn it off.

Stupid. Stupid. Stupid. You are so fucking stupid.

The words keep rolling over and over in my mind. I don't want to go home. Getting away from everything and everyone is what I need, no talking, no being nice to anyone. I just want to hole up in a dark room, lick my wounds and console my hurt feelings with a whole lot of booze.

Chapter 29

Morgan

Gabriella drives away while I look on, helpless to stop her. I fucked up. I could blame it on being used to working with my own design team and changing things whenever I see fit, but that's weak as excuses go.

She's right, she's not my employee; she is a collaborating company. Knowing how meticulous she is in her work, I should have talked to her. It's just like her to have a back-up plan already in place if something might not work.

Although I had no idea it would hit her like this when I did it. I should have. I know what this business is like and how many assholes there are out there, but after seeing how Sparks was with her, I realize it's way worse than I thought.

Now I'm one of them. It's no excuse that I changed the drawings before that enlightening encounter with Sparks in Gabriella's office. I should have believed her.

I scrub a hand down my face. Fuck.

We need to talk this out. I pull out my phone and dial her number. It rings a couple of times, then goes to voicemail.

A second try gets the same result. I try for a third time and go straight to voicemail. She must have turned her phone off.

"Morgan!" my client calls from inside the building.

Fuck.

I want to blow this guy off and go after her, but I can't. We're building office complexes like this one in four locations in the metro, representing a sizeable piece of income for the company. I also know that Gabriella is too raw and too pissed to talk this out at the moment.

Once I gather up the papers she threw at me, I put them in my truck. I'll get rid of this guy, then go to her house once she's had a few minutes to breathe and let the initial shock pass. Then I'll sit on her until she talks to me, and we work this problem out. I will not let my stupid mistake tear us apart.

It takes longer to get rid of the customer than I thought, or hoped, it would. I pull onto Gabriella's block a few hours later, just as the sun is setting. It looks like someone is having a party because I have to park almost a block away on the other side of the street.

That's probably best, so that she doesn't see me coming and run out the back door. I've tried calling her a few times, but it keeps going straight to voicemail, so she must still have her phone turned off. I have left several messages, but I have no idea if she's listened to any of them.

I knock on her door. There's no answer. Apparently, she's not going to let me in, no matter how much I was hoping she would. Thankfully, I have a key, and unlock the door calling out as I do, so I don't scare her. "Gabriella?"

The house is dark and silent. After turning on the light in the kitchen, I go straight to the door leading to the garage and open it. Her car isn't here.

Where could she be?

I go to her bedroom to find her closet open and a few pieces of clothing on the bed. It looks like she's packed a bag, so she is going to be gone at least overnight. I start thinking of ways to track her down.

It would probably be best if I left her alone to calm down. If she would just talk to me, I know we could work this out. My phone rings. I answer it without looking at who's calling. "Gabriella!"

"Sorry, Morgan, it's not Ella, it's Cait. I'm sorry to be playing go between, but Gabriella asked me to call and ask you to stop calling. She has left town for a few days to clear her head and wants peace and quiet."

"Cait. Sorry. Hi." I sigh. "I messed up with her."

She hesitates before replying, "Yes, you did. You pushed every button of self-doubt she has. Her life hasn't been exactly easy, and some things hit her harder than others."

"I know, but I'm going to fix it."

"I hope you do. Ella is a very special person, and she deserves someone who knows that."

"I do know that. I just...I did an idiotic thing because I didn't think." I let out a breath of frustration. "Do you know where she is?"

"All she told me is that she's in a cabin in the woods."

"I see. Thanks, Cait. I appreciate you calling."

"Goodbye, Morgan."

A cabin in the woods, huh? That sounds about right. She has mentioned going hiking more than a few times.

I'm worried about her out there by herself, though. Is she off by herself or is it a group of cabins? My instinct is to track her down, to protect her, to keep her safe.

But how can I keep her safe when she thinks I'm the enemy? Much less when I have no idea where she is?

I pick up one of the pieces of clothing from the bed. It's the shirt she had on earlier and as I hold it to my nose, her scent fills my head. I lay back on her bed and stare at the ceiling. How am I going to fix this?

Should I follow her, or should I give her the space she is asking for? The debate rages in my head, going back and forth, none of the options sounding overly positive. I start listing the pros and cons of each side of the argument.

I sit up in bed. I'm disoriented for a moment until I recall being in Gabriella's bedroom trying to decide if I should be a caveman and go after her to drag her back home or if I should let her have some space. It's probably a good thing I fell asleep because I was leaning toward caveman.

A board creaks somewhere in the house. Going still, I listen, trying to determine if it's just the settling of an old house or...another creak, closer this time. It sounds like someone moving through the house trying to be quiet.

I reach for my phone but have no idea where it is. It's probably somewhere on the bed with me, but there's no telling where. I slowly get off the bed and make my way to stand behind the door to the bedroom, trying not to make any noise. Another creak. They're in the hallway now.

"Fuck," a man's voice says low. "Not here."

I want him to step into the room far enough that I can hit him with the door, or even better, where I can get a grip on him, but he's still in the hall. There is a faint glow of ambient light in the house from the kitchen light I left on, but the bedroom is pitch black. Unless he has some kind of night vision gear on, he should be able to see clearly into the room.

This must be Gabriella's stalker! How the hell is he getting in?

Realizing she's not home, the man walks back through the house, less careful about making noise. He does what I did - goes to the garage door and opens it to see that her car isn't here. While he's moving, I move, too, counting on his noise to cover any I might make.

I'm listening to his movements and doing my best to stay out of his sight line, but something triggers him. He stops. I stop. I'm straining for the slightest noise. I know he can't see me, but something spooks him. He rushes through the house, and I hear the back door open.

I chase after him and make it out the door in time to see him going over the fence to the front yard. I follow. The fucker's fast. By the time I make it over the fence and into the front yard, I don't see him immediately. Motion two yards up catches my eye and I give chase.

Before I can even think of catching up to him, he ducks into a car and pulls out quickly, almost clipping the fender of a car in front of him. I'm too far away to get the tag number, but I recognize the car. I've seen it more than a few times.

The first was the night I saw her at the hotel bar. It pulled out from across the street and a few spaces back to follow her when she left the bar. It was a busy area, so I didn't think anything about it.

I've seen it more than once, though. More than twice, even. However, the car is a nondescript sedan and there are a million just like it on the road.

I go back to the house to see if I can tell how he got in, swinging by my truck to get a flashlight. He obviously came in through the back door, since it was unlocked when he left through it. I shine my light on the doorframe and don't see any evidence of force being used.

I look closely at the knob and deadbolt but don't see any scratches. He either has a key or a lock pick gun. Either that or he is very skilled with old-fashioned picks to not leave a single scratch on the face.

I go back to the bedroom and find my phone. My finger is hovering over my keypad to call emergency services, but I hesitate. There is zero evidence that there was anyone else here but me and I'm not exactly here with Gabriella's permission.

The cops will call her and make her come back. On the one hand, I'd love that. On the other hand, with no evidence supporting a break-in, she might think I made it up just to get her to come home.

As I put my phone away, a plan begins to come together in my mind. I lock her back door, confident the stalker isn't likely to come back again tonight. So that I can get a good look to see if the guy left anything behind, I turn on all the lights in the house.

Once I've gone over every inch of her house three times and found nothing, I lock up and head out to my truck.

Chapter 30

Gabriella

I sit on a stone outcropping looking over the lake. It was an easy enough hike to get here, but being surrounded by nature is soothing to my soul. It always has been.

Morgan had promised me a trip where we'd go camping and hiking, but this is the first weekend that has had decent temperatures without a bevy of thunderstorms. I hope the moderate temperatures with no rain last for a couple of weeks. Maybe we could take another trip.

I didn't get drunk last night as I had intended. There was some drinking involved, but the drive up to the state park helped me settle down quite a bit. The walk through the woods this morning has helped even more. It's early enough that I even saw a few deer in the woods, starting their day of foraging.

I take a deep breath, close my eyes, and revel in the feeling of the warmth of the sun and the soft breeze. In addition to not getting drunk and wallowing in my sadness, I finally turned my phone on late last night and listened to Morgan's many voicemails. He admits he made a mistake. I don't think I can hold that against him.

As much as I want to, I think that's my fear talking more than anything. I've never felt about anyone the way I feel about Morgan. He wants to work it out.

I want that, too. If he can be big enough to admit he made a mistake, I can be big enough to admit that I may have overreacted yesterday.

I texted him this morning just to let him know I was okay and would be out of town for a couple of days because I needed to clear my head and cool off. To clue him into my mindset, I also let him know I want to talk when I get back.

He offered to come to me, but I assured him it was better if he didn't. I know it was probably hard for him, but he said okay and asked that I call him when I was back in town.

The one thing I'm sure of is that I need to make some changes, but they are more about the business than about relationships. With a sigh, I let out the breath and open my eyes to a smooth flat stone by my foot. I pick it up, stand, and with a side arm fling, try to skip it across the surface of the lake.

It plops and sinks. I sigh again. I've never been able to skip stones.

The Universe is probably trying to tell me to stick to what I do well and stop trying to master the things I suck at. That's my life lesson for the day – focus on your strengths and quit trying to master your weaknesses. It will be a difficult transition, but it's needed.

My stomach growls, so I start back to my cabin to fix some breakfast. Once I eat, I'll go for another walk. While I'm here,

I might as well take advantage of the location. I won't stay another night, though, because I want to get back to the City to see Morgan.

Even though it hasn't even been twenty-four hours, I've missed him. Since the first time we made love, we've rarely spent a night apart. I've gotten so used to his warm body next to mine that it's difficult to sleep without him.

It is amazing how my entire world has shifted to encompass Morgan. This fight has helped me in a lot of ways, including recognize even more of my already innumerable issues.

I think part of me was waiting for it all to fall apart, so I leaped on the first time we found ourselves at odds. My old patterns kicked in and I ran away. I've always found it easier to run away and end things rather than staying to work it out. Deep inside, I believe that anything good is going to come crashing down someday, so I might as well crash it on my terms.

Did Morgan mess up? Yes. His messages said he was sorry. He finally showed me he is a real man and not a perfect Knight in Shining Armor. Perish the thought!

Considering all the stuff I've laid on him with my past, my ghosts, and my insecurities, I expected him to run away from me like everyone else has. But he didn't. Instead, he has taken me by the hand and walked through my trauma with me.

He has taken away much of the power of the ghosts that haunt me and freed me from my past. Not only that, but he has shown me the possibility of a future beyond what I ever dreamed. A future of love, happiness, and family.

Even after I go crazy in a whole new way, accusing him of purposely trying to take advantage of me, he is still holding fast to a future with me. That is amazing. I want that future with him, too.

After a bite to eat with some caffeine, I step back outside, ready to take another walk down a different path this time. I lock the door and start to step off the porch when I notice someone across the open space. It's a guy just standing there leaning against a tree at the edge of the woods.

He looks vaguely familiar, but I can't place him. Stalker is the first thing that pops into my head, and I feel a surge of panic stab through me. He doesn't look like the guy who came into the office that day, so I tell myself to calm down.

I kneel, pretending one of my laces is loose. Taking my time, I untie and retie one shoe, keeping the guy in my peripheral vision. He's still just standing there.

I wonder if he's waiting for someone. Whatever else he's doing, he's giving me the creeps. My phone buzzes in the pocket of my leggings. I pull it out and look at the face. It's Caitlyn. Instead of stepping off the porch, I move over and take a chair.

"Hey Cait!"

"Good morning, Ella! How is your trip going?"

I settle back in the chair. The porch is shaded so I know the guy across the way can't see my face clearly. I take advantage of that and look at him straight on. He's obviously watching me.

"It's going well. I think I have my head back on straight."

"Good. Have you talked to Morgan?"

"Not yet," I answer. I lower my voice so it doesn't carry. "I texted him this morning, but I think I'm coming back today so we can talk. You've got to think twice when a man is willing to admit his mistakes."

"That's true," she chuckles. "There's a lot to be said for a partner who's willing to learn."

"Exactly." I was going to keep it to myself, but for some reason I blurt out, "I think once I finish with the current projects that I'm going to let the business go, though. I'm just so tired of trying to swim upstream."

"Oh Ella! No!"

"It's okay. To do the part I love, I have to take on the part I loathe, and it's just worn me out so that even the part I love isn't enjoyable anymore."

"I'm sorry to hear that. What do you think you'll do?"

"I'm not sure. Maybe go back to school. Maybe do something completely different. I'm just going to see what doors the Universe opens."

Going back to school is something I thought about last night. It was a struggle to pay for school while trying to work, so I gave up. At such a young age, it's difficult to know what you really want in life and there aren't a lot of opportunities to just try things on.

"That sounds like a good plan. I'm glad you're feeling better. Let's get together next week."

"I'd like that. I'll call you when I'm back."

"Okay. Enjoy your day, Ella."

"You, too."

I act as if I'm still talking to Cait while I watch the guy across the way. He's still standing there against the tree. He isn't making it obvious that he's watching me, but it sure looks like he is.

I don't consider myself egotistical, but I don't know what else he could be doing. Maybe I'm just overly sensitive because of what's been going on at home.

I get up and go back into my cabin. When I come back out a few minutes later, the guy is still there. He's creeping me out enough that I decide to go over to the park office and report him.

There's a park ranger there as well as the information host. I tell the ranger about the guy, but also make sure he technically hasn't done anything but stare and make me uncomfortable. Afterward, I stay in the office a while looking at the brochures for area attractions, hoping that maybe the guy will be gone when I go back out.

I hear the bell over the door ring and the ranger greets the newcomer. A man's voice replies, low enough that I can't understand what he said. When I glance over, I see the man who had been watching me.

His back is to me so I get the attention of the ranger and mouth, *That's the guy!* The ranger gives me a subtle nod and I exit the office.

I hurry back to my cabin and grab the bags I'd packed in case I got a chance to leave without the guy watching my every move. Hopefully, the ranger detains him a while.

I jump in my car and take off, stopping only long enough to drop the keys to the cabin in the drop box outside the office. With a glance in the door, I see the ranger is still talking with the guy and looking at something in his hand. I hope they're checking the guy's ID.

Instead of heading straight home, I decide that since it's still early, I'll stop off at the shop of that gal that has a cooking show on television. I don't watch a lot of cooking shows, but it's not far from here and I've heard it's a neat shop. Once I park on a side street on the next block, I make my way to the shop, watching everyone, wondering if I'll see that creepy guy.

Once I'm in the store, I feel a little silly at my paranoia. I still can't remember where I know his face from, but I've seen him or someone who looks a lot like him somewhere before. Maybe that's it. He just reminds me of someone.

How would the stalker at home even know where I am? My paranoia slides away as I get lost looking at all the store's colorful wares.

I had intended just to spend time in the shop, but it doesn't take long for me to be carrying enough items that I need to go find a basket. It started when I found a t-shirt that made me laugh and think of Morgan, then a hand painted pitcher that would look lovely filled with fresh flowers.

By the time I was finished, I had a basket full of items and half my Christmas shopping done. Yes, I'm one of those weirdos that shops all year round for Christmas, keeping gifts squirreled away in a closet until it's time to wrap them.

After loading the bags in the car, I debate going to the shop's adjoining restaurant for an early lunch just because I've heard such good things about it. I'm not really hungry, but I could get something to-go. I decide not and slide into the driver's seat, ready to be home.

Chapter 31

Morgan

"Christ, Beckett, I thought you said this wouldn't take very long!" I check the time again.

We're supposed to be going to look at some car that he's thinking about buying, but he's either written the address wrong or someone is punking him. We've been driving around for hours.

If this takes much longer, I'm turning around and heading home. He only wanted me to go with him so I could drive my truck rather than him risking his car on these country roads.

"I'm sure it's just up here," he says, checking his phone for the millionth time. "Wait! Stop!" He squints into the shadows at an overgrown mailbox. "This, this is it."

I squint dubiously at the equally overgrown drive. "Are you sure? I'd hate to drive up this road and get shot."

"Go on, it'll be fine," he grins at me. "I'll duck if someone starts firing."

I shake my head at him as I turn into the drive. "Asshole. I sure hope this is worth it."

"If it's for real, it will be," he assures me.

"What exactly are you hoping to find?"

"I'm not sure. I was talking with a new kid on the Newman site the other day. He took a look at my car and said his grandpa had one similar to it in a barn. Similar to it, but older. I asked him to contact his grandpa and see if it would be okay for me to come look at it."

"You've been saying you're ready for a new project car."

"Yep, and I'm hoping the car gods are smiling down on me," he says with a grin.

We crest an incline, and a house appears out of the afternoon shadows. Set farther back on the property is an old, dilapidated barn. The entire property could do with a hefty dose of maintenance.

As we draw closer to the house, an elderly man steps out onto the porch with a shotgun in his arm, but before he can raise it, a young man comes out of the house. "There, that's Jimmy," says Beckett just before he leaps from the truck.

Jimmy waves at me, and I wave back. I recognize him. He's fairly new to the crew and starting out as a gopher, but he seems to be a good worker.

He's smart and extremely good natured. There's a lot to be said for a guy that can take the crap that's handed out on a construction site and end the day with a smile as big as it was at the beginning of the day.

Jimmy and Beckett start out for the barn, but the older man has taken a seat on a glider bench on the front porch. I take a moment to check my phone. There haven't been any more messages from Gabriella. I'm disappointed, but she said she would be back tomorrow and wants to talk, so that's a good sign.

I meander over to the porch and introduce myself to the man. As we talk, the sun starts to sink lower in the sky until the dark shadows overtake the yard. I think I'll see Beckett and Jimmy coming back at any moment, but I can see lights on in the barn.

Jimmy's grandpa excuses himself and heads inside saying that there's some television program on that he needs to go watch, so I start toward the barn. Halfway there, my phone pings. I pull it out and the notification makes my blood run cold. I run the rest of the way to the barn.

"Beckett, I'm leaving, now!"

His head snaps up. "What's wrong?"

"He's there again. I didn't think the mother fucker would try again, but he's there. I'm leaving now and if you aren't coming, Jimmy will have to take you home."

I turn and run back to my truck, hoping I can get back to civilization faster than it took to get out here. Beckett catches up to me. He's always been fast. We jump into the cab and take off, leaving a cloud of dirt and gravel in our wake.

"How do you know he's back?" Beckett is barely winded. The man never works out, yet somehow he's always in excellent shape.

"I put up a couple of our site cameras to monitor her front and back doors and programmed them to report to my phone instead of the usual computer at the office."

"Smart. What do you think he wants?"

"He wants Gabriella," I growl. "He's been messing with her and stalking her for weeks, if not months."

I focus on the road. It's dark and the last thing I need is for a deer or some other critter to dash out onto the road and cause a crash. Finally, we get back to paved roads and I'm able to go faster, but I still can't go all out. It takes almost thirty minutes before we hit a highway.

I hope he leaves when he finds out that she's not there, but by that reasoning, he should already be gone. My phone hasn't signaled any further movement, so he's still inside. Maybe he's waiting, hoping she will come home.

Thank God she won't be home until tomorrow. If he lays in wait for her, maybe we can get there and subdue him and call the cops. "Fuck, we're still thirty minutes out. I hope he sticks around."

I set my phone on the console between us and focus on the road. Although I'm well above the speed limit, I can't bring myself to slow down as I weave in back and forth amongst traffic to gain every inch I can. My phone dings. We're still fifteen minutes out.

"What is it? Is he leaving?" I hand my phone to Beckett, so I don't have to take my eyes off the road.

"Fuck."

"What? What is it?"

"Gabriella's pulling into the garage."

"What? What is she doing home? She's not supposed to be back until tomorrow!" I yell and pound the steering wheel.

"Could she know?"

"No, I don't think so. He was hoping to catch her sleeping last night. He had on something that allowed him to see in the dark. If she was involved with him, he wouldn't have needed to do that, and he would've known she wasn't there. I think he saw the light I turned on in the kitchen and assumed she was home."

"How did he know she'd be coming home tonight?"

"I can't say for sure that he did. It might just be a coincidence with him banking on her not being gone two nights in a row. Call Gabriella," I tell the truck's system.

"Calling Gabriella," a woman's computerized voice says.

The phone goes straight to voicemail.

"Fuck!" I pound the steering wheel again.

"Calm down before you give yourself a stroke," Beckett says.

"I can't calm down. I just found her; I can't lose her."

"We're almost there," he assures me, "and he's still there. That means it's extremely likely she's still alive. Pull yourself together and get your head straight."

When I'm a couple of blocks away, I call nine-one-one to alert the police of a break in. They tell us to stay out, but I tell them I won't risk standing around outside while he may be killing her.

I pull onto her block and turn off the lights. "Go around back in case he tries to run. Be quiet; I don't want to alert him to our presence too soon," I tell my brother. "I'm going in the front using my key. Once I assess, I'll try to surprise him when he's away from her."

"Got it," he replies.

We get out and close the doors quietly. Beckett darts around the house. I wait a beat and slowly slide my key in the lock and turn it as quietly as I can. My military training for breaching a structure with stealth kicks in, even if I haven't done anything like this for twenty years. I'm inside with minimal noise.

The house is dark except for her bedroom. I can hear a man speaking, but it's muffled. Moving swiftly but quietly to the back door, I unlock it to let Beckett in.

I motion for him to stay put. He hears the man's voice and frowns. He pulls out his phone and sets it to record. I don't know that it will pick anything up clearly, but I'm glad he's thinking straighter than I am.

The desire for one of my guns floats through, but that's wasting brain cells I need to focus. I'm completely unarmed, but that doesn't mean I'm helpless. I have no idea what kinds of weapons he might have, so I'll have to improvise.

I make it down the hall without alerting the intruder. His voice still sounds muffled, and I realize he's in her closet. I take a chance and duck my head around the corner, then draw it back quickly, waiting a heartbeat for my mind to make sense of what I saw.

Gabriella is laid out on her bed in her underwear, eyes closed and unmoving. I don't know if she's alive or dead, but I didn't notice any visible wounds. There is a bag, like an old doctor's bag, open on the floor next to the bed.

What the fuck is he doing in her closet?

He's still talking in the closet. This is my chance. I move into the room fast and cross to the closet door. He's coming out with a dress in his hand and he's wearing some kind of plastic suit. His eyes go wide when he sees me.

He throws the dress at my face. I grab for him, but I only get a handful of plastic and it rips away in my hand. "Beckett!" I yell.

The little fucker's fast. By the time I drop the plastic and spin, he's out of the room. Someone says, "Oof!" then there's a thud.

"Got him!" Beckett calls. "Settle down mother fucker or I'm going to beat the shit out of you."

Sirens sound in the distance.

Thank God, the police are almost here.

I go back to Gabriella trying to be careful not to disturb anything that might be evidence. I have to know if she's alive. With a shaking hand, I lean over her and put a finger to her neck, feeling for a pulse.

The beat is slow but steady. I sigh with relief and notice her chest moving, too. She must be drugged, but for the moment, at least, she's alive.

I go to the hall where Beckett has the guy pinned. Beckett was a wrestler in high school and college, so he knows how to keep someone down. "You got him?"

"Yep, he's not going anywhere."

"I'm going to the porch to let the police in and let them know what's going on so we don't get shot."

Just as I step out the door, police cars screech to a halt out front with lights spinning. At least they turned off the sirens. I raise my hands.

"I'm the one who called you!" I shout. "My brother has the intruder pinned inside and my girlfriend is drugged or something. Call an EMT if you haven't already."

"Mister Masters?" someone asks.

"Yes, I'm Morgan Masters."

"Guys, it's okay. I know this guy," the officer says.

When he comes closer, I see Manny Ortega. He worked for us in security for a time while he was going to school to get a degree in Criminal Justice.

"Can I put my hands down now?"

He grins at me. "Yeah. Is it Kellen or Beckett inside?"

"Beckett."

"Please stay put and let us take it from here."

Several officers go into the house and a few minutes later Beckett comes out. "They've got him cuffed."

An ambulance approaches. When they enter the neighborhood, they kill the sirens but leave on the lights. Manny comes out to meet them.

He talks low with them, but I can hear that he's rattling off information about Gabriella. Within minutes, they're wheeling her out on a stretcher.

"Do you need me to stay here, or can I go with her?" I ask Manny.

"I'll stay, you go," Beckett says.

Manny nods. "They're taking her to Integris."

"Thanks man. Thanks Beck, I love you, man." I take off running for my truck.

Chapter 32

Morgan

Hours later, I'm sitting by her bed in the hospital. I almost lost her. Whatever that mother fucker had dosed her with, he had given her too much and she died in the ambulance. I thank God, Goddess, the Universe, Odin and the little baby Jesus that the EMTs were able to bring her back.

Once they tested the contents of the vial that was found on the floor in her room, they were able to counteract the drug. I have been sitting here watching her sleep since they put her in a room, afraid to take my eyes off her. They said it could take up to six hours for her to come out of it and I want to be damn sure I'm here when she wakes up.

Beckett comes in with our mother. "How is our girl?" Mom asks quietly, coming to me with arms open wide.

"They're giving her something to deal with the drug he used to knocked her out."

I accept her hug and for just that moment, I let my fear pour out. I'm shaking as she hugs me. "We almost lost her, Mom. She died. She died in the ambulance, and they almost weren't able to bring her back."

She holds me and pats my back until I stop shaking. "But they did, son. She's here with us now and she's going to be fine."

"Come sit down, Mom," Beckett says, getting out of the chair I had been sitting in.

"What's the prognosis?" she asks.

"They said that other than the drug, they didn't see any other injuries. They also said it didn't appear that she'd been raped."

"Thank God," my mother gasps.

"Based on the drug he gave her, it could take up to six hours or so for her to come out of it and we're at about four hours now based on the time Beckett and I saw her get home."

"You'll be interested to know that Ford showed up before I left," Beckett says. "When he got a look at the guy's kit, he thinks the perp might be the serial killer he's been hunting. Cops showed up in force and are going over everything with a fine-toothed comb. They found his car and are impounding it. I only got a glimpse, but it looked like a black sedan."

I look up at that. It was a black sedan I saw the other night when I chased the intruder out of her house.

"I told them they could take the cameras you put out."

I nod, happy to provide any information that will help put the guy away.

"I don't know that my recording caught anything, but I forwarded that to Ford, too."

We all freeze and go quiet when Gabriella shifts in the bed. She settles again.

"He really thinks that's the guy?" I ask, lowering my voice even more.

"I told him the guy was rummaging around in her closet going on and on about being dressed to impress for a first date. He was looking for a specific dress but wasn't finding it, so he was trying to find something similar and debating out loud which one would be best," Beckett tells us. "I don't know what that has to do with the serial killer, but Ford got all excited when I told him. He also said that Cait will want to know what's going on with Ella and that you should call her."

"I'll call her once Gabriella wakes up."

We fall into silence as a nurse comes in to check Gabriella's vitals. She notes everything into a computer. She's about to take a blood pressure reading when Gabriella stirs. The nurse freezes. We all freeze.

Gabriella pulls against the cuff on her arm and when she can't pull free, her eyes spring open and she starts to scream and flail. The nurse drops the cuff and takes off.

I lunge for Gabriella and pull her into my arms. "Shhh, Baby, you're safe. You're okay. Shhh. I've got you. You're safe."

She's fighting me, but my words must sink in because she fists my shirt and stops fighting.

"Morgan?"

"Yes, Baby, it's me."

She breaks and sobs. "He...he...There was someone in the house. There was someone. He was in the house, and he pinched my arm. I couldn't move. He said he was going to kill me. He..." she breaks off, unable to speak as her body's wracked with sobs.

The nurse comes running back in with a syringe.

"Considering what happened to her, is that necessary?" I ask.

"This will just help keep her calm. It will make her drowsy but shouldn't knock her out. The doctors anticipated she might have an episode upon waking."

I nod as she introduces the meds into Gabriella's drip line. Gabriella's sobs turn to tears and her gasps turn to deep breaths. I keep holding and rocking her until she settles. When she's calmer, I pull back and wipe her tears away with the tissues Mom hands me.

She lays back in bed once the drugs have taken effect. She looks so frail. The dark circles under her eyes make them look haunted. "Here, dear," Mom says, handing Gabriella more tissues.

"Rebecca? I'm so sorry," Gabriella says.

"Sorry?" Mom asks. "What are you sorry for, dear?"

"For being so much trouble."

"Oh, honey, you're not any trouble at all. There was no way I was going to go back home after picking up Beckett. I had to come check on you and make sure you were okay first."

I'm so grateful that it looks like she's going to be okay. I can't stop touching her so I remain perched on the side of her bed.

"How are you feeling?" I ask.

"I feel like I weigh a million pounds. My limbs are heavy and my head's a jumble. I remember coming home and I wanted to call you, but my phone died. When I turned my back to the room to put it on the charger, I was pinched on the arm. I feel funny, like there's bunny slippers on my tongue. Are there bunny slippers?" she asks, sticking out her tongue for me to check.

"No, baby. They gave you something to help you relax, and that's what's making you feel funny.

She sinks back into the bed with a scowl on her face. "I don't like it. How did you know?"

"How did I know what, baby?"

"About the plastic man."

"We can talk about it tomorrow. You just need to rest for now," I tell her as I smooth her hair off her face.

"I'm still mad at you," she says drowsily.

"I know. We'll talk about that tomorrow, too." I lean down and kiss her forehead.

Mom pats my hand. "See, she's going to be fine. Why is she mad at you?"

"Because I'm an idiot."

"Well, dear, stop doing that and make it right," she tells me.

My laugh is mirthless. "Yes, ma'am. I'll do my best."

"I know you will. It's late, or should I say early? I'm going to take Beckett home and go home myself to get some sleep. Is there anything you need before I go?"

I shake my head. "Not tonight, but I do need a favor."

"Anything, dear, you know that."

"When they brought her in, she was only wearing underwear and I have no idea where those have gone. When you're up and about would you mind going by my house and getting some clothes for her? Because of the stalker, she's been staying at my house and has plenty of clothes there."

Mom has a key to my apartment, so I trust her to find what we need. In fact, as a woman, she'll probably do a better job of it than I would.

"I can do that, dear. I don't sleep much these days, so I'll see you in a few hours."

I lean down and hug her, kissing her cheek. "Thanks Mom. I love you."

"I love you, too, Morgan. Come, Beckett, let's go."

"Coming, Mother," he says with a grin. He gives me a guy hug and a slap on the back, then follows her out the door.

I return to the chair next to Gabriella's bed and slump into it, exhausted beyond belief. Her hand seems so small when I take it in mine. Things could have gone very differently tonight, and the thought of that makes my blood run cold.

If I had been a few minutes later, I could have lost her. I could have lost her forever. Lost her to a goddamn serial killer.

After all the shit she's been through in her life, she's targeted by a mother fucking serial killer. If I'd have known it when we caught him, I would have been hard pressed not to go vigilante on his ass and remove him from existence.

She keeps shifting in the bed like she can't get comfortable. I'm still holding her hand and she's got a death grip on mine. She whimpers. I can't stand it.

I take off my shoes and wedge myself onto the bed with her. There really isn't enough room for two, but I have to have her in my arms.

As soon as I wrap her up, she turns and burrows into me, her face against my chest and letting out a deep sigh. Her fidgeting stops. She doesn't whimper again.

I kiss the top of her head and say quietly, "That's it, baby. You just sealed your fate. You're mine, and I'm never going to let you go."

Chapter 33

Gabriella

S omeone's talking and they won't shut up. As my brain comes out of the fog of sleep, I realize it's two someones quietly arguing. One of them is Morgan.

I snuggle against his chest. "Be quiet, Morgan. It's too early to get up."

It comes out muffled. Closer still to being awake, I realize that my voice is muffled because my face is pressed against his shirt. "Why are you wearing clothes?"

"Hush, baby, go back to sleep."

"I'm trying," I huff and roll over in the bed.

A sharp pain jabs the back of my hand and I'm tangled in my clothes. Why am I wearing clothes in bed?

"Ow!" My eyes pop open to see an IV line in my hand. The tube is tangled up in the bedding and pulling on the needle. It all comes back to me then.

I'm in the hospital. Someone drugged me because they intended to kill me. Oh my God, someone wanted to kill me. How long have I been here? Did they catch the guy? I feel panic rising.

"Morgan?"

"I'm right here, Baby."

I relax. If he's here, I'm okay. "What day is it?"

"It's Sunday. They brought you in last night." I hear him groan as the bed shifts. "There, now you've got more room."

I look over to see a sour faced nurse scowling at Morgan. As soon as she sees me looking, her entire demeanor changes. She smiles and starts asking me how I'm feeling while she takes my vitals.

Morgan takes out his phone and calls someone. "She's awake" is all he says before hanging up and repeating the news to someone else. He does this three times before he puts his phone away.

"Who did you call? What happened?" I ask. "I remember some things, but it's all fuzzy and jumbled."

"Ford is on his way. He wants to talk to you first because he doesn't want me muddying the waters of your memory by telling you what I think might have happened. I called Ford, Mom, and Cait."

"I'm hungry," I announce as my stomach growls.

Morgan looks at the nurse. "I saw you all bringing trays around a while ago, so she missed breakfast, didn't she?"

"I can see if we have a leftover tray, if you like," she answers, apparently once he got out of the bed like she wanted him to, Morgan was no longer deserving of a scowl.

"That's okay," he replies as he pulls out his phone again and dials. "Mom, Gabriella's hungry and missed breakfast. Would you mind picking her up something on your way here?" He holds the phone away from his mouth. "What do you want?"

"I would kill for a chai latte, but other than that, it doesn't matter as long as it's something hot and terrible for me." The nurse nods and leaves the room.

"Did you get that?" Morgan asks. I can hear his mom speaking, but I can't make out what she's saying. "Okay, thanks Mom."

"Um, is it okay for me to get up?" I ask.

"I think so, why?"

"I've gotta go," I say, pointing at the bathroom in the corner.

"Then let's get you up." Morgan gets my IV untangled from the bedding and moves the stand holding the saline bag a little way from the bed so that I have room to stand.

I'm suddenly nervous. I still don't feel quite right and a fear of falling has me doubting whether I should even attempt this. As if he can read my mind, Morgan says, "It's okay. I'm right here and I won't let you fall." He holds out his hand to me.

The brief trip to the restroom wears me out and I can't wait to get back in bed. I am shocked at the person I see in the mirror. My eyes look sunken with dark circles and my normally tan skin tone is washed out and pale.

I finger comb my hair, but I still look horrible, which makes it so neato that there are people coming to see me. Morgan is fluffing my pillows when a doctor comes in, followed by Ford. The doctor is young but has an air of confidence about him.

"Ms. Carmichael, I'm Dr. Van Horn. How are you feeling?"

"Fine mostly. Sluggish and my head is still kind of fuzzy."

He uses his flashlight to check my eyes. "That's to be expected. You received a large dose of a benzodiazepine type drug last night. It was almost fatal, but thankfully, the folks in the ambulance were able to bring you back to us."

He keeps talking about my injuries and how much worse they could have been if Morgan and Beckett hadn't show up. Mostly I get that I'll be fuzzy brained for a while and might have hallucinations. Oh, and maybe even panic attacks and intense nightmares.

Wonderful.

"Do you have any questions?" he asks.

Considering I'm still processing what he said, thanks to the fuzzy brain, all I can think of is, "When can I go home?"

Morgan is here, so he'll know what the doctor said.

"We'd like to keep you for a while yet just to make sure there are no delayed issues from the drug or flushing it out, but you should be able to be discharged this afternoon."

"All right. Morgan, I'm not thinking clearly yet. Is there anything you want to ask?"

"Not right now, baby. Doctor, if we come up with any questions will you be available?"

"Yes, I'm on all day. If you want to talk further, just have the nurse call me down."

"Thank you," I tell him.

Morgan shakes his hand and the doctor exits.

Ford has been standing to the side waiting, but as the doctor leaves, he steps forward. "Ella, I'm glad you're okay. Cait sends her love and would love it if you would call her when you're feeling better."

I nod. "I will."

"Now, I know you're still not back to one hundred percent, but I'm hoping you can answer some questions. Do you mind if I bring someone in?"

"Sure, I don't mind," I say, thrilled that yet another person will see me in my current state. "I'll tell you everything I remember."

Ford goes to the door, cracks it open, and waves someone in. I'm surprised that it's a woman. I know Ford has a partner, but I always thought it was another man from the way Cait talked. Morgan moves to sit in the chair next to my bed and takes my hand in his.

"Gabriella, Morgan, my partner Bill is overseeing the processing of the evidence from your house back at the station. This is Special Agent Maxine Winters with the FBI. We asked for their help with the serial that's been operating in the City over the past year. When she heard about what happened to you, Gabriella, she asked to come with me to talk to you. Is that okay with you?"

"Sure," I reply.

"If it's okay, I'd like to record this."

I nod.

"Why don't you tell me what happened?"

"I came home, and my phone was dead, so I was trying to put it on the charger," I start.

"Came home from where?" Ford interrupts me.

"From Pawhuska."

"What were you doing in Pawhuska?" Ford asks.

"I went up there to clear my head."

"Why did you need to do that?"

"Because of the fight," I mumble. "I was mad."

"Who were you mad at?"

I look over at Morgan, but before I can answer, he says, "She was mad at me because I did something stupid. But I think we need to go back further. As you should know from the report she filed, someone has been messing with Gabriella for weeks."

"Okay, tell me about that," Ford says.

We're interrupted by Rebecca coming in with food and a bag of my clothes. Ford wanted to make her wait out in the hall. I told him it was my story, and I didn't mind her hearing it, so unless he wanted to wait until after I visited with her and thanked her for bringing me everything, he would let her stay.

He sighed and gave me a grudging agreement, then told me to continue. I caught Rebecca up as I unpacked my food and took a big swig of my latte. "This is wonderful. Thank you so much!" She brought Morgan breakfast, too, so he vacated the chair for her and sat on my bed so he could share my tray table. I told them the story between bites.

In starts and stops, I tell them about misplacing things at my house and pointed out that it never happened when I was at Morgan's. The specific example of the house porn book gives them an example of the kind of thing I was experiencing and how it freaked me out and had me checking all the locks again, only to find them unchanged.

"I was about to go to a hotel, but I saw a Masters Construction Security car out front," I say. "Morgan had sent someone to watch over me. After that, I've spent every night at Morgan's until Friday, but when he couldn't get to me at home, things started happening at work."

"Friday was the fight," Morgan says.

He said it as a statement, but I answered, "Yes. I was mad at Morgan, threw a fit, and ran away. I went to my house, packed a bag quickly, and looked up state parks with cabins available. That's how I ended up at the state park outside of Pawhuska to clear my head."

"Cait said you had planned to stay until Sunday. Why did you come back early?"

I told them all about the strange man at the campground and stopping to shop. They asked me follow-up questions about the man, and I told them he didn't look like the guy who came to the office that I figured was the stalker, but I thought the ranger checked his ID.

I couldn't remember the ranger's name but was able to give them the time and a description of the ranger. They said they would talk to him.

"By the time I realized my phone was dead, I was on my way home. I didn't have a charger in the car, but figured I'd charge it and call everyone when I got home. I came in and was fiddling with the charger when I..." I frown trying to remember.

Rebecca takes my hand in hers and pats it. "Take your time, dear."

When she moves my arm, there's a twinge in my biceps. I reach over and touch it with my free hand.

"I heard a noise and felt someone pinch me. Or I thought they pinched me, but I guess it was when he gave me the drug. It took a few minutes for me to pass out and he kept talking about how he would be my last first date because after he was done, I would be part of his collection and dead."

I shiver.

Ford turns to Morgan. "And how is it that you just happened along while the suspect was here?"

Morgan sighs and tells his side of things, including falling asleep at my house, interrupting the intruder, and chasing him out of the house.

"The little fucker was fast. He was around the house and up the block before I could catch him. Knowing her house would be empty, I got some of the motion activated cameras we use on job sites to cover the main entries. I got an alert and saw the guy entering. I wasn't alarmed until the alert went off again, showing Gabriella coming home."

"Did you report the first break-in?" Ford asks.

"No. The guy was gone. There was no proof, and I figured if I reported it, someone would call Gabriella and that would make her come home, but I wanted her to have the time away she needed. She may have even thought I made it up to make her come home."

"You still should have reported it," Ford admonishes, but I can tell from the look on Morgan's face that he'd do it the same way all over again. I put my foot on his thigh and he squeezes my toes.

Even when I was mad at him, had blown up and thrown things at him, he was watching out for me, taking care of me. I had been horrible to him and thought the worst of him.

He's cared for me in a million different ways. Instead of talking to him about it when I felt wronged, I went off the rails even as I was accusing him of not talking to me about something. How could I have been so stupid?

Ford asks a few more questions. "Do you think you could identify your attacker?"

I shake my head. "No, he had something over his face, but I could identify the guy from the campsite or the guy that came into the office if that helps."

Ford continues. My energy is flagging but I try to answer as best I can. By the time Ford and Agent Winters leave, I am working hard to stay awake. Morgan walks them to the door, and that's the last thing I remember before sleep overtakes me.

Chapter 34

Gabriella

I hear hushed voices as my awareness starts to rise to the surface. It's Morgan talking again. Morgan and his mother, Rebecca.

At first, I wonder why they're talking while I'm sleeping, but then I remember I'm in the hospital. I don't know how long I've been asleep, but I hope Rebecca hasn't been waiting around here long. I'm sure she has better things to do.

"How much longer do you think they'll keep her?" Rebecca asks.

"The doctor said that depending on how she's doing, she could possibly go home this afternoon."

"That's good. Do you think the police are through with her house yet?"

"I don't know. She and I still need to talk about what happened Friday, but as far as I'm concerned, she's staying at my place until we find out what's happening with the guy they have in custody. If she's still mad at me, she can sleep in the second bedroom, but I will not allow her to stay somewhere alone until I know she's safe."

I know I shouldn't eavesdrop, but I keep my eyes closed and stay quiet, curious to hear the conversation.

"You two will work it out, I'm sure," Rebecca says. "If she insists she doesn't want to stay with you, she can always come and stay at the house with your father and me. We have plenty of room."

"We've got to work it out. She's it for me, Mom. I know it has happened fast, but I love her. I haven't told her because I didn't want to spook her by moving too quickly, but the only way she's going to get rid of me is if she tells me flat out that she doesn't want me."

"I know," she replies. "I could tell how you felt about her when you brought her over for Mother's Day. For what it's worth, I think she feels the same way about you."

"I hope so. I can't lose her. The whole time I was racing to get to her I was so scared that I would get there too late, and she'd never know what she means to me."

I turn onto my side away from them because I'm afraid I'll give myself away. The urge to laugh vies with the one to cry. I do love him.

Not only because he's taken care of me and helped me exorcise my ghosts, but he's a truly good man. He's honest and loyal and he's the kind of man the world needs more of.

They stop talking. Footsteps sound on the tile floor. Morgan is coming around the bed. He pauses, then smooths my hair out of my face. I decide to give up the farce and flutter my eyes open.

"Hey," he says, his face even with mine.

I smile shyly. "Hey."

He cups my cheek and leans in to kiss my forehead before he stands from his crouch. I turn onto my back in bed. "Hi Rebecca."

"Hello, dear. How are you feeling?"

"Gritty and gross and ready to fly this chicken coop."

She laughs.

"At least you don't have bunny slippers on your tongue anymore," Morgan teases.

"What?" I ask.

"When you first woke up, you said you thought you had bunny slippers on your tongue because it felt funny." His lips are tilted up on one side.

"I did not!"

"You sure did. Mom can back me up; she and Beckett heard it, too."

I look over at Rebecca, and she's grinning from ear to ear.

I pull the blanket up over my head. "How embarrassing!"

"You were on a lot of medications, dear. Nothing you said can be held against you," Rebecca says.

I sigh and pull the blanket back down. "Yeah, but he's never going to let me live it down."

"Probably not," she says, "and Beckett will be even worse."

I groan.

"Well, I'm going to go now," Rebecca says, patting my hand. "I just wanted to stay until you woke up again to see how you were feeling. You seem to be just fine. From the sound of things, you two have a lot to talk about, so I'm going to get out of the way. If you need anything, dear, don't hesitate to let me know."

"Rebecca, thank you so much for your kindness. I can't tell you how much I appreciate it."

She hugs me, then hugs and kisses Morgan on the cheek. He walks her to the door, thanking her for everything. She's so sweet.

Morgan's whole family is so wonderful. Well, maybe except for Kellen, he's a bit of a cold fish. But all in all, they're the kind of family I always wanted, and Rebecca's the kind of mother a girl should grow up with. She's going to be a great grandmother.

Morgan closes the door behind Rebecca. His shoulders slump and he's quiet for a long moment. This is the first time we've been alone that I've been awake since I was brought to the hospital.

"I almost lost you," he says. When he turns around, I can see the toll that it's taken on him.

I look at my lap. "I know. I'm sorry."

He starts to speak, but I interrupt him.

"I'm sorry I ran away instead of talking to you. If I hadn't taken off alone, he wouldn't have had the opportunity…"

"Stop that right there," he says, his voice firm. I look at him and his eyes are bright and intense. "This is in no way your fault. He was watching and waiting. If he hadn't done it last night, he would have seized an opportunity as soon as one arose. He's been watching you for a long time, probably even more closely once you started staying with me so he could capitalize on any opportunity."

I nod. "I know."

He comes and sits on my bed, taking my hands in his. "So, back to Friday. You were right; I should have talked to you before I made changes to your drawings."

When I try to interrupt him, he puts a finger to my lips.

"If I had stopped to think about it for one minute, I would have realized that you probably already had a back-up plan in place because that's just like you to have all the bases covered. I'm sorry. I was an idiot, and you were right to be upset with me."

"I'm sorry, too. I flew off the handle and ran away instead of talking to you about it. I won't do that again. Not that I won't get mad and with me being both Spanish and Irish, there are likely to be times I yell, and maybe even throw things, but I won't run away again."

He chuckles. "I can handle you yelling at me when I'm an idiot, but yeah, you leaving was hard to handle." He pulls me into his arms, holding me so tight it's almost painful. "Dammit, woman, you scared me. Let's not do that again."

We sit there like that for a while. "I love you Gabriella," he says.

"I love you, too," I say against his shirt. "That's been true for a while now, but I didn't say it because it scared me."

"You don't have to be afraid with me, Gabriella. You're it for me. We can get through anything as long as we're willing to talk to each other and work it out."

My throat clogs with emotion and all I can do is nod against his chest.

Chapter 35

Gabriella

"Are you sure you want to go to work today?" Morgan asks.

It had been early evening by the time the hospital released me. Cait had come by to see me, and I had napped off and on, but Morgan never left my side. I knew he was probably exhausted, so when we went by my house, all I picked up was my purse and cell phone.

I had enough clothes at his house to last me several days. The doctor said it probably wouldn't be a good idea for me to drive for at least a few days, so we left my car there as well.

Morgan said he would be happy to play chauffeur and if there is something he can't do, his mother or Cait are willing to help. His mother had even left food in the refrigerator for when we got home.

"Yes. I think I'd go crazy sitting around here all day with nothing to do. I need to work."

At least I think I need to work. I want to need to work. I'm so conflicted, but Morgan has bent over backwards for me and the sooner I can get back the normal, the better it will be for him. I just need to buck up and muddle through. I'll be fine.

It'll be fine.

Really.

I hope.

As if he can read my mind, he says, "Don't push yourself. You can take it easy for as long as you need to."

"I'll be okay." I see him fiddling with my phone. "What are you doing?"

"I'm programming Mom's cell number into your phone, so you have it."

"Okay, I'm ready, let's go."

Morgan takes me to my office and goes in with me. He lingers before leaving. "What time does Hailey get here?"

"She has class on Monday mornings and will be here around eleven," I tell him.

He frowns. "I don't like this. I think you're moving too fast."

With my hand on his chest, I force a smile. "I'm fine. It'll be fine. If it's not, I'll call someone to come get me. I've managed to make it to thirty-four on my own just fine. I think I'll be okay for the next eight or nine hours."

"Listen, I know you're tough and I know you are capable. You don't have to do it alone anymore, Gabriella. It's okay to let people care for you."

"I know. But I think some normalcy will be good for me. The guy is in jail, so I have nothing to worry about, right? I'm safe and Hailey will be here in a few hours."

His frown turns to a scowl. "Okay." He kisses my forehead. "I love you. Call me if you need anything, and I mean anything."

"I love you, too, cariño. Now go to work."

I walk him to the door and wave as he backs out to leave. Returning to my office, I turn on my computer. I really don't have anything pressing, which is why I thought today would be a good day to try the office. Just a nice, peaceful day to show myself that I can do this and that I don't have anything to be afraid of.

I want to do some research, but first I need to prioritize the week. First, I open our project tracking software, make some updates and print a report. A shadow crosses the wall, making me jump.

I laugh at myself and shake my head. "It's just someone out on the sidewalk walking by. Calm down," I say to no one but myself.

I make notes on the report, then set it to the side of my desk. There are two sets of drawings I need to get started on, but they're not urgent. Neither homeowner wants to get started for at least a month.

I pull out my notes on each and set them with the report, intending to read through them later today. Someone else crosses in front of the office sending their shadow skating across the wall. My hand begins to shake.

You should go lock the door.

I resolve to ignore the voice telling me I need to lock myself in. Just to be safe is what I tell myself. I move my computer screen so that my back is to the front of the building, thinking it will keep me from seeing the shadow play along the wall that stretches from the front window to the back wall.

Next, I start doing my research, making notes on a notepad, but having my back to the open room is unnerving. Someone could sneak up on me. An ember of fear sparks deep inside.

Stop it. You're being ridiculous.

I take some deep, cleansing breaths.

You should go lock the door.

"Gaaaah!" I cry out in frustration, throwing my hands up in the air. I get up and pace back and forth in my office. My hands are shaking. My heart is pounding.

I should call Morgan. This was a mistake. He was right.

I go to my purse and pull out my phone. I press his contact to dial and move the phone to my ear as it starts to ring.

My whole body is shaking now, the ember of fear growing.

Ding!

The ember of fear surges into an inferno of panic.

He's here! He's here! He's here! Hide! Hide! Hide!

"Hey, baby. It's okay, you're safe. It was just a panic attack. Take a deep breath. That's it."

I look up to see Morgan crouched in front of my drafting table. The drafting table I'm huddled underneath, my back wedged into the corner.

"Maybe this was a bad idea," I say, my voice small. "I'm sorry."

"It's okay. I know you had to try, and you don't need to be sorry for that." He extends a hand to me and helps me crawl out from under the table.

I see Hailey standing by my desk, a worried look on her face. When I stand up, I smooth down my pants and shirt, unable to look her in the eye. "Oh, Hailey. I'm sorry I frightened you."

"Are you all right?" she asks.

"Panic attack," I offer by way of an explanation.

"No worries," Hailey says. "It's understandable, considering what happened."

"Baby, why don't you have a seat while I talk to Hailey?" He guides me to my desk chair. I sit down and he goes out to the lobby with her. I can hear them talking in low voices, but can't make out what they're saying.

I pull over the report and folders I had set aside earlier and start reading through my notes in the top folder.

Morgan puts a hand on my shoulder, and I jump. "Hey, easy there. I said your name from the door, but you didn't hear me. Come on, let's close up."

I nod and shut down my computer, then gather up the report and folders along with my things. My body feels like an automaton. As long as he tells me what to do, I can keep moving.

"I know you don't want to be at home alone," he says when we get into the truck, "so why don't you come to my office? You can hang out with me, or I can even rustle up a free drafting board if you'd like to do some drawing."

I nod.

He reaches over the console and takes my hand in his. "Baby, it's going to be okay. It's just going to take some time."

The Masters Construction offices are huge by my standards. "How many employees do you have?"

"I'd have to ask Kellen to be sure, but I think we've got around a hundred."

"Wow, and I thought six was a lot to handle." I grab his hand, needing a connection with him. He pulls our hands up to his mouth and kisses the back of mine.

"Do you want a tour, or would you rather chill out a bit first?"

"I think some quiet would be good as long as I'm not alone. Being alone is what got me this morning."

"The doctor said that panic attacks could happen as your body readjusts to dumping the drug out of your system. It could have been just that, and if that's so, there's nothing you did or didn't do to cause it."

He leads me in and introduces me to the receptionist, then takes me to his office. The offices are nice, but not over the top luxurious. There seem to be people everywhere; some in cubicles, some in offices, some scurrying around like squirrels on a mission.

His office suits him in its practicality and essence of man reflected in the dark wood and lack of anything frivolous. There is no art on the walls, but there is a bookcase along one wall with several framed photos.

"Go ahead and do whatever you need to do. Don't mind me," I tell him.

He sits behind his desk, and I start perusing the photos. There are mostly pictures of his family. Some of him and his brothers when they were younger.

A couple of photos of them with their parents and a couple of just his parents together. There are a few shots of him when he was in the Marines; he looks so young.

I wonder how that young man would compare to the man he is now. Personally, I was a hot mess when I was seventeen and fresh out of high school. Clueless is a good descriptor because I had no idea of who I was or what I wanted. That doesn't seem like something Morgan has ever been afflicted with.

I sit on the sofa on one side of his office, pull out my folders and go back to reading the notes. As I read, my mind conjures a 3-D vision of what the drawings should look like, and I'm itching for a pencil and some paper. I look up to see Morgan watching me.

I smile, feeling shy. "You said there might be a drafting table I could use?"

"I tell you what, Mom's bringing lunch in a bit, so why don't I give you a tour so you can get the lay of the land, then after lunch I'll turn you loose in the design area. Does that sound good?"

"That sounds excellent."

Chapter 36

Gabriella

After the tour and lunch with Rebecca, I'm feeling better. Everyone I have met has been very nice and they all seem to love Rebecca. She had to shoo them out of the kitchen to keep them from eating the food she brought. Masters Construction is impressive, and they have a lot to be proud of.

I am not only impressed, but a little intimidated by their design area. I've never thought of myself as old, but apparently, the way I do things is considered old-school. The two young designers I meet, Trent and Stephanie, do everything on computer.

Computers are good, but there's no soul in them. For basic designs with a lot of right angles and smooth surfaces, they're great, but some of my stuff can only be visualized with a pencil in my hands. Brenda, the woman who is out on maternity leave, seems to do a bit of both. Her office holds the drafting table Morgan says I can use if I want.

I think I'm going to take him up on that, even though I really want to just stay here in his office with him. When I'm with him, I feel safe. However, I can't be by his side twenty-four hours a day.

Working in Brenda's office with plenty of people around and Morgan nearby seems like a better way to start trying to work. If I can do that, maybe I'll be able to try my office again.

I return to Morgan's office once I wash up after lunch. He's looking at my construction report. "Hey nosy parker," I tease.

"Yep," he replies with no shame.

"I'm going to go draw in Brenda's office."

"Okay, baby. Do you remember the way?"

"I do, thank you." I lean up and kiss him. He pulls me into his arms and deepens the kiss. "Does that door lock?"

He laughs and lets me go. "Don't tempt me, woman."

I grin at him. "I was being serious!"

He swats at me, but I dodge out of the way with a laugh. I grab the top folder from my stack and make my way back through the offices.

"Are you ready to go?"

I turn around and see Morgan leaning in the doorway. "What?"

"It's five o'clock woman, I'm starving."

"No, it's not! There's no way it can be five. I've only been working for an hour or so."

He points to the wall where a clock shows five. He comes over and looks at the drawing I've been working on. "Wow, you got all of that done this afternoon? I think you're faster than the computer kids."

"Let me just gather up my drawings. I'll need to finish them tomorrow."

"Why don't you leave them here? You can work here again tomorrow."

I hesitate. Do I want to work here again tomorrow? What about my office? What about Hailey? "Um…"

"Leave it here for now and think about it," he says. "It's just some paper, so if we need to grab them and take them somewhere else, that's easy enough."

I nod. "Okay."

I can't move. He's here! He has drugged me again, but with something different this time. I'm awake but I can't move. Oh God! I can't move!

He lays my blue dress out on the bed next to me, then climbs on top of me, straddling my waist. His hands go around my throat, and he begins to squeeze, all the while telling me what he's going to do to me after I'm dead. Oh my God! He's sick!

I'm gasping but I can't breathe! I try to kick and buck him off, but I can't make my body obey. My ears are ringing. I try to scream, but my vocal cords are crushed. My eyesight starts to dim, and blackness closes in.

Morgan, I'm so sorry! I'm sorry I wasn't strong enough. I'm sorry…I'm sooo…

"Gabriella, wake up! Come on baby, wake up."

I come awake screaming, flailing, and kicking. Morgan gets me under control by wrapping his arms around me and pinning my arms to my sides. My screams turn to sobs as I go limp.

I should have known that it was all going too well. I had a productive afternoon working at Morgan's offices. We had a nice dinner and made love for the first time in four days.

"It's okay, baby, you're safe. I've got you. It was just a nightmare."

"I'm sorry," I sob against his shoulder. "I think there should be only one freak out allowed per day after being attacked by a psycho."

"Or maybe the more you have in a day, the sooner it works its way out of your system."

"It still sucks."

"It is what it is, baby. We'll get through it, so don't stress."

My tears subside. My shaking stops. I take in a deep breath and let it out with a sigh. "Be right back," I say as I get out of bed.

I go to the bathroom and throw some water on my face. I don't know how I'd get through this without Morgan and his family. Without Morgan and Beckett, I'd be dead.

I go back to bed, but I know I won't be able to sleep, so I prop myself up on pillows. Morgan has fallen back to sleep, but when I slide in on my side of the bed, he wraps his arms around my waist and lays his head on my chest.

I sit there in bed, riffling my fingers through Morgan's hair while I watch him sleep. And I think way too much. The guy...I wish I knew his name because it feels weird to just keep calling him "the guy"...is in jail. He can't hurt me anymore. I just need to focus on that.

I heard Morgan say that this guy might be the one who has been killing women over the past year. How crazy would that be if I somehow landed on the list of a serial killer? I wonder how that happened. Why me? What did I do?

My mind is roiling with a million different questions. I'm not going to figure anything out sitting here spinning my wheels.

Maybe I should meditate. Or perhaps I should go get a double shot of whiskey to help me sleep. Maybe I need to find a therapist to help me sort this shit out.

One thing I'm sure of is that Morgan is putting up with this shit right along with me, so I need to make it as easy on him as I can. I'll work at his office again tomorrow so he won't have to worry about me being at mine.

Hailey will need to be notified. I'll also have to figure out how I can do my site visits because I doubt Morgan will let me go to those alone. I'll talk to him about it tomorrow.

"How are you doing?" Cait asks.

Morgan had to be out on job sites today, so he suggested I might enjoy having lunch with Cait. I have a feeling they are conspiring behind my back, but I'm happy with the results, so I can't get too bent out of shape.

"I'm working through it. Yesterday, I made it through the whole day without a freak out. However, I had a panic attack and a nightmare on Monday, so I think I overused my quota and now I'm just waiting for my freak out availability bank to refill."

She chuckles. "I hope you don't mind, but I invited Demi to join us."

"No, I don't mind." Although I do. Just a little.

Cait keeps in close contact with all the members of our Society quint. I like them, all of them, and I know Demi better than the other two women.

However, I know Cait will want to talk about what happened, and I don't know if I'm comfortable doing that in front of Demi. If I'm not, I'll just have to say that I'm not and ask them to change the subject.

I was wondering why she wanted to drive all the way to Moore for lunch. Demi's office is in Norman, so this was a way to meet in the middle. Sneaky woman. Cait is the nicest person you'd ever want to meet, but she has her own magic way of getting people where she wants them. Funny thing is, I'm usually happy about it.

Maybe Cait is thinking that Demi will be able to help me because she's a therapist. However, I know that Demi's specialty is working with couples with sexual issues and that's an area Morgan and I definitely don't need help in. But, like I said, there's usually a method to Cait's madness, so I'll relax and see what happens.

"Sorry I'm late," Demi says as she takes the chair across from mine. I jump because I hadn't heard her coming. "I apologize, Ella. I should have announced myself."

"No, it's okay," I tell her.

"No, it's not. I know better."

I'm not sure what she means, but I nod in acceptance of her apology.

Once we've placed our orders and are waiting for our food, Demi dives right in. "I'm sure you're wondering why Cait brought you all the way down here to have lunch with me. I know you know I'm a psychologist, but I also know you're aware of my specialty. While the training helps, it's not the main reason."

When she grins at me, I know the confusion must be plain on my face.

"I don't talk about it a lot," she says, "but one thing that caused me to become interested in psychology is the fact that in my first year at OU, I was kidnapped and brutalized by five men who wanted to gang rape me."

She says it so matter-of-factly. I wonder if I'll ever be able to talk about my incident so coolly.

"When I woke up in the hospital," Demi continues, "I had cracked ribs, a sprained ankle, and my face was so swollen from being hit so many times that they had to wait several days for the swelling to go down enough to ensure there wasn't any damage to my orbital socket. The first moment I was alone in the hospital, I had my first panic attack."

Okay, that's what I get for making assumptions.

"So, no pressure," she continues, "but if you want to talk, I'm available. It doesn't have to be in a professional capacity, it can be just as friends."

I fiddle with my silverware and before I realize my hand is shaking, she places her hand over mine and squeezes. "You're going to be fine," she says.

"How did you get past it?" I ask.

"Time, mostly. I have some wonderful friends who helped me, watching over me, being willing to listen, and helping maintain some normalcy in my world. I still have times when I can feel a panic attack creeping up, but it's very rare and mostly when I'm too stressed out."

"I can see how stress would be a tremendous factor," Cait says.

"It is," Demi confirms. "I meditate, which helps me to stay grounded in the now. Exercise also helps keep me balanced and I take Krav Maga classes so that if anyone tries to hurt me again, I can kick the shit out of them."

I almost spit water all over the table when I laugh.

Chapter 37

Gabriella

"How was lunch?" Morgan asks when he comes to get me at the end of the day. He comes over to the drafting table and stands behind me, putting his arms around my waist as he looks over my shoulder.

"It was enlightening."

"How so?"

"Well, I had no idea, but Demi was kidnapped and attacked when she was at OU. They beat her up pretty badly. She had panic attacks and nightmares, too. Said it's partly why she got into psychology. She also said that she is available if I wanted to talk either professionally or just as a friend."

"How do you feel about that?"

"I am surprised, but I think it will be good to talk with someone who's been through something similar," I tell him honestly. "She also had some other suggestions, like reducing stress, exercise, and meditation."

He kisses the top of my head. "Speaking of reducing stress, I did something today that you might get mad at me about."

I stiffen.

"I know you were worried about doing your site visits, so I took your project list and Alejandro, and we did your site visits today. A couple of them are lagging, so Alejandro is going to keep an eye on them for you for the rest of the week."

"I want to be mad at you for not talking to me first, but in reality, I'm relieved."

"So, with that settled, and speaking of exercise, and your drawings not being needed for a few weeks, what do you think about getting out of town for a few days?"

"I'm listening," I reply, leaning into his embrace.

"I have a friend who has a cabin out in the woods. It's close to Robbers Cave State Park where there are lots of hiking trails and close to Eufaula Lake where he keeps a boat that we can use to go fishing or swimming or just lie around in the sun drinking beer all day."

I turn and face him. "You're really going to go hiking with me?"

"Absolutely! I figure we'd go up tomorrow morning and come back Sunday night or we can stay longer, if you want."

"You are the best boyfriend ever. I love you, Morgan Masters!"

"Love you, too, baby." He kisses me and kisses me some more and just as it's really starting to heat up...

"Well, excuuuse me," Beckett says.

"Why did I have to have brothers?" Morgan says, putting his forehead to mine.

Unfazed, Beckett goes on. "I heard you guys are going to Dave's cabin. Mind if I come out and go fishing Saturday morning?"

"So much for a romantic weekend," Morgan says.

Beckett waves a hand. "Romance schmomance. Y'all got the rest of your lives for romance, but it is a rare occasion that I get to go fishing."

"It's up to you," Morgan tells me.

"We'll still have a few days alone together, so I'm okay with it. It's the least I can do for his help in saving my life."

"Yes!" Beckett says with a fist pump.

"We're going out tomorrow morning. If you want to go fishing, you'd better get there Friday night so we can get on the water early Saturday," Morgan says.

"Done. I'll drive out after work tomorrow night. Now, what's for dinner?"

The next morning, we are just passing out of Oklahoma City when I blurt out, "I think I'm going to close my business."

I've been thinking about it since my fight with Morgan almost a week ago. I love seeing my vision come to fruition, but I don't like dealing with the build outs. If I could find someone to be a construction manager, I would be okay with it, but that hasn't worked out for me so far.

"Okay. Tell me what you're thinking."

"As you know, I don't like the construction stuff. I never wanted that to be part of my business, but felt like I had no choice. It's becoming such a large part of what I do that it's making me fall out of love with design and drawing. I want to go back to school and get either a degree in architecture or go the tech school route and do drafting and design. I enjoy doing things by hand, but I'd like to learn the software, too. I've only just started researching schools and degree options."

"Do you know where you want to end up?"

I shrug. "I'm not sure. I enjoy running my own thing so I'm not sure I'd want to work for someone else, but being in your office the past few days has been fun. It's nice to have people to talk to. That has allowed me to see where collaborating with a team and drawing on each other's creative ideas would be something I'd enjoy."

"I've been thinking the last few days, too."

"Oh?" I ask.

"Actually, for a bit longer than the last few days. What if you could have the best of both worlds?"

"What do you mean?"

Morgan pauses as if he needs to organize his thoughts.

"As you know, our lead designer is out on maternity leave. I pretty much knew it was going to happen, but last week she informed us she won't be returning."

"So you want me to take her place?"

"No. I mean, not exactly. Brenda was good, but needed a lot of input, especially for technical specs and even with guidance, we had to cover the same ground several times because she wasn't retaining it. Beckett wanted her to run the design department, but she never stepped up in a way that made us confident she could handle it."

As he's speaking, my mind is whirring, trying to put the puzzle together before I even have all the pieces.

"It's nothing against her," he says. "Some people simply aren't manager material. So, I was thinking that maybe we could buy your company and you could come work for Masters Construction and run the design department."

"What about my customers?"

"We could go ahead and bring you in and finish up your current projects, then you could focus on just design. If you want to go back to school, your hours could flex around your classes and you would have exposure to designs beyond just residential."

"People would think I just got the job because I'm your girlfriend."

"Even if you weren't my girlfriend, if it was just you applying for a job, you'd get it. People can think whatever they want, but your talent would become clear quickly and they wouldn't say that anymore. However, like I said, it wouldn't be just a job. We'd be buying your company to shore up an area where our company is lacking. We've been good at design, but you could make us great."

Wow. I did not expect that at all. I think through the ramifications of his offer.

"What about Hailey and my crew?"

"We could offer them positions with Masters Construction and it would be up to them whether they wanted to take them or move on somewhere else."

We drive in silence for several miles. My mind is spinning with thoughts, and I need to get them into some sort of order before I can give an answer.

"You don't have to decide right now," he says, as if he's reading my mind. "It's just an idea I've been toying with, and since you brought up wanting to make changes, I wanted to throw it out to you. It's something to think about."

"Okay, I'll think about it."

Chapter 38

Mr. Smith

As soon as I walk out of the courthouse, I pause to take a deep breath of fresh air. Maybe I should say free air because there's nothing fresh about it with all the smokers sitting on benches just outside the door.

I'm surprised there are no reporters, but they're probably out front. Thankfully, my attorney knows about this side exit that empties onto an alley that is used by employees for their breaks.

The employees have plastic badges that allow them to re-enter when their break is over, but for me, it's an exit only. Fine by me. I have no intention of going back in there. Ever.

Moving down the block to a less populated area away from the stink, I take out my phone and call home. The missus will need to come retrieve me and she'll need to do it quickly. I have things to take care of. There's no answer.

Hmmm...that's interesting. I wonder where she could be because I made sure she wasn't locked in her box since there was no telling whether the police would search the house.

Perhaps she, like the police, thought I would be remanded to the tender loving care of the county jail for the duration until I had my day in court. They were so smug when the judge handed down the astronomical amount required for me to be released. I could almost hear the bail bondsmen coming in their pants when they heard it.

I could have written them a check for it, but my check was no good. Oh, I have plenty of money, but the archaic court system requires cash or a cashier's check. They really need to get with the times and accept transfers of funds.

After a random choice of a service provider to post the funds, my belongings are returned to me and I am released. I don't even get slapped with one of those ankle monitors. Halle-fucking-lu-jah. Having my movements tracked would put a real kink in my plans.

There's unfinished business to finish, and then I'll carry out my exit plan. I knew I wouldn't be able to carry on forever, so of course, I have a plan to disappear. These past few years of being invisible have been excellent practice for the day when I will cease to exist and a new version of myself will come to life with a new name in a new place.

It's all set and the documents which will allow my transformation are located somewhere those bumbling cops would never have found them. I'm not stupid enough to store them at my house or my office.

The task at hand is to go home and wash off the vile atmosphere of the disgusting, over-crowded jail, but first, I need to get there and with the missus not responding, that means I'll need to acquire transport.

That's easy enough. There's a hotel around the corner where cabs are continually lined up awaiting visitors to our fair city who may need to go somewhere. In a few brief moments, I'm on my way.

The house looks like a tornado has been turned loose inside. Those fucking cops. For a moment, anger surges up, but I remind myself that once I shower and change, I'll be on my way to finish what has been left incomplete.

That's what I need to focus on. I need to add that cunt Gabriella to my collection and then I'll fade into the woodwork. With that cheerful thought in mind, I make my way through the house to the master bedroom.

The missus is nowhere to be found. When I discover many of her things are missing, I surmise she has left. Seeing her wedding rings placed conspicuously on top of the dresser, where they were impossible to miss, my suspicions are confirmed.

Oh well. I was tired of her, anyway. For a moment, the thought of going after her once I'm finished with Gabriella flits through my mind. But no. Instead, I'll leave her be. She'll know I'm out there, somewhere, and will live the rest of her life in fear, looking over her shoulder, and wondering when I'll show up.

After a few years with me, she'd become a broken doll, not even worthy of adding to my collection. Most likely, she's turned traitor and hopes to parade her nasty ass into the courtroom to spill the details of all the delicious punishments I meted out to her.

It makes me smile that she'll never get the chance. By the time anyone realizes I'm gone, I'll be two states away at the house I paid cash for over a year ago, where my new identity awaits.

For now, I need to get clean and dressed and get ready to go hunting. A thrill runs through me with the thought. First things first, though.

I take my time in the shower, enjoying the high-end multiple head experience. My new house doesn't have one of these, but it's definitely something I need to remedy once I'm settled in. Once I'm clean, steamed, and massaged within an inch of my life, I step out and put on a robe.

All I could think about in the shower was the hunt. To see where my target has gone to ground, I open the app on my phone. Surprisingly, she's not in the metro. It looks like her and that neanderthal of a boyfriend have decided to do a little vacation in the woods.

At least it looks like woods on the satellite maps. It looks like a cabin on a dead end road not far from Lake Eufaula. They've done me a favor by going there because witnesses will be few and far between. How sweet of them!

While considering which mask I want to wear for this next part of my journey, I go to my home office. It's been ransacked like the rest of the house, but my secret storage place is untouched. Not even the missus knew about this location and, based on her exodus from our home, I'm glad I never showed it to her.

Inside is an unregistered gun, some money, and the trappings of the absent-minded professor I had on when I visited Gabriella's office. That was a great day.

My cock gets hard at the recollection of the look of confusion on her face that soon morphed to fear and had her locking the door. I turn to go back to the bathroom, but considering the state of the house and the fact that the police already have my DNA, there's no need to bother.

Opening my robe, I stroke my cock, imagining how it will be with Gabriella tonight. There will be no dressing her up. No posing her. Tonight will be about completion and closing this chapter of my life.

I will put my hands around her neck until the life seeps from her eyes. Then I will strip her naked and fuck her like the whore she is. But first, I will let her see the bullet hole I put between her rescuer's eyes.

She'll know there's no Knight in Shining Armor coming for her this time. This time will be her last time and she'll be mine.

My cock explodes, spewing all over the carpet and wall. Once I've emptied myself and wiped the head of my cock on a pillow that used to be on the sofa, I begin to pull my things from the cache.

I need to get going before the reporters come looking for me, which they surely will once news of my release spreads.

Chapter 39

Gabriella

"**D**o I need to put you in bed?" Morgan asks.

We're curled up on the sofa watching a movie on DVD and I keep dozing off.

"No," I tell him. I try to focus on the screen, but my eyes are going a little fuzzy. "Maybe."

Headlights arc across the front windows, causing me to tense.

Morgan squeezes me in reassurance. "It's probably just Beckett. It's about the right time for him to be arriving."

He gets up and goes to the front door. "Yeah, it's just Beckett."

"Just Beckett? Since when am I ever just anything?" His steps sound on the deck. He comes inside carrying a small bag.

"Hi Beck," I call from the couch.

"Hey gorgeous, how are you enjoying playing hooky?"

"I think I overdid it today; I'm having trouble staying awake," I reply.

"She decided she was up for a five-mile hike after we got here and unloaded everything," Morgan chimes in.

"Gawd," Beckett says. I can hear the grimace on his face, and it makes me smile. "You and I have very different ideas of what vacation means. If I'm going to get all hot and sweaty, it's not going to be from marching around in the woods."

"Um, TMI, thank you," I tell him. "Plus, wandering around in the woods is good for the soul."

"Until you get eaten by a bear, or a mountain lion, or something. There's only one way I want to be swallowed down."

"Eww! TMI Beckett!" I throw a pillow at him, aiming for the shit-eating grin on his face. It lands short and hits the floor. He looks down at it and up at me and raises an eyebrow.

Morgan just shakes his head.

"Where am I staying?" Beckett asks. "I'm ready to get comfortable. I'm glad I went and got one of the company trucks. Felicity would not have liked these gravel roads."

"Felicity?" I ask, confused.

"That's his name for his car," Morgan tells me. "We're in the master. You can have your pick of the other bedrooms. David's wife gave the rooms a once over and aired everything out yesterday."

"Well, I'm headed to the opposite side of the house then, in case she gets a second wind and decides to jump your bones. I do not need to hear that."

Morgan follows Beckett to his bedroom. Their voices are low as they talk in the other room, so I can't make out what they're saying. I hope he's not discouraging Beckett from being playful with me. His wicked sense of humor tickles me.

Morgan returns and settles next to me again, pulling me close under his arm. "What did I miss?"

"Nothing," I tell him. "I paused it." I unpause the film. The movie stars one of the female MMA fighters I'm familiar with. She's kicking ass and taking names as she tries to find her husband who has been kidnapped. "If I can fit it in around classes and work, I'd like to take Krav Maga."

"Krav Maga?" Beckett asks, reentering the room.

"Yeah, Demi recommends it," I say.

"Who is Demi and is she cute?" he asks.

"She's a friend. Cait and I know her through the Society. I had lunch with her and Cait on Wednesday, where Demi told me she was attacked several years ago. She says that learning Krav Maga and how to handle herself is one of the things that helped her overcome the aftermath of the attack."

Beckett sits on the other side of me and squeezes my ankle when I burrow my cold toes under his thigh.

"I see," he says. "Maybe I don't care if she's cute. It sounds like she could kick my ass if I got out of line, and I always get out of line."

I laugh. "She's cute. She's very nice too, and she's a sex therapist."

"Hmmm...Maybe she could teach me a trick or two."

"That's a possibility," I agree.

"Will y'all shut up? I'm trying to watch the movie to get an idea of what my future might look like with a woman who can beat me up," Morgan says.

Beckett and I look at each other and grin, and then we shut up.

I wake up the next morning with no memory of going to bed. It's still dark outside and I can hear the men talking in the kitchen. Morgan sticks his head through the door. "Good, you're awake. Get a wiggle on because daylight's burning."

"It's dark outside."

"Exactly, the fish are just about to start biting."

I roll out of bed and head to the bathroom and make it to the kitchen in record time.

"Did you put your suit on? It will be warm enough to swim after the sun's up," Morgan asks.

I raise my shirt and flash him my red bikini top. Beckett gives me a wolf whistle.

"Woman, I'm the only one who's supposed to see that," Morgan grouses.

"He's going to see that and more if we go swimming," I retort.

"Ooh la la," says Beckett, "I can't wait."

Morgan kisses my temple. "You have everything you need?"

I hold up a small drawstring bag. "Book, sunscreen, bug spray, and sunglasses."

"Let's hit the road, then," Morgan says, handing me some food wrapped in a paper towel. "Beckett and I have already loaded the truck."

We file outside and Morgan locks the cabin up. I let Beckett sit in the shotgun seat and I sit in the back. I'm sure they'll want to talk, and I like to be quiet in the mornings for a while. We pull onto the road and Morgan closes a gate behind us.

Sure enough, they start talking so I tune them out and watch the dark forest going by. The road is winding with trees on both sides most of the time, but as we traverse hills, there are times when there is a steep incline up or down on one side or both. Morgan slows the truck and stops.

I'm about to ask why we're stopping when Morgan looks at me in the rearview mirror and says, "There's a deer in the road. It looks like someone hit it, so I'm going to go see if I can move it. Stay put."

He and Beckett share a look, and Beckett nods.

I go back to inspecting the trees. On the passenger side is thick forest and on the driver's side, there is no shoulder. It goes down in a steep rocky decline. Although it's dark, I can make out that the road looks messed up and there's a faint glow over the edge. I sit up in the seat trying to see down the hill. When I can't, I get out of the truck.

"What are you doing?" Beckett asks.

"I think there's..." I step closer to the edge and gasp. "Morgan, there's a car down there."

"Baby, stay away from the edge."

Beckett is suddenly next to me with a flashlight that he shines down the hill. He looks over the edge, then looks at Morgan.

"See if your phone has service. If it does, call nine-one-one," Morgan says to his brother. "It looks like they lost control when they hit the deer."

He surveys the side of the hill and starts down. The car smashed into the trunk of a large tree after mowing down saplings and bouncing over rocks. Beckett hands me the flashlight before going to get his phone.

"Morgan..." I say, concern lacing my voice.

"It's okay. I'll be careful, but I need to check on the car to see if there's anyone still in there and if they need help. Stay there."

I watch as he slips and slides down the hill, grasping saplings and trees to keep his balance. He reaches the car and has to pull hard on the door to open it. Beckett comes to the edge to watch next to me as he talks on his phone to the emergency operator.

Morgan holds up a finger. "There's one person in the car," Beckett relays.

Morgan reaches inside the car with one hand, then looks up at Beckett and shakes his head. "And they're deceased," Beckett relays again. "Yes, we can stay until someone gets here."

He repeats our location and disconnects the phone. "They're on their way," he tells Morgan.

"Good," Morgan replies. I hold the flashlight and watch as Morgan makes his way back up the steep incline. "Baby, will you do me a favor and look in the blue tub and get me one of those wet wipe things? I'd like to wipe my hands off."

I look down the hill, frowning. "That poor person." I shiver, then turn to go to the truck.

"Why don't we go wait in the truck, baby? It's going to be awhile before the police get here."

He gets in the back seat with me, putting me on the side away from the wreck.

"Damn it!" Beckett exclaims.

"What happened?" I ask.

"Nothing, I ran out of birds."

"What?"

"Angry Birds," Morgan tells me. "He's addicted."

"Seriously?" I laugh. I quickly stop myself. It seems wrong to be laughing when someone is dead just a few feet away.

"So, enough about me," Beckett says. "Morgan, when are you going to pop the question and lock this lady down?"

"If the police weren't on the way, I'd give you a beat down you tactless ass," Morgan replies.

"I'm too pretty to hit," Beckett assures him. "I mean, you're both crazy about each other. I've heard the L word from both of you, and you've been practically living together for weeks, so what's the holdup?"

"When are you going to quit playing around and get serious?" I ask him.

"Never! Here comes the po-po."

I look out the front window and see red and blue lights reflected in the brightening sky. Morgan gets out of the truck to meet the arriving officers. I start to follow him, but Beckett puts a hand on my leg.

"Let him go. He'll feel better if you wait here."

I frown.

"He's in protective mode right now."

"What?"

"Listen, Morgan is the oldest child, so he has the typical leader traits that come with that. He will never, ever clip your wings to keep you from flying or being who you want to be, but he will do whatever it takes to keep you safe from the horrors of the world. If you go out there, he's going to be worried about you getting too close to the edge or heaven forbid, getting a glimpse of the dead body they're going to haul out of there. He's extra sensitive where you are concerned right now because he feels guilty that you were hurt."

"Yeah, I might have gotten hurt, but you two kept me from being dead. Being hurt is nothing compared to that."

"I know, but while he knows he can't save the entire world, you and the rest of us he loves are his world to protect and keep safe."

I look over at Morgan talking to the officers that remain on the road. A couple of them went down the embankment to the car. Every once in a while, Morgan will glance over his shoulder at me, and I can see in his eyes what Beckett is talking about.

"I'm sorry you won't get to go fishing," I tell him.

"It's okay," he shrugs. "We can still go out on the lake and hang out. Blow off some steam. Soak up some sun. Have a few laughs."

I watch Morgan through the window. "I do love him, you know. He has saved my life in more ways than just what happened last week."

"You saved him, too. It's been a while since he's been with anyone, and he was starting to get a little bleak and a lot stale. He has smiled more in the last month than has in the last year."

"Morgan offered me a job. Sort of."

"Did he, now?"

"Yeah, Brenda's position."

"Are you sure? Seems to me like he intended to buy your company and have you run the department, which is a lot more than what Brenda did."

"You knew?" I swat his arm.

"Of course I knew," he shrugs. "You'd be working in my area, so he ran the idea by me a couple of weeks ago. He says you are one of the best designers he's ever seen and that's saying something because he's worked with a lot of them over the years. Do you think you'll take it?"

"Probably. It really would be an ideal situation for me."

"I know, because you'd get to see me every day!"

I laugh. "Yeah, that's the most important thing."

I settle back in the seat, unable to stifle a yawn. Beckett pulls out his phone and starts playing his game again. I watch the scene play out on the road and wonder what they're saying.

Chapter 40

Morgan

The Night Before

"Where am I staying?" Beckett asks. "I'm ready to get comfortable. I'm glad I went and got one of the company trucks. Felicity would not have liked these gravel roads."

"Felicity?" Gabriella asks, confused.

"That's his name for his car," I tell her. "We're in the master. You can have your pick of the other bedrooms. David's wife gave the rooms a once over and aired everything out yesterday."

"Well, I'm headed to the opposite side of the house then, in case she gets a second wind and decides to jump your bones. I do not need to hear that."

I follow Beckett to his bedroom. Once we're out of earshot, he asks me, "Does she know?"

"No. I don't think it has hit the news yet. The only reason I know the bastard made bail is because of Ford. He texted me when Felton was leaving the jail with his attorney."

"That's the guy's name?"

"Yeah, Andrew Felton," I tell him. "He runs a retirement and financial planning group in Edmond."

"Do you think he'll come here?"

"I don't know," I say honestly. "I can't think of any way he would know where we are, but I would rather be safe than sorry."

"What are you going to do?"

"I have the cameras that I used at Gabriella's house and extra sim cards in the truck to replace the ones the police took. The last turn off on the road leading to the cabin is three miles back. Once someone passes that point, they're either lost or coming here. I'm thinking about posting the cameras on the road so that if anyone is coming, I'll get an alert."

"What are you going to tell her?"

"Nothing if I don't have to. She's wiped and already having trouble staying awake, so she'll be out soon. Once she's asleep, I'll hoof it down the road, so she doesn't hear the truck starting and set the cameras. If she wakes up, I can tell her I went for a run. Plus, you're here tonight to keep an eye on her while I'm gone."

"Sure, sure, that sounds like a good plan."

"Thanks, Beckett."

"Anything for family. You know that, and as far as I'm concerned, Ella's family."

I return to the sofa in the living room, pulling Gabriella next to me, tucking her under my arm. "What did I miss?"

"Nothing, I paused it," she says as she holds up the remote and hits play. I'm only halfway paying attention to the film because I'm thinking about setting the cameras and how far out I should put them.

"If I can fit it in around classes and work, I'd like to take Krav Maga," Gabriella says. I guess she's inspired by the woman on the screen who seems to have no problem beating up anyone that gets in her way.

"Krav Maga?" Beckett asks, reentering the room.

"Yeah, Demi recommends it," she says.

"Who is Demi and is she cute?" he asks.

"She's a friend. Cait and I know her through the Society. I had lunch with her and Cait on Wednesday, where Demi told me she was attacked several years ago. She says that learning Krav Maga and how to handle herself is one of the things that helped her overcome the aftermath of the attack."

Beckett sits on the other side of her, right up next to her. He has no designs on Gabriella, he just enjoys yanking my chain. "I see," he says. "Maybe I don't care if she's cute. It sounds like she could kick my ass if I got out of line, and I always get out of line."

Gabriella laughs. It's a beautiful sound. "She's cute. She's very nice too, and she's a sex therapist."

"Hmmm...Maybe she could teach me a trick or two."

"That's a possibility," she agrees.

"Will y'all shut up? I'm trying to watch the movie to get an idea of what my future might look like with a woman who can beat me up," I joke.

Just as I expected, Gabriella falls asleep soon after restarting the movie. I carry her to the bedroom and tuck her in with a kiss to her forehead then put on my boots. With a flashlight and keys in hand, I stop by the truck to prep and grab the cameras.

I tuck a pair of gloves in my back pocket out of habit and take a pry bar from my toolbox just in case. You never know what you might run into in the woods in the middle of the night.

The moon is full, so I don't really need the flashlight as I jog down the gravel road. The road snakes back and forth on its way up a hill. I'll put the first camera at the top. It's a couple of miles from the cabin, so it will be an excellent location that will give a few minute's notice of someone approaching.

I reach the apex and am choosing a tree with the right size trunk when I see lights across the small valley as a car tops the hill on the other side. I watch to see if it takes the last turnoff before the road sign shows that it turns into a dead end. The car keeps coming.

It could be coincidence, but my instincts tell me it's not. I start running back to the cabin. Quickly, I get to the curvy portion of the road and decide to cut across where I can.

In one area, it's fairly flat on one side, but with a steep decline on the other. I pull out my flashlight and step into the woods. It's slower going because I have to watch my footing, but I'm still making better time than I would on the road.

I'm just about to connect back to the road when I come upon a herd of deer grazing. They either hear me or the car coming, because their heads pop up to assess the threat. The car is close. I can hear the crunch of the tires on the gravel road.

I need to move. There's no way I can beat the car to the cabin, but if it's Felton, I doubt he pulls right up in the driveway. Cautiously, I start to work my way toward the road. The deer spook and go racing off in all directions. I see the car just as its lights illuminate a large doe racing into its path.

Gravel goes flying as the car brakes and tries to avoid the creature. The headlights disappear and I hear it crashing through the trees before it comes to an abrupt stop with the screech of twisting metal.

I race to the road and across to the other side. The car has hit a large tree, and the front is crumpled and twisted. It's a black sedan, just like Felton supposedly drove.

I set the cameras and pry bar down on the edge of the road, then flip on the flashlight to see if there's a way for me to get down the hill. Using trees to keep from sliding, I make my way over the terrain, a mixture of dirt and boulders. One misstep and I'll end up at the bottom of this hill with a host of broken bones, or worse.

With a hard pull, I get the door open and see the car has one occupant. The man is slumped over the steering wheel and passed out. I put a finger to his neck to check for a pulse. He's alive and when I touch him, he rouses.

"Hey man, you've had a wreck. What's your name?"

"Wh...what?"

"What's your name?" I ask again. I'm looking him over. He's banged up, with a gash on his forehead oozing blood.

I'm not sure if the car doesn't have airbags or if they mal-functioned. A large sliver of wood from one of the trees he hit is sticking through the windshield and has impaled his shoulder. He's bleeding a lot from that wound.

"A...A...Andrew. Andrew Felton. Can you help me get out of here?"

I pause for a breath. The name matches the man who Ford believes has killed seven women and tried to kill Gabriella. If someone doesn't stop him, he will keep killing and Gabriella is number one on his twisted list.

"Sorry, you didn't make it," I say, pulling the gloves out of my back pocket. I could leave him here and hope he bleeds out, but with a little effort, he could make it out of the car and to the farm in the valley for help.

"Huh?" He looks up at me, confused. When I see his face clearly, it matches the one in the photo that Ford had sent me. That further seals his fate.

I put the gloves on and reach into the car, putting one hand on the back of his head and one on his chin. With a hard jerk, a sickening crack sounds as I break his neck.

I will do anything to keep those I love safe.

I close the car back up, trying to make sure I've left everything as close to how I found it as possible, then make my way up the hill trying to keep to my same footsteps. I gather everything up and jog back to the cabin. Beckett is sitting in the living room with all the lights off when I return.

"Did you get them set?" he asks when I come into the house after putting everything back in the truck except the gloves.

"No. Come with me," I tell him quietly as I walk through the cabin and out the back door.

As I'm gathering everything I need, I tell him what happened. Once a small fire is going in the firepit, I throw the gloves in, squirt them with lighter fluid, and keep the fire going until the gloves are completely consumed.

"It would have been better if the wreck had killed him. I'm sorry you had to do that, but I would have done the same thing. I hope the bastard is rotting in hell," Beckett says.

We go back in the house, and I pour us both a double shot of whiskey. I throw mine back. "We'd better get some sleep. We'll need to be up in a few hours to go fishing."

"Yeah," Beckett says, after swallowing his.

I take a shower before sliding into bed with Gabriella. When I move behind her, she turns and snuggles against me. She feels cold, so I wrap her in my arms to warm her. She melts against me, and I thank God, the Universe, or whatever is out there that she's mine.

I stick my head into the bedroom and see Gabriella is awake. "Good, you're awake. Get a wiggle on, daylight's burning."

"It's dark outside," she says in that sexy sleepy voice I adore.

I'm tempted to go climb back into bed with her, but think better of it. We've got to find the car and put our footprints all over that road to cover up my footprints from last night.

"Exactly, the fish are just about to start biting."

I head back to the kitchen and fix her some breakfast to go while Beckett pours coffee into a thermos. Much more quickly than I thought possible, Gabriella appears, ready to go.

"Did you put your suit on? It will be warm enough to swim after the sun's up," I ask her.

She raises her shirt and flashes me her red bikini top. Beckett gives a wolf whistle.

"Woman, I'm the only one who's supposed to see that," I grouse, but she knows I'm teasing.

"He's going to see that and more if we go swimming," she retorts.

"Ooh la la," says Beckett, "I can't wait."

I kiss her temple. "You have everything you need?"

She holds up a small drawstring bag. "Book, sunscreen, bug spray, and sunglasses."

"Let's hit the road, then," I say, and hand over her breakfast. "Beckett and I have already loaded the truck."

I lock the cabin up as they get into the truck. She lets Beckett sit in the shotgun seat and takes the back. That's probably for the best, because she'll likely fall back to sleep once we're on the road.

We reach the site of the accident where the deer is still on the road. I hadn't paid much attention to it last night, but it's in the middle of the road. I look at Gabriella in the mirror.

"There's a deer in the road. It looks like someone hit it, so I'm going to go see if I can move it. Stay put."

I look at Beckett, and he nods. He knows I won't want her seeing what has happened to the deer. She has a soft spot for animals. I doubt she will be able to see the car from where we stopped.

She chooses that moment to show me I don't know everything and gets out of the truck. I hear Beckett say something to her and she replies, then calls out to me, "Morgan, there's a car down there."

I look over to see her peering down the hill as she stands on the side of the road. "Baby, stay away from the edge."

Beckett moves up next to her with a flashlight that he shines down the hill. He looks over the edge, then looks at me. I nod in affirmation that this is the same wreck I told him about last night.

"See if your phone has service. If it does, call nine-one-one," I tell him. "It looks like they lost control when they hit the deer."

I come to the side of the road and look down at the same scene from last night. I start down the hill trying to step into the same footprints I left last night and use the same trees as handholds.

"Morgan..." Gabriella says. I hear her worry.

"It's okay. I'll be careful, but I need to check on the car to see if there's anyone still in there and if they need help. Stay there."

I reach the car and pull hard on the door to open it again. I can hear Beckett's voice as he talks to the operator. I hold up one finger to tell him there's one person in the car, although he already knows that.

"There's one person in the car," Beckett relays.

I reach inside the car and check for a pulse, relieved there's not one. A broken neck doesn't kill every time, and I couldn't have been positive that he would bleed out. Most of all, I touched the body last night, so I needed to touch it again in case my fingerprints are discovered. I look up at Beckett and shake my head.

"And they're deceased," Beckett relays again. "Yes, we can stay until someone gets here."

He repeats our location and disconnects the phone. "They're on their way," he tells me.

"Good," I reply. I make my way back up the steep incline. "Baby, will you do me a favor and look in the blue tub and get me one of those wet wipe things? I'd like to wipe my hands off."

I have blood on my fingers from checking his pulse. The blood from his scalp wound had run down and covered most of his face and neck.

"That poor person," Gabriella says.

"Why don't we go wait in the truck, baby? It's going to be awhile before the police get here." I want to get her away from this scene. If she sees too much, the police will want to question her and I want to keep her insulated from that.

I get into the back seat with her, putting her on the side away from the wreck.

A few minutes later, Beckett exclaims, "Damn it!"

"What happened?" she asks, startled out of a doze.

"Nothing, I ran out of birds."

"What?"

"Angry Birds," I tell her. "He's addicted."

"Seriously?" she laughs.

"So, enough about me," Beckett says. "Morgan, when are you going to pop the question and lock this lady down?"

"If the police weren't on the way, I'd give you a beat down you tactless ass," I tell him.

"I'm too pretty to hit," Beckett assures me. "I mean, you're both crazy about each other. I've heard the L word from both of you, and you've been practically living together for weeks, so what's the holdup?"

"When are you going to quit playing around and get serious?" Gabriella asks him.

That's my girl.

"Never! Here comes the po-po."

I get out of the truck to meet the arriving officers. Gabriella starts to follow me, but Beckett puts a hand on her leg.

"Let him go. He'll feel better if you wait here."

I go from wanting to hit him to wanting to hug him. He's not obliviously tactless. I honestly think he enjoys shocking people and seeing their reaction.

Two cars pull up. I stand in front of the truck and wait for them, keeping my hands in plain sight. The first guy that gets out is older, probably mid-fifties. His partner looks to be about twelve.

I have learned not to guess ages anymore. Most of the guys working on the job site look like they're twelve, too, so I just make sure their IDs are checked before turning them loose with power tools. I chalk it up to getting older.

"Mister Masters?" the older cop says.

"One of them," I answer. "My brother is the one who called you."

The younger cop goes and peers down at the car.

"I'm Officer Nichols. Can you tell me what happened?"

"We're staying in my buddy's cabin at the end of the road and were headed over to Eufaula early this morning to do some fishing when we came upon the deer in the road. I got out to see about moving the deer and my girlfriend got out because she noticed how the road was messed up."

I point to the skid marks in the road and going over the edge.

"She came to the edge of the road and spotted the car. My brother called y'all while I went down to see if someone was in the car that might need help. There's one man in the car. I touched his neck for a pulse and didn't find one, so I closed the car and came back up to wait."

"Whose cabin are you staying in?"

"My friend's name is David Whitaker. He lives over in McAlester and works at the armory," I answer.

"How do you know Mr. Whitaker?"

"We served in the Marines together about twenty years ago."

He nods. "I know David."

The officers from the second car have joined the kid at the edge of the road. Nichols says, "Bobby, stay put. You'll break your neck if you try to go down there. Mitch, you and Chris go down and see if you can find some ID. Bobby, call a wrecker and the coroner."

"Got it" and "Copy" come from the men while the kid says, "Awww, man!"

Mitch wrenches the car door open and his lip curls at the sight of the dead man. He leans in and several minutes later, pops back out.

"I've got a wallet." He opens the wallet and looks inside. "The guy's name is Andrew Felton," he calls up.

I stiffen and Nichols notices. "Do you know him?"

"Only the name. A man named Andrew Felton has been stalking my girlfriend for weeks. He attacked her a week ago and if it hadn't been for my brother and me interrupting him, he would have killed her. They think he might be the serial killer that's been killing women in the City. A detective on the case is a friend of a friend; he texted me yesterday morning and let me know Felton had made bail. I have no idea how he would have known where we are. I thought maybe he had been tracking her car, but it's sitting in a parking garage in Oklahoma City."

"What is the name of the Detective?" Nichols asks.

"Ford Pickering," I answer. "I may have one of his cards." I pull out my wallet and a small stack of business cards. I flip through them, finding Ford's about halfway down and give it to Nichols.

"I'd like to cover all my bases and speak to your brother and girlfriend and get the story from them."

I nod. "I understand. Gabriella doesn't know the name of the man who attacked her, and she didn't see his face. When he was arrested, it was only for her attack. They believe it's the killer based on the things he had with him during the attack, but they're still building a case. I'd rather be the one who breaks it to her that he was coming after her. At least, that's the only reason I can think of for him being out here."

"That won't be a problem. I'll just talk to them separately and get the details of what happened this morning."

"Thanks." I wave to the truck and Beckett gets out.

"Uh, Mr. Masters, how long will you be staying at the cabin?"

"Gabriella and I will be staying until tomorrow afternoon. My brother will be going back to the City later today."

Beckett comes over to where I'm talking to Nichols. "Gabriella went back to sleep," he informs me.

That makes me smile. Her body is still adjusting after the drugs he gave her. "I'll go wake her up while you talk to Officer Nichols."

I open the back door to the truck and shake Gabriella awake. "Hey, baby, the cops want to talk to you, too. They just want to get everyone's viewpoint of what happened this morning."

"Okay," she says as she yawns and stretches.

She gets out of the truck but before she can go over to Nichols, I lean against the truck and pull her back against me. "He wants to talk to you separately, so hold up here for a minute."

I put my arms around her shoulders, and she leans her head back against my shoulder. I kiss the top of her head. She hooks her hands on my forearms.

"I sure do love you," she says.

"I love you, too, baby."

Chapter 41

Gabriella

We're on the boat and headed out on the water a couple of hours after finishing with the police. Something about that car wreck is bothering me, but I can't put my finger on what.

As we stood there talking with the police and watching a glorious sunrise, something was niggling at the back of my brain. I finally realize what it's been trying to tell me.

"Where do you think he was going?"

"Who?" Beckett asks.

"The guy in the car wreck. He was past the last turn off, so he was either lost or he was coming to where we're staying."

I've been gazing out over the water, but when neither of them answers me, I turn to see Morgan and Beckett sharing a look.

"What?" I ask.

Morgan steps away from the wheel and lets Beckett take over. He comes and squats in front of me where I'm sitting and takes my hands in his. "The man in the car was named Andrew Felton, and he's the one who attacked you last week. I think he was coming to find you."

I blink at him, trying to process what he's told me.

I frown. "I thought he was in jail."

"He made bail yesterday morning. Ford texted and let me know. I got the notice when we were buying groceries."

"And you didn't tell me?" Anger starts to percolate. How dare he keep something like that from me!

"I wanted you to have a relaxing weekend away from all that, and I knew that if I told you, it would just frighten you. Plus, I had no idea he'd be able to find us. I thought that before, he had some way to track your car, but I don't know how he found us this time."

Okay, how can I be mad at that? He was trying to protect me and he's right. If he had told me I probably would have freaked out and we would have had to leave. I wouldn't have thought he'd be able to find us either, but I still would have been watching over my shoulder the whole time.

I sigh.

"So, he's dead?" I ask.

"Yes. He had a couple of wounds that bled a lot, so he must have lost too much blood before we found him, but they'll do an autopsy to find out for sure."

"At least he won't be able to hurt anyone else."

"That's right. He won't be able to hurt you or anyone else ever again."

I nod. "Good."

Call me cold-blooded, but I am glad that he is dead. If he is who they think he is, he killed seven women and intended to make me number eight.

If he hadn't died in that wreck, it would have taken a long time for him to go on trial. He would have kept coming after me and if he got me, I'd be dead, and he would start looking for number nine.

Morgan holds my eyes, and I hold his right back so he will know I mean it. Then I lean forward and peck him on the mouth before I settle back on the bench.

I pull one of my hands out of his and pull the breakfast he made me out of my bag. He snorts as his mouth tips up on one side, then rises and goes back to the wheel of the boat.

"It's a good thing we bought groceries," I tease when we return to the cabin.

"Woman, don't make me turn you over my knee," Morgan threatens.

"Promises, promises," I retort. I walk behind him to put the remaining beer in the fridge and run my hand across his butt.

"If we had been there on time this morning, we'd be eating fish for days," Beckett says as he comes in with the other ice chest.

"Will you be staying for supper, Beckett?" I ask.

"It depends. What are we having?"

"I was going to grill some steaks," Morgan says.

"Steak, grilled potatoes, and a salad," I add.

"Oh, you do know how to make a man's heart go pitty pat," Beckett says. "Yes, I'll stay to eat, but I've got to get back to the City tonight so I won't stay late. Therefore, if y'all want to have wild monkey sex all over the house, there won't be anyone here to cramp your style tonight."

I bark out a laugh. "Beckett!"

Unfazed, Morgan says, "That's good. Go start the charcoal so I can get you fed and out of here."

"I'm going to go shower right quick to wash the lake off and I'll be back to fix the potatoes," I say. "Want to join me?"

"Yep," Morgan says as he grabs my hand and pulls me toward the bedroom.

Both of us strip quickly and get into the shower. He pushes me against the wall and presses his body to mine, his knees wedging in to spread my thighs. His cock begins to harden against my stomach.

He takes my wrists in one of his big hands and holds them above my head. With his other hand, he brushes the hair from my face, then lifts my chin. My eyes meet his intense blue gaze as he studies me. He looks as if he wants to eat me whole.

He leans in and my eyes flutter closed in anticipation. His lips brush mine, making me whimper against his mouth, wanting more. He gives it to me. His tongue slips into my mouth, finding mine, and he deepens the kiss and doesn't stop until I'm panting with need.

"You've been teasing me all day in that bathing suit. I had to fight the urge to take it off you and have my way with you."

Before I can answer, his mouth is on mine again. He leans down and lifts me. I wrap my legs around him as he lowers me onto his shaft. "What about Beckett?"

"I don't give a fuck about Beckett right now. I couldn't go another minute without having my hands on you. This is probably going to be quick because I've been hard for you all day, but consider it the appetizer baby and you'll get a proper fucking once my knucklehead brother is gone."

He starts to move, impaling me over and over on his length. I try to be quiet, I really do, but it feels so good.

I move in time with him, undulating against him which makes his body rub my clit in all the right ways sending me racing toward the edge. When the orgasm rips through me, I sink my teeth into Morgan's shoulder to keep from crying out.

"Christ, Gabriella," he grits out and with a few more powerful thrusts, he empties himself into me with his own orgasm.

Morgan takes more care of me by washing and conditioning my hair, then lathering up my body. I love the feel of his rough hands on my skin.

He's just starting to stoke the fire in my body back to life when he rinses me off and kicks me out of the shower. "Out woman. I can't spend all night servicing you. We'll run out of hot water."

"Tease."

"You heard me. Proper fucking later."

I laugh as I go into the bedroom to dress.

Chapter 42

Gabriella

"Sounds like someone got a tune up," Beckett says when I enter the kitchen. "Needed a little something to tide you over until I leave, huh?"

"You are so bad!"

"You know it!"

I start prepping the potatoes while he monitors the charcoal. "Tell me about Kellen," I say.

"Thinking you've got the wrong brother?"

"No!" I swat at him with a dish towel. "He's just such a mystery. I feel like I'm getting to know everyone else in your family, but not him."

"No one really knows Kellen except Mom. He talks to me some, but it's not like it is between Morgan and me. He was a bit of an oops baby. There are seven years between us so by the time he came along, I was already firmly established as the fuck up youngest child, so he became like a second first born kid or really almost an only child. He has always been serious, but he doesn't have Morgan's drive or ambition to lead. He's good at what he does, but I honestly have no idea if he's happy doing it or what he likes to do for fun, if anything. He's very private."

"Hmmm."

"Scoping out the family to see if you want to spend the rest of your life tied to us?" he asks.

"Not really. I was just curious. I think your mom and dad are wonderful and Morgan is by far worth putting up with you as a brother-in-law."

"I am the best brother-in-law and future uncle to your children you could ever hope for."

I'm still laughing at him when Morgan comes in to prep the steaks. His hair is wet, and he's only wearing a loose pair of shorts. My pulse ratchets up seeing the well-defined muscles in his chest and arms earned through years of physical labor.

His tattooed arms are also on display. I remember our first meeting when his tattoos intrigued me by peeking out from under the cuffs of his sleeves. Now I know every line, every detail.

I wrap the potatoes in foil and wash my hands. Beckett takes them out to the grill.

I sidle up to Morgan and put my hand down the back of his shorts and cup his ass. "Now, who's being a tease?" I ask.

"I don't know what you mean," he says with mischief in his eyes.

"Mmm hmm," I reply, letting him know I don't buy his feigned innocence.

Beckett comes back in, so I give Morgan's butt one last squeeze before I pull my hand out.

"Do you want a beer, cariño?"

"Yes, please, one of the stouts," he answers with a wicked grin. He knows he's getting to me.

I pull one out and open it for him.

"Beckett, beer?"

"Nah, I'll take a pop, though. I'll have a beer with dinner, but I'd better lay off the booze since I'll be driving a couple of hours tonight. I would not look good in an orange jumpsuit."

A couple of hours later, we stand on the front porch, Morgan behind me with his arms around my waist, and watch Beckett get into the big construction truck. It doesn't suit him like his sports cars do.

I couldn't imagine him restoring one on his own until I saw a photo of him in Morgan's office with his head under the hood and grease up to his elbows. He was grinning from ear to ear, clearly doing something he loves.

I wave as he starts to turn around, and he beeps the horn at me. I love that man. He is right, though. I can't imagine a better brother-in-law.

We watch until his taillights disappear down the road. Morgan nuzzles my neck, sending shivers down my spine. "Is it time for dessert?" I ask.

"Dessert?" He starts kissing his way up and down my neck.

"You said," I gasp when he hits the magic spot below my ear. "You said the shower was the appetizer. I would think the proper fucking would be the dessert." I wiggle my hips back against him.

He slides his hands underneath my t-shirt to cup my breasts. When he encounters my bra, he growls and pushes it up, freeing the flesh that he wants to touch.

"I love your hands on me," I tell him as I reach up to cradle his head and run my fingers through his hair, pushing my breasts deeper into his hands.

"Do you want your dessert here on the porch or inside?"

"As much as I would love an open-air encounter, I would prefer not to get a mosquito bite on my coño." He tweaks both nipples between his fingers as he shapes and molds my breasts. "Oh that feels good."

"Inside it is." He stoops and picks me up like I weigh nothing, but when he gets to the door, he stops. "Damn I'm getting old. Woman, get the door because if I try to, I'll probably drop you."

I laugh and reach out to turn the knob and push the door open. He kicks the door closed behind us once we're through and moves through the house to the bedroom. I lightly scratch my nails through his stubble. "I like this, too."

He drops me on the bed, making me laugh more. Quick as a flash, he strips off his shorts and is on me, pulling at my shirt. "Too many damn clothes, woman."

It comes off over my head. He tosses it aside and goes to work on unbuttoning my shorts. I help him by taking my bra the rest of the way off.

He grips the waist of my shorts and panties and pulls them down my hips and thighs, then sends them the way of my shirt. I'm lying there on my back completely naked with him kneeling between my legs as if I am his altar and he is a devotee ready to worship.

His blue flame gaze rakes over my body. "You are so beautiful."

I squirm under his spotlight.

"Gabriella, look at me," he commands.

I raise my eyes to his. "You are beautiful. In body, mind, and spirit, you are magnificent, and I am a lucky man."

I smile at him, but he is all seriousness. He pushes my knees apart, exposing my most sensitive parts to his scrutiny. His hands stroke my inner thighs, raising gooseflesh all over my body. I watch his sex as it stiffens.

I did that. Just the sight of me fills him with desire so great that his body can't help but respond. He leans over me; on all fours he hovers as he lowers his mouth to mine and his kiss sets my blood aboil.

I reach up to touch him. He snatches my hands and puts them above my head. "Grab that headboard and don't let go. Do you understand me?"

"Yes, cariño, I understand."

"Good girl."

He kisses my forehead. Then each eyelid. Each cheek. He lowers his mouth and stops so close that his lips brush mine when he says, "I am ravenous for you, and I intend to touch and taste every inch of you."

I bite my lip.

His mouth and hands move over me, stoking the heat higher with every stroke, every lick. His fervid exultations draw him lower and lower until he is bowing at the heart of his temple. He utters an oath then laves me with his tongue in a long, slow stroke, savoring the proof of the desire he has ignited in my body.

His ministrations draw gasps and moans from me as I roll my hips against his mouth. He is licking and sucking, teasing and nibbling. The divine and the carnal become one, pushing me to the realms of rapture, my body exploding with holy fire.

The feeling is so intense that I have to grit my teeth as every muscle contracts and ripples with profound pleasure. Morgan watches as I tremble with the effects of his stewardship. I am weak with the aftermath, but I am far from sated.

"I need you," I gasp.

He is already moving over me. I see the evidence of his ardor standing thick and weeping at the apex of his thighs. He lowers himself and enters me with one sharp, forceful thrust of his hips.

I cry out with comingled pleasure and pain, his possession stretching me so tight. I quiver from the impact, my body returning to a state of heightened sensitivity.

He slams into me again, harder, seeking to invade me to every extent of his ability. His mouth meets mine, stealing my breath away. My fingers keep a death grip on the headboard, trying to maintain leverage as I move against him in time with his punishing thrusts.

We are beyond coherence; the sounds accenting the noise of our bodies crashing together are guttural grunts, groans, and moans. It is so raw and animalistic and perfect.

I want to scratch my nails across his back, marking him as mine, but I don't dare loose my hold. Instead, I make do with leaning up and sinking my teeth into the pectoral muscle that has been hovering over my face tempting me.

He hisses in response. His penetrating assault increases in speed, becoming unrestrained. Wild. Primal.

I have no more control. A scream tears from my throat when the orgasm rips through me, tearing me asunder, leaving only bits of shrapnel where my body used to be. Morgan utters a hoarse grinding growl as he is overtaken with absolution.

I release the headboard as he rolls, putting me on top, our bodies still joined. His heavy breaths waft through my hair. I look up at him, taking in his beautiful visage draped in pleasure and love.

It's hard to believe this magnificent man is mine. Never have I felt so loved, so cared for, so cherished. It's so overwhelming that I feel tears well.

I turn my head and lay my ear against his chest before the moisture in my eyes finds purchase and starts to flow. His heartbeat's strong tattoo is comforting, grounding me.

Hours later, or maybe minutes, he takes a deep breath and kisses the top of my head. His fingertips begin to stroke and play along my spine.

"So, what do you think about what Beckett said?" his voice is a vibrating rumble against my cheek that makes me giggle.

"About which what that Beckett said? Beckett said a lot of things, as usual."

His chuckle bounces me which makes me giggle again. "That's true. What do you think about getting married?"

I turn my head and prop my chin on my hands to look up at him. "Morgan Masters, are you asking me to marry you?"

His whole disposition changes, becoming almost boyish as he shrugs and looks away. "Hell, if I'd had my way, I would have proposed weeks ago. From the moment we first met three years ago, I knew there was something between us, but the timing wasn't right yet. We were both involved with other people, no matter how casually."

He shifts and looks away from me, his voice barely a whisper.

"That day in Delores, when I pulled you back from the brink, I knew you were mine. Everything since has only deepened that knowing. I didn't want to move too quickly and spook you. If you're not ready, I understand, but I wanted to talk about where you're at in this whole thing to see if you're headed the same way."

I tuck my arms back around him and turn my cheek to his chest again, luxuriating in the feel of him. "Well, Mr. Masters, when you're ready to ask, I can tell you my answer will be yes."

The End

Get a **FREE** copy of a bonus scene where Morgan finally agrees to take Gabriella camping.

https://dl.bookfunnel.com/rpt77l7dhg

If you enjoyed A Murderous Intent, do me a solid and leave a review! It's not a book report; it's okay to keep it short. Have fun! Be honest!
https://mybook.to/MurderousKitMcKenna

Thank you loves!

XOXO

Kit

About the Author

Kit McKenna writes romance books that are dreamy, dirty, and sometimes have a splash of darkness and danger set against the backdrop of Oklahoma.

Kit is a born and raised Oklahoma gal who has lived here her whole life except for a brief detour to hang out in the mountains for four years. She is an artist and free spirit who loves roaming around in the woods and finds great joy in the unusually and sometimes darkly beautiful. Kit has worn a lot of hats in her life, a server, a factory worker, nightclub manager, office administrator, state drone, and business owner.

A bit of a dichotomy, she loves all things positivity and light, but still loves to play in the dark. Her favorite book offerings range from authors like Eckhart Tolle to Stephen King. Her favorite movies are horror and holiday is Samhain (Halloween) but she still loves a good romance. She's a huge sucker for a story where the underdog comes out on top.

If the bar doesn't have a good cider, she'll opt for a fine whisky.

She comes to writing later in life after tiring of reading books that seem to only focus on perfect, perky, barely legal heroines.

Her stories are about real people who have their own demons, drama, and challenges to overcome.

You can find her on online at:

Website – www.kitmckenna.com

Facebook – @authorkitmckenna

Instagram - @kitmckennaauthor

TikTok – @kitmckennaauthor